Rise of the Enemy

Rob Sinclair

Vesey Manor Publishing

First published by Vesey Manor publishing in 2016

ISBN: 978-0-9956933-1-9

Find out more about Rob and his books at:
http://www.robsinclairauthor.com

Books by Rob Sinclair

Dark Fragments

The Enemy Series:
Dance with the Enemy
Rise of the Enemy
Hunt for the Enemy

In loving memory of Joan Sinclair, xxx

Prologue

Dance with the enemy and your feet will get burned. An old friend once said that to me, many years ago. The same old friend who was now sitting in front of me, across the table of the café. I think he'd misquoted the saying, but it always stuck with me nevertheless. And recently, his words had come back to bite me with a vengeance.

I'd made the mistake of getting too close to people I thought were friends. People I trusted. Angela Grainger was one of them. We'd had a connection like I'd never had with anyone before. I still thought about her every day. Mostly, despite myself, I still thought of her fondly. But she'd betrayed me. Betrayed my trust. I'd let her get too close and my feet had been burned.

The man sitting before me was another one. Grainger's betrayal was something I would never forget – it still dominated my mind. But in many ways the betrayal of this man hurt the most.

He was the person I had trusted more than anyone else in the world.

I never imagined that we would end up like this. Talking in this way. The accusations. The insinuations. Speaking to each other like we were natural enemies rather than two people who had worked so closely together for nearly twenty years.

They wanted me to kill him. Until a few days ago, the mere suggestion would have been laughable. Something had changed, though. I didn't know what and I didn't know why, but our lives would never be the same again. The fact we were sitting here like this told me that.

And if it came down to it, I would do it.

I would kill Mackie. My boss. My mentor. My friend.

Because it might be the only way for me to get out of this mess alive.

Chapter 1

Yuri Zhirkov. That was the name on the passport that I handed over to the security guard. He was sitting behind the booth in front of me – a big man, broad shouldered with a scarred and pockmarked face and deep-set, brooding eyes. He looked like he meant business. This was no rent-a-cop. All of the guards here were ex-military. In fact, it was a safe bet many of them were still military given what the site was used for.

At least, given what we *thought* it was used for. The official story was something quite different.

The guard took the passport and opened it to the picture page. The picture was of me, but he had no way of knowing I wasn't Yuri Zhirkov, but Carl Logan, a British agent working for the secretive JIA.

Dmitri, a double-agent who worked for the Russian FSB and the man I'd been working with on the case, was standing next to me. He had a similarly fake passport in his hand, ready for the guard's inspection, in the name of Andrei Veronin.

The guard pulled over a piece of paper attached to a clipboard. He held it at an angle and I couldn't make out any words. I guessed it listed the day's planned visitors. Yuri Zhirkov and Andrei Veronin would both be on there. That was for sure. It had been carefully arranged that way by the man we would be meeting here, Viktor Grechko. The two passports were fakes but the names were real; two low-level analysts working for the Ministry of Defence of the Russian Federation. Nothing unusual about two staff from the Ministry visiting.

The guard carefully compared the details on the passport with the list in front of him. Without looking up, he started to speak. In

Russian. He spoke quickly. His accent was strong. I didn't catch all of the words straight away. I could speak Russian almost fluently, albeit with a heavy English accent. This wasn't my first foray on Russian soil. At the start of the operation my language skills had been somewhat rusty, but after four months of living here and speaking barely a word of my native tongue, my Russian was now better than it had ever been. But the guard's words had come out as one long mumble.

My mind raced as I tried to process what he had said. One second passed, then another. I looked over at Dmitri, who stared at me expectantly. He nodded his head to indicate for me to look up. I did so and saw the security camera in the corner of the room, up behind the right shoulder of the security guard. I finally translated the man's words in my mind.

'*Look up at the camera for me, please.*'

It had taken me three full seconds to process. Not good enough. If I kept that up, we would be found out before we even got into the building. They weren't hard words to decipher. It should have been automatic. The first sign of nerves creeping in.

Nerves. There'd been a time not long ago when I didn't even understand what that meant.

'Okay, that's fine. Thank you,' the guard said, handing the passport back to me.

This time I understood his simple words straight off. The guard took a plain white plastic card and placed it into the machine in front of him. The machine whirred and the card popped out again with a picture of my face on it.

'Wear this around your neck at all times,' the guard said, placing the card in a plastic wallet, which he handed to me.

He then went through a well-oiled diatribe. I missed some of his words again. The gist was that the card he had given me identified me as a visitor, signified by the red cord that ran through the wallet. The card wouldn't give me access to any internal doors. I would have to be accompanied at all times. Staff wore green or blue cords, according to their security clearance within the building complex. I noticed that the security card around the guard's neck had a black cord – the skeleton key of security cards, I presumed.

'Your passport, please,' the guard said, holding his hand out to Dmitri, who promptly gave him the passport bearing the name of Andrei Veronin.

The guard repeated the same procedure again. The security here was tight, methodical. Deliberate. But then we knew that would be the case. We were at the headquarters of RTK Technologies, Russia's biggest manufacturer of military technology.

At least that was the official line.

This part of it, the red-corded wallet dangling from my neck, was merely the cherry upon the icing upon the cake. Just to get this far we'd had to get past the outer gated entrance, which was fortified with armed guards. There, a brutish man in military-like fatigues had checked both our passports against a list. He had called something in on his radio, only opening the barrier for us after another colleague, driving a Jeep, had arrived to meet us from somewhere within the as-yet-unseen inner sanctum.

From there we had been escorted to the visitor car park, which consisted of just four spaces in front of the Portakabin-style building that we were sitting in. The cabin stood directly in front of a wire fence, nine feet tall with balled barbs at its peak, a near-identical construction to the outer perimeter fence that lay some thirty yards further out. In between the two fortified fences was some sort of no man's land. The only visible signs of life and activity within it were the visitor car park and the cabin. For all I knew the whole thirty-yard strip was booby-trapped with land mines. In fact, it wouldn't surprise me at all.

I really didn't want to find out, though.

'Okay, please take a seat over there,' the guard said, having satisfactorily concluded his review. 'Mr Grechko will be with you shortly.'

Dmitri and I turned in unison and walked over to the two plastic chairs that were facing the guard's desk. We sat down and waited.

We had targeted the man we were meeting, Grechko, some two months previously. A leading biochemist for RTK, he had high security clearance that would provide him with access to RTK's most confidential files and papers. And *we* had leverage.

We'd snatched him for the first time almost three weeks ago, just after he finished his business with a prostitute I'd paid off. Before he'd had a chance to buckle his belt back up, I'd been holding a gun to his head. From there it had been simple. Grechko was a civilian, a civilian with a questionable role no doubt, but he wasn't trained to withstand the threats we'd made. It'd been easy to get him to do what we wanted. And for the finale, all we had to do was make him escort us into RTK, where we could get the information we needed and get out.

After five minutes sitting on the hard plastic chairs I was beginning to get edgy and wondered whether we had already been rumbled. I thought over the options if the guards had discovered that we were imposters. I didn't like any of them much.

I heard the deep rumble of another Jeep approaching the cabin. The noise grew louder and I could feel the vibration in my seat as the vehicle approached. The whole cabin seemed to shake from the reverberations of the growling diesel engine. My heart rate quickened and I squeezed my fists together tightly, channelling my energy, trying to remain calm and unfazed, at least on the outside. Whatever was going to happen, it was going to happen soon.

How many more guards would there be in the Jeep?

I heard the grind as the parking brake was engaged. The opening of a car door. Footsteps approaching the cabin. Only one set. That didn't mean we were in the clear, but I suddenly felt at least the odds were still in our favour. I looked over to Dmitri. His face was a picture of calm. I hoped that mine was too, despite the nerves that I was feeling inside. That was the way it always had to be.

I turned my head at the sound of the cabin door opening. In stepped another thick-set guard.

'Please come with me,' the man said. 'Mr Grechko is ready for you now.'

No onslaught. No ambush. No bullets or poisoned darts flying. No reason to panic.

Yet.

A wave of relief rushed through my body and I unclenched my fists. The game was still on.

I got up and casually walked to the door, Dmitri close behind. Outside we followed the guard to the waiting open-topped Jeep.

Another guard was sitting in the driver's seat. I took the seat behind him, and Dmitri sat next to me. The driver reversed the Jeep out of the parking space so that we were facing the security gate that led into the compound. The barrier lifted up and we moved through.

We drove past endless rows of parked vehicles and turned corners lined with dense trees until finally the buildings making up the expansive complex came into view.

First we passed a sprawling two-storey office block, tens of windows long. Then an oversize industrial warehouse loomed into the sky, as high as eight or even ten storeys. Next came a series of smaller offices and workshops, and a giant chimney with dark smoke billowing out of its peak that swirled into the cold grey sky, becoming congruous with the dull clouds. The structure looked like an incinerator.

I wondered what they were burning.

We had driven for what I thought was close to a mile before we came to a stop. The building before us was a gleaming glass structure, four storeys tall. It looked out of place against what had so far been brick and corrugated-iron erections. More modern. Less aggressive. Less threatening almost.

'Please follow me,' said the guard from the passenger seat as he got out of the Jeep.

Dmitri and I stepped out and followed the man up to the large double doors that fronted the building. I caught a glimpse of myself in the glass in front of me. My six-foot-three frame looked misshapen by the edges of the glass and my green eyes sparkled from the reflected light. Dmitri and I were both wearing casual work attire: shirts, trousers, shining black shoes; no need for overcoats yet in the mild autumnal weather. My mousy brown hair was trimmed short and parted neatly. We looked every bit the office workers we were pretending to be.

I noticed to the left of the doors a gold plaque with black writing that said in Russian *Advanced Technologies.* Words, I expected, that told very little about what went on there. But I knew enough.

Two words: biochemical weapons.

The guard swiped his black-corded security card against the pad underneath the plaque, eliciting a clicking and then a rolling sound as the locking mechanism on the doors released. He pulled a door open and ushered us through. Inside was a shining-marble-floored atrium. Two black leather sofas stood in the waiting area off to our left, clustered around a coffee table strewn with magazines and corporate paraphernalia. In front was a reception desk with a young and quite attractive brunette.

'You're here to see Mr Grechko?' the receptionist asked.

'*Da*,' Dmitri said.

'Okay, please take a seat. Someone will be with you shortly.'

The drawn-out process was becoming tiresome, but we did as we were told. We made our way to the coffee table and sat. The guard stood watch over us, not showing any intention of letting us out of his sight. That was fine by me. If the time came for action, having a guard with us might not be a bad thing. I had spotted some time ago they were all armed. And I wasn't.

Not yet.

We didn't have to wait in the reception area for long. Within two minutes the door off to the receptionist's right wheezed open. In stepped a suited man. He was slick, tanned and well-groomed with jet-black hair neatly parted at the side. His navy-blue suit was complemented by a heavy white shirt and a blood-red, thick-knotted tie. He had a broad smile on his face – not pleasant, but knowing, calculating. A smile that showed he was in charge and he knew it. He strode over to us, maintaining eye contact with me the whole way.

I had never seen the man before. I didn't know who he was. But I could feel my heart thudding in my chest. I clenched my fists again and my mind raced, thinking over less-than-satisfactory options for our next steps.

Because whoever this man was, he wasn't Viktor Grechko.

Chapter 2

'Gentlemen, welcome to RTK!' the man said in Russian, his words articulate and clear. He held out his hand and his smile widened to reveal dazzling white teeth. 'I'm Mikael Semshov, CEO of Advanced Technologies.'

Dmitri got to his feet and shook Semshov's hand. 'I'm Andrei Veronin,' he said. 'And this is my colleague, Yuri Zhirkov.'

Semshov turned to me and I shook his hand. He had thick, strong fingers and the firmness of the handshake took me by surprise.

'Pleased to meet you both,' Semshov said, releasing my hand. 'Please, come through.'

Semshov turned and began to retrace his steps past the receptionist's desk. Dmitri and I followed. We exchanged a quick questioning look. Grechko had assured us that we would be meeting with him. His absence wasn't a good sign. Not at all.

As we approached the open doorway I noticed yet another fatigues-clad guard standing on the opposite side.

'Is everything all right with Viktor?' Dmitri asked. 'Only we thought we were meeting with him.'

'Ah, Viktor? He's fine,' Semshov replied without turning to face us. 'He just got called out to a meeting. You know how these things are. He should be back within half an hour, but I thought I'd extend my courtesies to you. It's always nice to meet our customers. I can give you a tour of the facilities too if you like, but let's wait for Viktor in my office.'

It sounded plausible enough, but I didn't buy it. Maybe we had been too trusting of Grechko. But we still had our job to do. We'd just have to wait for things to play out.

We followed Semshov through the open door. The guard on the other side waited for us to pass before setting off in tow behind us. The guard from the Jeep was also following. We rounded a corner and came to what looked like an airlock – a glass pod with a thick door bisecting it down its centre. We were led through it, one at a time. This wasn't colour-coded necklaces anymore. This was serious security. It would make our exit all the more difficult; we had no way around that. But all these precautions also meant we were getting closer to where we needed to be.

We were taken down a short corridor, passing closed doors on our left and right that gave no indication of what lay behind them. As we reached the end of the corridor, Semshov stopped to open a large oak-panelled door on which a chrome plaque displayed his name and title.

Semshov stood in the doorway and ushered me and Dmitri through. Inside it could have been the office of any corporate chief in any industry in any country in the world: plush carpets, oversized bookshelves filled with various ornaments, knickknacks and photo frames, a large desk and executive leather chair. Not bad for a scientist.

'Please take a seat,' Semshov said, walking around us and pointing to the two less-impressive chairs at the near side of the desk.

We again did as we were told, at least partly content that we were finally deep in the bowels of RTK – exactly where we wanted to be. Though the absence of Grechko was certainly a worry. I noticed that the room had only one window, directly behind the large desk. The view was unspectacular, the office looking over the neighbouring building, a nondescript brick structure that was only about ten yards away. On the other side of the office, behind where I was sitting and off to my right, I had noticed a closed door. A toilet or shower room perhaps?

Or an alternative method of escape if our visit here turned south?

My eyes followed Semshov as he came around and sat at his desk. Both guards were out of my peripheral vision but I heard shuffling feet as they stationed themselves somewhere behind me. Semshov had a smirk plastered across his face. I fought hard to keep my calm exterior. I wasn't getting good vibes.

'So, gentlemen, where were we?' Semshov asked rhetorically. 'Perhaps you could tell me a little more about what you were hoping to get from your visit?'

'Yes, of course,' Dmitri said. 'As you know, the Ministry has just recently agreed its budget for research expenditure for the next five years. As a longstanding and trusted…'

Semshov held up one hand in the air, palm pointed outwards, stopping Dmitri in his well-rehearsed tracks.

'No, no, no,' Semshov said, shaking his head. 'The truth, please.'

I stared straight ahead at Semshov. My heart was pounding in my chest. I could feel blood and adrenaline racing through my body. The collar of my shirt felt tight and stifling, practically choking. Because I knew what was coming.

Semshov dragged the silence out, the malice in his smile growing. I sensed movement behind, the guards moving closer, and heard them drawing their weapons, the tell-tale sound of metal on leather as they pulled the pieces from their holsters. I knew that the barrel of a gun would now be pointed at the back of my skull.

'Why don't you start with who you two really are,' Semshov said. 'Because I know you're not from the Ministry.'

Chapter 3

Clearly the game had changed. But it wasn't yet over. Dmitri and I weren't just there to steal information, we were there to leave a mark. We certainly hadn't planned for our visit to pan out like this, but we could still achieve our aim. Fake passports and stolen identities had got us into RTK, but the plan had never been to leave covertly.

Why?

Because for the last nineteen years I had worked for the Joint Intelligence Agency, the JIA. A secretive intelligence agency, controlled jointly by the USA and the UK, the JIA's agents ran specialist operations away from the scrutiny of the mainstream law enforcement and other intelligence agencies. It was policing, espionage and elite armed forces all rolled into one.

And the JIA, together with the British and American governments who oversaw us, wanted RTK, wanted Russia and the other governments that were sponsoring RTK's research, to know they had been hit. That was the real purpose of my visit. We wanted them to know that we knew what was going on there. Think of it kind of like government-to-government blackmail. Simply a matter of strengthening our own hand.

All of that explained why at that moment, when Semshov revealed that our cover was blown, when I heard the guards behind me drawing their weapons, I didn't react. I waited.

All five people in the room remained silent for a few seconds longer. Without looking behind I didn't know exactly where the two guards were stationed. And I told myself I wasn't going to look. You don't want to go making too many sudden movements in a situation like that. For all I knew they were only inches away, guns trained on my head and Dmitri's, and any movement from me might have been my last. And I couldn't have just sprung out of my chair and tried to tackle them to the ground. If they were too far away, I would have been an open target and it would have been nothing more than suicide.

So I waited.

'How did you figure it out?' Dmitri asked.

His voice was still calm and casual. I knew he wasn't interested in the answer to the question. He was just buying time, doing the same thing I was. Not trying to figure out how we were going to escape from the predicament, but figuring out how we were going to get what we came for and *then* escape.

'What, you thought we wouldn't know about you turning Grechko to your side?' Semshov said, smiling. He was enjoying every second.

'So where is he?' Dmitri asked.

'Come on,' Semshov said, laughing. 'You are Russian, aren't you? What do you think we'd do with a traitor like that?'

'You killed him?'

Semshov didn't answer. But we all knew that Grechko was dead. The trap had been laid for us and we had walked right in.

I heard more shuffling of feet from behind, could now hear the breaths of a guard standing only inches away. I should have been feeling sick with trepidation. But the reality was that the situation hadn't changed. If they had wanted to kill us, they would have done it already. In fact, I was feeling more confident than before. Because having heard the guard's movements, I had a better feeling for how close he was.

Not close enough.

'You need to understand something,' Semshov said, his smile now gone. 'I know a lot more than you might think about how these things work. There's no need for me to kill you both. What I want is to know who you are and why you've targeted us. We want to know who our enemies are. All this secretive running around in the dark – it's degrading. So I'll make this quite simple for you. You can tell me now, straight up, or we can force it out of you.'

Neither of us said a word. I heard more movement from behind and felt light pressure on the back of my head. A gun barrel being pressed against my skull. I knew that Dmitri would be feeling the same.

Was it the end for us?

No, it was going to be the opportunity. Because I now knew exactly where the guards were. Striking distance.

'You don't want to talk? That's a shame. You know, I actually feel sorry for you two, your masters having sent you here like this. What does that make you? You must be the cheapest labour they have, no? Dispensable. You're just like pet dogs. Loyal, obedient. But I like that. I actually like dogs. It's your masters that are the real problem. They're the ones who risk your lives. They're the ones that want to destroy us for no better reason than they don't fully understand what we do. And that we work for Russia and not them. But unfortunately, your masters aren't here. And you are.'

Semshov nodded to the guard behind Dmitri. A gunshot rang out. I flinched at the sound, but I knew immediately that the shot hadn't been from the guard standing behind me. The scream that came through Dmitri's gritted teeth told me that. I didn't know where he had been shot, but the fact he was screaming at all meant that it hadn't been intended to kill him.

I rotated my head slightly to get a look. Blood was pouring out of a hole in Dmitri's right shoulder. The bullet had gone straight through bone and tissue, in and out. Dmitri was panting heavy breaths, his nostrils flaring, trying his hardest to control the pain, to retain his focus.

We had bluffed our way so far, but it would take us no further. Now was the time to react. Dmitri looked over at me. We both knew what to do.

I stared at Semshov, who had a look of such arrogant confidence on his face. He opened his mouth to speak. But before he could say a word, I leaned forward. Just an inch or two. I strained my legs and pushed down hard on my feet, readying them to take my weight. I moved my hands down to my sides, resting them on the seat, next to my thighs. Then, in one swift motion, I used my legs, my arms, my whole body weight to propel the chair backward, crashing it into the legs of the guard directly behind me.

I heard commotion to my left and was aware that Dmitri would be doing the same; I hoped he had the strength and concentration to pull it off. In the blink of an eye I rushed in a narrow arc around the chair, moving up behind my bemused guard. If he was an amateur, he would probably start pulling on his trigger in desperation, aiming at where I had been. If he was in any way decent, he would be moving away and into a defensive position while he determined what was happening. I didn't hear any more shots, so maybe he wasn't an amateur. But he still wasn't good enough.

Before the guard had the chance to manoeuvre away, I twisted my left arm around his neck and grabbed hold of his right ear. My right arm snaked around my left and I clasped my right hand over his jaw. I used the grip to pull his head backward and upward, twisting in a sudden anti-clockwise motion.

I heard his neck snap and released the grip. His limp body slumped onto the plush carpet below.

Only a few seconds elapsed between hurling the chair and hearing his body hitting the floor. A split-second later a similar thud told me Dmitri had accomplished the same feat. Not bad with a gunshot wound to contend with.

Semshov was halfway to a desk drawer, his hand reaching out to it. Was he going for an alarm? A weapon?

'Put your hands where I can see them!' Dmitri shouted.

I turned to see Dmitri, his left arm held out, fingers gripping a Glock 17 pistol that he was pointing at Semshov. The gun belonged to the dead man at Dmitri's feet.

Semshov looked up, his hand still outstretched toward the desk. He had taken on a ghostly look. Shocked at how the balance of power had so quickly changed.

'You'll never get out of here alive,' Semshov said. 'Whatever you do to me, it's nothing compared to what we'll do to you.'

I noticed the slightest of twitches in his right arm. A piercing alarm began to sound. And that same wicked smile that he had first greeted us with began to creep across Semshov's face once more.

'Fuck!' Dmitri shouted.

I tried to stop the inevitable. 'Dmitri, no!'

But I was too late. Dmitri pulled on the trigger of the Glock twice. A quick double-tap. The two slugs hit Semshov in his chest, less than an inch apart, right at the centre of where his heart would be. He writhed in his seat for a second, a look of disbelief wiping away just a sliver of that confidence.

And then he was gone.

'Why the hell did you do that!' I shouted.

I wasn't upset that Semshov was dead. Just that he was dead before we'd got any of the information we needed. He could have been useful. A hostage may even have helped us to get out.

'Eliminate all threats,' Dmitri said.

'But not until we get the files! You'd better not hit any roadblocks getting the information, otherwise we're screwed.'

'Don't worry about me. I know how to do my job.'

Dmitri took his briefcase and placed it on Semshov's desk. He opened it up and went to the concealed compartment that held all of his equipment. I wouldn't know where to start with all the high-tech gizmos that he used, but I knew the basics. The tools of the trade that Dmitri had mastered would allow him to copy the entire hard drive from Semshov's computer in just minutes, simultaneously transmitting it wirelessly to our remote field office. We had planned to take Grechko's hard drive, but that wasn't going to happen now – perhaps Semshov's would be more fruitful anyway.

On top of that, we had already obtained Grechko's security details. While the hard drive was being copied, Dmitri would be able to roam free through RTK's server data for anything else of interest.

At least that was the theory.

But all of that took time. And with the alarm blaring, I wasn't sure we had much.

'How long do you need?' I asked as I watched Dmitri attach leads from Semshov's desktop to a handheld device that looked to me nothing more than an extravagant mini-tablet.

'Longer than we have,' he said.

'Shit.'

'Give me five minutes. I'll see what I can do.'

I wasn't sure we really had five minutes. Guards would surely be swarming us on all sides already. But we had to try.

'Are you able to do it with your shoulder like that?' I said.

'Just let me get on with it!'

I walked over to the guard I had killed and took the gun out of his hand – a Glock 17, just like the one that Dmitri had. I checked the magazine. Still full. Seventeen rounds. The chamber was loaded with another. I searched through his pockets, looking for anything else of use. I found another full magazine, a mobile phone, a radio. I took them all. I also took his black-corded security card from around his neck. Just in case. Though I had to expect they had us on lockdown already.

'Rather than looting the dead, why don't you figure out how we're going to get out of here?' Dmitri said.

I didn't like how he said it.

'Just let me get on,' I said. 'I know how to do my job as well, remember?'

'I'll be done in two minutes. At least check the doors and windows, figure out which way we're going to go.'

'I'm not opening that door until you're ready. No point in inviting an onslaught.'

Dmitri huffed. I got on with what I was doing. The alarm was piercing. The pitch made my insides curdle. It had been going for a few minutes already. Back-up had surely arrived nearby. The only questions were how many men, how well-equipped, where the hell they were and, more importantly, what their orders were.

I headed over to the other internal door, hoping that there may be some good fortune through there. There wasn't. The door led into nothing more than a small cupboard. We weren't going to get out that way.

I began to creep over to the window, cautiously, not wanting to create a target for anyone stationed nearby. I stopped before I got too close. I could see vehicles and bobbing heads lining up outside. But as long as the glass was breakable, the window had to be our best bet for escape. The door we had come through would only take us through narrow corridors. And back to the airlock. Even if those doors hadn't already been locked down, they would take far too long to clear and we'd be nothing more than sitting ducks.

'Please tell me you're nearly done?' I said.

'Just...hang.' Dmitri held up a finger at me. 'Done! Now, get us out of here.'

'Bullets or chair?' I said, staring over at the window.

Dmitri shrugged. I took aim with the Glock.

There was an almighty crash as one of the window panes exploded. Thousands of neat pieces of safety glass flew through the air and crashed to the floor.

Dmitri looked at my gun as though what had just happened was impossible for such a low-calibre firearm. And it was. Because I hadn't even pulled the trigger. This fact dawned on both of us just a second later.

'Get down!' I screamed.

I threw myself to the floor on the near side of the large desk, away from the now open and exposed window. Dmitri began to move, but before he could get to me an explosion erupted, so loud it felt like my eardrums had shattered to pieces, just like the window had moments earlier. With it came a bright white flash of light that seemed to burn and burrow its way into my head – I was completely blinded.

I knew what it was. A stun grenade. Non-lethal, but incapacitating.

But knowing that didn't make the effects any less severe. For a number of seconds my brain was fuzzy and my body felt like a dead weight. A result of the shock caused to the stabilising ability of my inner ear. I tried to stand but fell into a heap on the floor, my face scraping painfully on the thick weave of the carpet. I knew the effects would pass, but by then there could be ten guards in the room, guns at the ready.

I pulled myself along the floor, toward the cupboard door. I didn't really know why, other than it took me further away from the window where the grenade had come from.

My vision started to return. The spinning in my head began to subside.

'Dmitri. Are you okay?' I said, turning around.

No answer.

I heard shouting from outside. I wasn't sure whether they were shouting at us or giving each other orders. I stayed where I was, on the floor.

'Dmitri?'

Still nothing.

I finally got my sight back, though everything seemed to be spinning around me. Dmitri was lying on the floor, next to the guard he had killed. I went to get up, again failed. My legs were like jelly.

Only then did I feel the searing pain tearing through my legs, my arms, my torso. I gave myself a once-over. No blood. My brain quickly went over the possibilities. There was only one. It hadn't been just a stun grenade but a sting grenade too. The stun grenade incapacitates by delivering an incredible flash of bright light together with a bang. It temporarily blinds you and makes your head hazy and confused, just like mine was. A sting grenade is likewise not lethal, but its method is altogether different. It contains hundreds of rubber balls that disperse upon explosion, again designed to incapacitate rather than kill. Like being hit with a hundred paintballs at once.

I fought through the pain, got to my feet and rushed over to Dmitri. I turned him over. He was breathing, but he didn't look good. Without the desk to protect him, he would have taken many more hits than I had from the rubber balls. His arms and face were covered in bright-red welts.

'Come on. You need to get up.'

He responded to my words, pulling his legs into his body, as though testing that he still had use of them. I put my hands into his armpits and tried to haul him onto his feet.

'Let's take the door,' he slurred.

'No way. That's what they're expecting. We go out the window.'

'Straight into them?'

'How many of them can there be?'

But just then the door burst open. Before I could react a volley of gunfire rang out.

I was down again, flat on my back, before I knew it.

I rolled onto my side, momentum more than anything, but that was as far as I got. It felt as though my body had left me. I opened and closed my eyes, drifting. Such a surreal feeling. I remember thinking how different it felt from the last time I had been shot.

In fact, hadn't one of the bullets just hit me in the head? Why wasn't I dead already?

As I lay on the floor, wanting to move but unable to, watching the steel-toe-capped boots gathering around me, I saw the reason. A bright-blue rubber bullet lay next to me. One of many. Fired through the open door to put us down, but not out.

As my eyes slowly opened and closed, the movement becoming more strained each time, I thought I heard voices.

'Take him.'

'No, that one first. She's already waiting for him.'

And in those last few seconds before I lost consciousness, I knew with absolute certainty that they'd wanted us alive. A stun grenade. A stinger. Rubber bullets. Like riot police. No lethal force.

The only question was: why?

Chapter 4

Three months later

I was running. I didn't know where to, but I had to get away. I couldn't see more than ten yards in front of me. Every direction I looked in was simply a wall of white. I ran as hard and fast as I could. I avoided trees at the last second as they finally came into my view. But I was unable to escape the pot holes and undulations in the ground, which were completely obscured by the thick covering of untouched snow, just a few inches deep in places, as much as two feet in others.

Impossible to really run in conditions like that.

More than once I stumbled when my foot went further into the soft white powder than I anticipated, falling flat on my face in the process. At least the falls were cushioned. But they slowed me down and that wasn't good.

It was cold. How cold, I don't know. Whatever temperature my brain thought, it would be colder. Take off another five or ten degrees centigrade at least to account for the heat building up from me running and the masking effect of the adrenaline flowing through me. It wouldn't have surprised me if the temperature was as low as minus fifteen, minus twenty even.

It didn't matter.

All that mattered was that I get away from there. I could worry about the cold after.

I had on a pair of thick leather boots, one size too small, over my bare skin. I'd commandeered them just minutes earlier. My feet were probably red-raw, the skin scraped off from the constant friction. But I couldn't feel any pain. Maybe my feet were numbed by the cold already.

The uniform I was wearing fitted me nicely. The overcoat I had on, although weighing me down, would be essential later on when I eventually stopped running. I knew that my hands and face were too exposed, but at least the blood pumping quickly through my body was keeping the cold at bay for now.

I put a foot down, expecting the ground to give by six inches or so as it had done for every other step. But it didn't. My foot hit hard ice, just below the powder surface. The unexpected step sent a jolt through my ankle. I stumbled, my body fell forward, my chin cracked off my bent knee, which was higher than it should have been. I rolled into a heap in the snow.

Dazed, it took me a couple of seconds to regain myself. A fire ripped through my left ankle. The numbness from the mixture of cold and adrenaline had quickly dissipated. But I could still move and twist my foot. The ankle wasn't broken. I felt a warmth on my chin, wiped at it with my hand. Blood. I had bitten into my lip when my knee struck my chin. I cursed before lifting my heavy body upright again.

Without thinking twice, I continued my sprint.

A thick mist surrounded me. I knew I was in a forest because of the trees. A pine forest. The sharp, pungent smell from the trees, unmistakable to me, fired pleasant memories in my head of past holidays. Memories that were completely out of place given my predicament.

Because of the darkness, the trees and the mist, I couldn't sense what else was around me. For all I knew a road or even villages lay directly at either side. But they would be completely lost to me in the cloud of white. I didn't even know whether I had merely been running in circles. Although the moonlight seeping through the trees allowed me to make out nearby shapes, the eerie haze all around meant I couldn't locate the moon itself or any stars in the sky to give me any kind of direction. I had to rely on my instincts and nothing else.

I thought I had been running for about twenty minutes, but I had no way of knowing for sure. Taking account of the terrain, my fatigue, my clothing, I couldn't have been averaging more than five miles an hour, even though I had been going as fast as I could. That would take me close to two miles from where I had started out.

I didn't know whether they were chasing me yet. They could have been as little as a few hundred yards from me for all I knew. But I couldn't hear any voices shouting after me, or footsteps close behind.

Maybe they weren't looking for me at all.

No, I couldn't think like that. I had to assume they were out there somewhere. And I had to get away.

But how many men would there be? Did they have vehicles? Dogs?

It didn't matter. Hiding wasn't an option. I had to run.

During my training many years ago I had been put through survival exercises countless times. Often in terrains not at all dissimilar to this. The rule of three was something that had always stuck with me. Humans cannot survive more than three hours exposed to extremely high or low temperatures. Humans cannot survive more than three days without water. And humans cannot survive more than three weeks without food.

The theory was as basic and unscientifically proven as you could get. I had survived many more than three hours of exposure. You hear miraculous stories of people who have survived far longer than three days without water. For starters, numerous other factors are relevant: the temperature, whether you are at high or low altitude, the humidity level, how otherwise healthy you are. And you see numerous claims by monks and the like of fasting that has lasted for weeks, months, even years.

But the basic rules apply. You need food, water and shelter from extreme temperatures to survive.

And I had none of those.

Running was against every basic rule I had learned. The exertion would be burning my body's energy supply, my water, far more quickly than being stationary. I knew that. And it started to play on my mind. The doubt crept in: was I doing the right thing?

For the first ten minutes of my run, I had been so focused on getting away, the adrenaline had been pumping so hard, I hadn't stopped for even a second to think about what I would do next. But now my legs were becoming heavy, my muscles becoming tight from exhaustion and cold. Every step was an effort, like I had on a pair of lead boots.

And I started to question whether what I was doing was actually a huge mistake.

What if nothing was out there?

How long would I run through this vast nothingness?

Wasn't I best sticking to what I had learned? Find myself shelter. Start rummaging for food. Start a fire. Get out of the cold and reserve my energy. There would be plenty of food I could forage for. Plants, leaves, even small animals were abundant in terrain like this. Reindeer lichen, a type of moss, is so called for the very fact that it grows in vast, icy wildernesses like the one I was in. Virtually every tree trunk around would have it growing around its bark.

Those were all the sensible things I should have been doing. But then, stopping to find food, water, shelter might have been just as much a death sentence as running to the point of collapse. Either way, when I stopped, they would find me. I had to believe that.

And at least running wasn't giving up. Stopping and burrowing away from the cold would be akin to waving a little white flag. People with extreme hypothermia are known to exhibit what is called terminal burrowing. A last show of despair where they look for confined spaces to hide in. Sounds sensible, right? But even after people have been rescued they burrow. Hiding in cupboards in their own home, under their beds, anything to get away from the feeling of cold and isolation. The brain takes over, animal instinct returning. But it's a feat of desperation. Literally crawling into a corner to die.

That's why stopping would feel like giving up. Because if I stopped, I would end up doing just that: terminal burrowing.

But my legs weren't listening. No matter how much I wanted to keep going, my legs were about to give up.

I stopped running, slowing to a walk. Within a few steps forward progress had been halted altogether. It was the end, I knew. Like in marathon running. You've got to keep going, because the second you stop it's a signal of defeat to your brain. All the hard work that you've done to convince your body that your legs can take it disappears in that instance. Your toes will hurt, your ankles, calves, shins, knees, thighs. The wall.

And I had just stopped. I had just hit my wall.

I sank to my knees. Exhaustion finally taking over. Not only from two miles of running through thick snow, but from the ordeal of the previous three months. And yet I felt more than just fatigue. A feeling of abject failure, of doom, washed over me. I had come this far, only to give in so quickly. So easily.

But my body was no longer responding. I couldn't go on.

Having only stopped for a few seconds I could already feel the sub-zero air cooling my reddened face. Within minutes my circulation would readjust. Wanting to conserve warmth, my body would no longer pump my blood close to the skin. The network of veins and arteries would close off the pathways to my extremities: hands, feet, face. It wouldn't be long before they turned blue from cold. Frostbite would come next. I knew all that, and yet my body was no longer responding to my will. It had left me. I was more alone than I could have imagined.

With my own heavy breathing subsiding, I could, for the first time, hear the forest around me. The gentle rustle of branches swaying in the chilly breeze. The whistling as stronger gusts forced their way through the narrow passages created by the vast trunks.

But that was it. Those were the only sounds of life.

Other than that, I was all alone.

Abandoned.

I bowed my head down into my chest. Not to escape from the cold, but because of the melancholic feeling that was sweeping through me.

Nobody was coming for me. Not my own people. And not *them*. Perhaps they didn't even care that I was gone. My own people didn't, so why should *they*? I almost wished I could hear their voices. Hear their footsteps, the barks of the dogs. See the beams of their torches scattering around the trees toward me.

But there was nothing.

And that was why I began to cry. Because I was out there alone and it wouldn't matter to a single person whether I lived or died.

Not even to me.

But suddenly I looked up, eyes wide open and alert. At first I didn't understand why. Then I heard it again. The not-too-distant hum of machinery. I got to my feet, my face creasing from the pain that was spreading through my body from head to toe. The humming got louder, feeling almost deafening compared with the near-silence that had come before it. I thought I could actually feel the vibrations moving through the ground and up into my body like electricity.

The humming turned into a roar. I knew then that I was listening to a vehicle. A powerful four-by-four or maybe even a truck. I spotted the outline of headlights in the distance. They swept across in front of me from left to right as the vehicle turned, moving up and down as it passed over uneven ground. The beams weren't strong enough to fully break through the thick mist, but I knew it wasn't far from me.

Relief. That's what I felt at first. Relief that I wasn't alone. I wasn't going to die in some makeshift shelter, forever lost to nature. There was life out there. A road. Maybe a village or a town.

But after the relief came a dilemma over what my next step would be. Because chances were those lights would belong to the very people I was running from. And I would be faced with one of the greatest choices in the animal kingdom since time began.

Fight, or flight.

Chapter 5

I had been dreaming of Angela. I often did. The small piece of happiness in a wasted life. The only time in my sorry existence that I had ever felt such hope, passion, kinship toward another person. Felt so alive. I'd had casual lovers in the past but they'd never meant anything to me. Angela had been different. The attraction I had felt for her had been pure chemistry, a force that couldn't be stopped.

My life had gone off the rails some twelve months before I'd met her, following my failed assignment to bring a violent terrorist, Youssef Selim, to justice.

Selim had captured me, held me prisoner. He'd tortured and very nearly killed me. In the aftermath, I'd been a mess. Nineteen years of working and thinking like a robot came to an abrupt halt. I'd suffered severe post-traumatic stress. I didn't know if I could go on. But five months later I'd been back on the job, assigned to track down Frank Modena, America's Attorney General, who'd been kidnapped in Paris. Selim was the main suspect. Mentally, I hadn't been ready. But Mackie, my boss, had brought me back anyway. Brought me back to finish Selim off.

Along the way I'd met Angela Grainger, an FBI agent. A woman I had been attracted to like no other person before or after. Angela had come seemingly from nowhere and helped me to turn my life around. To get back some sense of normality in an utterly abnormal existence. My saving grace.

She helped me to track down Selim and I killed him. Thus ending what had seemed like the sorriest chapter of my life.

And yet even my time with Angela had come to a miserable end. She'd lied to me. She'd used me. She'd betrayed me.

27

She'd shot me!

Angela had been the one behind the plot to kidnap Modena all along. Her aim: to use the Attorney General to identify the man who'd killed her father. Innocent people had lost their lives. And as the plot ran perilously out of control, she used me to help her rectify the situation, all the while having me believe that she was helping me to bring to justice a madman – Youssef Selim – who had taken Modena hostage for his own nefarious purposes.

It would be an understatement to say I felt bitterness toward Angela. And yet, bizarrely, that didn't take away the sweetness of our time together. That would always remain. The one good thing that could never be taken away from me.

Even in my dreams, where the good times were retold, I knew that she was gone. Knew that when I woke up she wouldn't be there lying next to me.

But I knew that one day I would find her again.

My latest dream had been a replay of one of our best times together – a hotel in Paris where we'd spent two nights barely leaving our bed.

I wasn't sure what I was expecting to see when I finally opened my eyes. It always takes the brain a few seconds to recalibrate after dreaming, to remember where you are and why. But this time, a whole lot more confusion than normal coursed through my mind.

I hadn't even managed to make out the room that I was in before I was forced to close my eyes again because of the searing pain in my head. I held my eyes tightly shut, waiting for the stabbing to subside. It didn't go away entirely, but after a few seconds, once it had dulled, I tried again to open my eyes.

What I saw was accompanied by a flash of memories. Semshov's office. Dmitri lying on the floor, blood pouring from his shoulder. The feet gathering around me as I lay on my side. The voices.

At that moment it dawned on me where I was.

A cell.

No windows, no lights hanging from the ceiling. The only illumination was from the neat slivers of light outlining a door in front of me – enough to show the shape of the room. A square. Less than four yards wide and long. The walls looked black and wet in the dull light. The room was bare except for a large pot in the far corner.

I was lying on the ground, up against the wall at the back of the cell. I slowly, painfully, hauled myself to my feet, only then realising that I was naked. My whole body ached. Possibly from the rubber bullets. A beating from the guards too, maybe. Sleeping naked on the cold, hard floor certainly wouldn't have helped. I gave myself a once-over. Other than the aches and pains and a few areas of bruising, I had no serious injuries.

I hobbled up to the door and put my ear against the cold metal to see whether I could hear anything on the other side.

Nothing.

I could shout out. Maybe Dmitri was in a cell next to or opposite mine. Maybe a guard was stationed out there who could tell me where the hell I was. Why I was here.

But I didn't.

I wasn't desperate. I had been in cells like this before. I had always got out in the end. And it had never once been through begging.

I would sit and wait for them *to come to* me.

I moved back over to the far corner and slumped down onto the cold floor. I held my hands up to my face. I could barely see them in the dim light but I knew from the awkward sensation that they were shaking. It had been months since that last happened to me.

The post-traumatic stress I'd suffered following my encounter with Youssef Selim was something I'd tried my best to ignore, deny even. I'd fought hard for months before finally accepting the problem. The pain I felt in those days had dissipated after I met Angela. After the two of us tracked down Selim and I put a bullet in his head.

But in the cell, some of those painful feelings of isolation and despair from the last time I'd been held prisoner were already creeping back into my mind.

Luckily, with the feeling of doom quickly descending, I didn't have to wait long. I reckoned a little under two hours since I'd woken up. If I'd been them, I would have left me for much longer.

I heard their footsteps approaching. Two sets. Their boots sounded thick and heavy against the hard floor. Next came their voices. But they were almost whispering and I couldn't make out any words.

A flap in the door opened, sending a bright stream of light into the room. I winced as my eyes adjusted to the sudden change, holding up an arm to my face. I saw the barrel of a gun poked through the flap. A handgun of some sort. I doubted it would be a regular firearm. Why would they shoot me now after such a deliberate effort to bring me here alive? My guess was that it held tranquiliser darts.

'Move to the back of the cell. Put your hands above your head,' one of them said.

I was surprised that I was being spoken to in English. A broken English, but English nonetheless. I wasn't certain what the accent was. I had presumed that I was still in Russia. But on hearing the man's voice, the slightest doubt crept into my mind.

I didn't move, as I had been told to. I spoke in Russian to the guards.

'Where are we?'

They didn't answer. Had they understood me?

'Step back,' one of the voices said, sterner this time. 'Or we'll shoot you.'

I still didn't move.

'Do you even understand a word I'm saying, you dumb fucks?' I said, still in Russian.

'Yes. We understand you just fine,' was the simple response that I got, in Russian this time.

I heard a dull thwack and felt a light, stabbing pain in my thigh. I looked down to see a dart sticking into my leg, a trickle of blood escaping from the small, plugged wound.

I collapsed to the floor.

Chapter 6

I decided on fight rather than flight. I guess it's just my nature. I stood and watched as the lights from the vehicle came to a stop, off to my right, possibly fifty or so yards from where I was.

Because of the dense mist, I still hadn't had proper sight of the vehicle at all. Or who was in it. The engine remained idling, the purr from it loud to my ears. And the lights remained on, though pointing away from me.

Now that I had a target, a focus, the feeling of defeat that had been washing over me only seconds before had disappeared. I wasn't alone. Whoever the vehicle belonged to, I had a chance to get away from this place. And my body was responding to my renewed motivation, a strength and drive returning to my sore limbs.

I wasn't sure whether the people in the vehicle had spotted me or not – or even whether they were a threat – but I wasn't going to stand and wait to find out. Whoever they were I certainly didn't want them driving off before I got to them, leaving me to my death in this frozen wasteland. I crouched low and began moving forward, slowly. Not directly toward the vehicle, but around the back of it so that I could approach from behind. With my muscles exhausted and my body now trying its best to conserve heat, every step I took was an effort.

Two steps later and the engine stopped. Then the lights went dead. There was darkness all around and a creepy silence once more. I slowed up. With the engine off, they weren't going anywhere in a hurry. Best to keep my advantage and approach with caution.

I kept my eyes busy, darting from one side to the other, looking for any sign of life. I had a mental picture in my head of where the vehicle should be, off to my right. But in the darkness I began to doubt my own senses. I wondered even whether maybe it had driven off, the engine not turned off but the sound simply fading into the distance.

The next step I took was onto something other than snow. Something hard and black.

A road.

A single carriageway, cutting its way through the trees in front of me from left to right. The snow had been cleared from it and was piled up on either side in small mounds every few yards. As I walked out onto the tarmac, the mist seemed to thin. The moonlight for the first time gave me a sense of direction. Of scale. And as I looked up the road, to the right, I saw it. Just a few yards from where I was standing. A military-style Jeep.

It had to be *them*. No-one would come out for a leisurely drive and stop here, in the middle of this desolate space. Wherever the hell here was.

I ducked back into the trees, back into cover. Every step that I took was now critical. I had no doubt that they were armed. I could handle that. But I had to get close to give myself a chance.

I stooped down, brushing away the snow around my feet. Looking for a branch or something, anything, that I could use as a weapon. I found nothing. Just frozen leaves and wilted foliage.

I took a step forward, kicking the snow as I went, still looking. And I hit lucky. A log. About two feet long, three inches thick. Frozen solid. Like picking up a block of ice. I could immediately feel the cold from it penetrating my right hand, which was now shaking violently – from adrenaline or cold or anxiety, I wasn't sure. Regardless, the log was exactly what I needed.

I went to straighten up, then froze when I heard a crunching sound only a few yards behind me. I crouched back down again as silently as I could, turning my body as I did so.

At first I didn't see anything. But then, through the mist, I made out the outline of a person. A man. He was facing away from me, taking long, slow steps. He wore camouflage, grey and white. Each time he stopped moving, with the snow and fog around him, he blended into the scenery. But with each stride, his form was unmistakeable.

He was also armed. A large automatic weapon held in both hands. At the ready.

I knew there would be more than one of them, but I didn't know how many more. Again I had a decision to make. He hadn't seen me. He was still moving away. I could track behind him and attack. I was certain I could do it before he noticed me. But one of the others might see me doing it. It would be sensible for them to be spotting one another. And they were dressed for the occasion. I wasn't. The others could be within a few feet of me and I might not even know it.

And most importantly, the goal wasn't to take them out. The goal was to get their vehicle.

Still holding the icy log, I began to creep further away from the man. With each step I paused for a short moment, listening. Nothing. I couldn't even hear the man I had just seen anymore. I crept forward another step, pulling up against a tree trunk that was wide enough to obscure my entire body from the Jeep, just a few more paces from me.

I peered around the trunk, looked toward the vehicle. I didn't see him at first, but another man was on the far side, similarly dressed to the one I had just crossed paths with. He was out of the vehicle, but it looked as though his orders were to stay and stand guard. He was slowly walking back and forth in front of the bonnet.

Moving forward further, I soon reached a point where I was adjacent to the back of the Jeep. I moved out of the tree line and onto the smooth and slippery tarmac, pulling up alongside the rear of the vehicle. I bent low, looking for sight of the man. He was across on the opposite front side, his feet pointing away from me. I moved around the near side, staying low, stopping every half-step to check on his position.

When I reached the front tyre, I looked one last time. He was still there, and I saw now he was armed, his automatic gun pointing down at the ground.

I sprang up, the log held back, ready to swing. I took one lunging step forward to take me close enough...

But just at that moment, he turned around.

Our eyes met.

A look of surprise crossed his face. He began to raise the barrel of the weapon toward me. I swung the log back further, right around my neck like a baseball bat. He lifted his gun, pointing it at my chest. As my arms began to recoil, the log swinging forward in a wide arc, I sidestepped, trying to get out of the firing line. I heard the crack as he pulled on his trigger. Once. Twice.

But he missed.

He never got the chance to fire a third time. The log smashed against his head, the cracking sound it made as it crushed his skull almost as loud as his gun had been. The log snapped in half on impact.

If the man wasn't dead from that single blow, he wouldn't be far off.

But the noise had surely alerted his friend. And any others I hadn't yet seen.

I quickly got down and took his weapon. A Russian-made PP-19 Bizon submachine gun. A good weapon. I'd had doubts about whether I was still in Russia at all. This wasn't definitive proof, but it was certainly an indication. The PP-19 was commonly used by the FSB, Russia's internal security service; the new name for the KGB. The people who had been holding me for the last three months.

I was about to check through the dead man's pockets when I saw movement off to my right. Just inside the tree line. The gunshot caught me by surprise; the clunk as the single bullet lodged in the bumper of the Jeep, only a few inches from my face, was the first indication I'd had. I threw myself to the ground, putting the front left tyre of the vehicle between me and where I calculated the shooter had been.

I hadn't heard the shot at all. Was it a sniper firing from a distance? Maybe I just hadn't been concentrating.

On my belly, I slid back so that I could look and aim from underneath the car. Maybe the shooter would stay in position. Waiting for sight of me. Or maybe he was already moving, flanking me.

Because of where the shot came from, I now knew at least three men were out there. The first man I had seen was probably still somewhere behind me. He couldn't have covered enough distance in such a short space of time to be the shooter. Which meant one man was either side of me.

Which meant I was now a sitting duck.

They should have been able to pick me off with ease. But the shooter was too impatient. I saw more movement, and made out camouflage as it passed in front of a dark tree trunk. Taking just a moment to aim, I squeezed off three shots. I think they all hit. The shape slumped to the ground without a noticeable sound, the soft white snow cushioning the fall.

Unfortunately my weapon hadn't been so silent. I needed to get away. I sprang to my feet, rushed over to the driver's door and pulled it open. The key was in the ignition. I had to hold back a smile. I wasn't in the clear yet, but commandeering the Jeep would make my plight a whole lot better.

If I'd had the time, I'd have checked both of the dead bodies more thoroughly. They may have had a whole multitude of things of interest. Things that I needed like money, food, identification, weapons. But with the third man still out there, possibly more, that was a luxury I couldn't afford.

Without another second of hesitation, I jumped into the driver's seat and turned the key. The engine groaned into life, the cold air straining the process of combustion. It was a miracle it started first time. I pushed the gear lever into first and released the handbrake.

As I pulled away, I looked up into the rear-view mirror. From the darkness, thirty or so yards behind me, a man stepped out. He was dressed in camouflage, his weapon held in both hands, trained on the ground. The man who'd walked right past me not long before. He didn't raise his weapon toward me. Didn't fire off in desperation. Just looked on, defeated.

As I watched his figure disappear into the distance, I wondered whether he knew the rule of three.

Out there, I didn't fancy his chances.

Chapter 7

I opened my eyes. A bright beam of light was shining in my face. Reflexively I jerked my right arm, trying to bring my hand up as cover. But I couldn't move it. Looking down, I saw I was naked and secured to a chair by my wrists and ankles. The small hole where the dart had pierced my skin was sealed with dried blood, the bruising around the puncture site only just evident. I couldn't have been out for long.

I squinted into the light. I could make out the form of a desk in front of me. But with the angle of the beam directed at my face I could see nothing of who or what lay beyond.

I tried to rock on the chair but it didn't move. The legs were bolted to the ground.

'Well, now that you're awake, why don't we get started?'

The voice was a man's. Calm and assured. I couldn't see his face but the sound had come from the other side of the desk. He had spoken to me in English. Just like the guard had before. Except this guy's English was perfect. No hint of a foreign accent. It only added to my confusion as to where I now was.

My job with the JIA had seen me operate in many countries across the world, including Russia. I had made many enemies in the process. So it wasn't unthinkable that I had already been moved to another country as a means of settling old scores. Or simply to better hide me from my compatriots, whom I could only hope were looking for me.

I heard the rustling of papers, then he said, 'Please tell me your name.'

I didn't answer him. I stared directly in front of me. Directly toward where he would be sitting, even though I couldn't see his face. I wanted to make a stand, however futile it might have been.

The man waited for a good thirty seconds. Didn't repeat the question. Didn't push me for a response.

'What is your name?' he said eventually. His voice still calm, matter-of-fact.

Again, I didn't answer.

'Where were you born?' he asked after what I counted as another thirty-second pause.

I pursed my lips, breathing through my nose. A feeble show of strength. But I wanted to make it clear that I wasn't going to be giving him anything.

'Who do you work for?' he asked.

No answer.

'Why were you in Russia?'

Did the past tense of the question mean I no longer was in Russia?

'Why were you at RTK Technologies?'

I remained silent. After a longer pause, I heard more rustling of papers.

'What is your name?' he asked again.

He proceeded to repeat the same questions for a second time. And then a third and fourth. A set thirty seconds between each question. I didn't say a word. His voice remained placid, emotionless even, throughout. No intimidation, no threats.

The situation was unnerving. Disturbing. I didn't know who they were. I didn't know what they wanted from me. But I knew then that they were going to try to break me. I couldn't let that happen. My whole life had been about the JIA. Mackie, in particular, I felt great loyalty to. We'd worked together for more than half my life. He was a commander in the JIA; I was his agent. I couldn't talk. I couldn't fail now, let Mackie and everyone else down. Put their lives at risk.

But I knew that this timid questioning would just be the start of my ordeal. Things were going to get a whole lot worse from here. They didn't need to intimidate or threaten me to tell me that. I just hoped, in the end, something would give.

I had never been broken before. But everyone has a breaking point. I just hoped they wouldn't find mine.

'Okay. We're done here. Take him away.'

I heard footsteps approaching me from behind. I hadn't even known anyone was back there. How would I have?

Before I knew it, my world once again turned black as a thick cloth bag was placed over my head.

Chapter 8

I didn't know where the road led, but I kept going. Putting as much distance between myself and where I had come from as I could.

The Jeep was a lifesaver: not only was I mobile but I was kitted out with snack food, a flask of hot tea, a torch, a first-aid kit and a wallet full of cash. Roubles. Those, and the Russian branding on the snack food, told me I was still in Russia. I still didn't know where I was in the vast country, but it was a start.

Given the terrain and the weather, my best guess was Siberia. The very same place I had started out from, some months ago now, in the city of Omsk. That was where I wanted to get back to. The safe house that Dmitri and I had been staying at was there. More than that, Omsk was a place I knew. Somewhere I could feel comfortable while I figured out what to do next.

I should have been eager to contact my people, my boss: Mackie. We'd worked together from when I had just been a teenager. He was loyal to me, had shown his faith in me countless times when others had wanted to hang me out to dry.

But the truth was, I really wasn't sure whom I could trust anymore, Mackie included. I gripped the steering wheel tightly, my knuckles turned white. Even just thinking about my long-term commander and mentor in that way made me feel alone and vulnerable. Scared. Because without Mackie, I wasn't sure what else in the world I had.

I tried to block out the gloomy thoughts. Tried my best to cast off the tension that was gripping me. I hoped Omsk would hold some answers as to what had happened to me. But Siberia covers ten per cent of the world's entire land surface. It's a massive area.

Even if I was correct and that was where I was, I could still be thousands of miles from where I wanted to be.

I had been in the Jeep for several hours already. When I had first got in, I had put the air on cool, just sixteen degrees. The lowest it would go. I didn't want to warm my shivering body too fast. A sudden jump in temperature could have sent me into shock. Even that low temperature had felt like a Saharan wind to start with. By the time I had felt warmed through, some hours later, I had raised the bar to twenty-two. The warmth, together with the food and drink, made me feel somewhat normal again.

That is, as normal as one could be after three months of what I had been through. Scratch that, make that nineteen years of what I had been through.

I passed several signs of almost-life on the trip: signposts that gave the names of various places I had never heard of, a solitary petrol station that was closed up for the night, maybe for the entire season. I had even seen three other vehicles going in the opposite direction to me. But I'd seen nothing that I could use to pinpoint my position. The petrol tank had been three-quarters full when I got in. In the two hundred miles that I had covered since, the tank had dropped to just over a quarter full. If I didn't find somewhere to stop, a town or a village, or at the very least a petrol station, I would soon be out in the cold again.

But just as I was pondering how things might pan out, I finally hit lucky. A signpost told me Taishet was only sixty miles away. The first place name I had recognised, and the first one that was actually within touching distance. More than that, though, I knew Taishet has a railway junction that the Trans-Siberian railway passes through.

My ticket back to Omsk.

In the end, I found the station easily. The town was tiny, seemingly only in existence to cater for the railway. The Trans-Siberian covers almost six thousand miles. Taishet, I knew, was roughly halfway across the line. It would take me maybe three days to reach Omsk. I was prepared to lie, beg or steal to get back there. But I hoped the wallet full of cash meant I wouldn't need to. Hell, what was I talking about: I already *had* stolen that.

The station was open when I arrived. A half-dozen other people were milling around. Dawn had come not long before. The darkness had made way for bright sunlight that had quickly cleared away the night-time mist. I could feel that the temperature had improved slightly, but it was still some way below zero. It wasn't until I saw the clock in the terminal building, though, that I actually knew the time.

Ten minutes after nine.

It may sound odd, but knowing that made me feel a little more alive. It's so easy to become disorientated when you don't know what the time is. What day it is. For weeks and months on end. Just having those simple reference points can make a whole lot of difference to your outlook.

Which was the very reason I had been deprived of such things.

I could see on the simple electronic board that the next train was in two hours. I bought a ticket. The teller forced me to splash out on a four-berth cabin. It was the only available ticket in second class and I wasn't going to pass up the chance to be on the train. It used up nearly all of the available cash. But it was lucky that I had any at all. For the first time in a long time, I felt like things might just start going my way again.

I'd left the PP-19 in the Jeep. As much as I wanted to be armed for the journey ahead, there was no way for me to carry such a weapon inconspicuously. I would find something more suitable before long, though knowing I was unarmed made me feel just that little bit more vulnerable.

The station had a sheltered waiting area but I didn't head there, preferring to wait in the far corner of the frozen platform, out of sight. I had to assume people were still after me and it probably wouldn't take a genius to figure that I would head for the railway. That was one of the reasons I had driven the Jeep straight past the station and dumped it discreetly on the outskirts of the town.

It was cold and my body didn't appreciate my passing up the opportunity to stay indoors, but it had to be the safest option. With my ticket in hand, I huddled deep down into my coat and waited.

Chapter 9

When you get down to the basics, there are two reasons for torture. The first is simply to inflict as much pain and suffering on another person as you can. Victims are horribly mutilated, brutalised, raped. Very often they end up dead, quickly. The human body can only withstand such torment for so long. And the tormenters rarely have the ability to pace themselves. The second is for information. The goal isn't to kill the victim. It's to get them to talk.

The people holding me wanted information from me, that was clear. Which meant they weren't about to disembowel me before my eyes and they weren't going to pull the skin from my face. Not yet anyway. That made me feel better. Because as long as I retained my wits, I also retained the position of strength. I had what they wanted.

How long I could keep it up for, I wasn't sure.

I knew what they were doing to me. And that, to some extent, helped. I had experience as both a giver and receiver of torture. But that meant I also knew the effects of what they were doing. And I didn't know how much longer I would be able to hold out.

I thought I had been held for something close to nine days, but I had no way to know for sure. I had no reference point. I didn't know how long I had been out for when I first arrived here, or each time they shot the tranquiliser dart into my thigh to remove me from my cell. And on the very rare occasions that I slept, I had no way of knowing whether I had ten minutes, one hour or ten hours.

When I was awake and alone I could count time easily. In fact counting time was something I could at least do to take my mind off the ordeal. But I hadn't been given that luxury often. And counting endlessly would probably send me insane.

I needed to try to retain some focus.

My brain was beginning to succumb, that was for sure. At times I wasn't sure whether I was awake or asleep. The world before my eyes was like a dream that I wasn't even a part of. They had been deliberately depriving me of sleep. I had been shut in a room with white noise blaring. I'd had my eyelids forced open, spotlights pointing at me so bright that it burned my skin after a few hours. I'd been put into one stress position after another after another.

Much like I was now.

Blindfolded, I was standing in a half-squat, my arms held out in front of me. The white noise was still going. I didn't know how long I had been here. A few hours for sure. But my mind was starting to play tricks on me. Every so often it would take me away somewhere else. Sometimes to a king-sized bed in a five-star hotel. Sometimes to the cell. More than once I'd drifted off to be with Angela, though unlike in my real dreams the time with her was sinister, nightmarish.

Any time that I moved, if my arms fell down, or if my legs gave in, they would whip me. One lash. Enough to break the skin. Most of the time enough to bring my mind back, to pick me up off the ground. A few times it took more than one crack.

And now I was nearing the point where I wasn't sure I could stay in position any longer.

My arms were in spasm and heavy, as though lead weights hung from my wrists. My legs were on fire; my thighs in agony, feeling like thousands of pins were being pushed into them. Every part of my body ached.

I gritted my teeth. Tried to count the seconds away. Tried not to think about the pain. Tried to buy myself a few more minutes.

But the inner fight didn't last long this time. I was too far gone.

I gave in.

I fell to the ground in a heap.

'Get up,' the voice said from behind me, almost immediately.

I now recognised the voice. Not the man from the questioning room. One of the guards. He had a husky, accented voice. I didn't move. *Perhaps I tried to. I'm not sure. Even if I did try, it hadn't worked. I stayed on the ground. Enjoying the feeling of release washing over my body. Not thinking about the consequences of what I was doing.*

'Last chance. Get up, now.'

I closed my eyes. The world seemed to calm, the gritty noise from the speakers fading away from me. The walls around me were changing, the pillow beneath my head warm and soft.

The crack from the whip brought me back around, back to my confines. I cried out. I imagined I could feel the skin on my back splitting as the leather cut across me.

'Get up.'

But I couldn't move. Not this time. I just lay there, quivering, grimacing. Wanting something to take me away.

Another crack.

I shouted out again, kept my eyes closed. Squeezed them shut. Willing, hoping, that I could get away.

Crack.

My whole body flinched. I squeezed my eyes shut even harder.
Crack...Crack.

It was working. My mind was taking me away. I wasn't even sure that I could feel the whip anymore.

Crack. Crack. Crack.

I stayed on the floor. Still aware of the sensation of the whip as it cut into my skin, aware of the pain, but no longer caring. No longer able to care. I could barely hear the sound, even. My world was changing. The sound and the pain were fading fast. Before long, they were completely gone.

Chapter 10

I slept for a solid twelve hours. But it hadn't been good sleep. My body, at least, felt somewhat revitalised, but my head was swimming.

During my waking hours I tried hard not to think about what I had been put through over the last three months. But in sleep I was a victim of my own mind. The physical wounds would heal. Many of them had already; it had been a number of weeks since the physical abuse had stopped. The mental wounds – well, they take much longer. I knew that from experience. The last three months weren't the only time I had been held against my will. But they had made me question myself, my life, everything I knew.

Every time I closed my eyes, my mind replayed my ordeal from the previous months. What they'd done to me. But it wasn't just the torture. It was the things they'd said to me.

I didn't believe them. *Couldn't* believe what they'd told me. And yet the doubts were there. Creeping into my thoughts at every opportunity. I didn't *want* to believe them. But I had to find out for myself. I had to get to Omsk.

And when I was there, safe, I would speak to Mackie. My boss. The man who'd sent me to RTK Technologies.

I got up off the bed and stretched, my aching muscles straining with the movement. I'd rested, now I needed to replenish. I left my cabin and walked through four long carriages to the restaurant car. As I walked in, I spotted the narrow bar area in the far corner, just four stools up against it. Numerous tables made up the remainder of the carriage.

The time was almost midnight. All the diners had long gone, but the place was bustling with drinkers still. Couples sat side by side or opposite each other. Larger groups took up several rows, with empty cans and bottles stashed high around them. The bar would stay open all night, twenty-four hours a day. I wondered how many of these people would last the pace through to the morning.

One of the large groups, a gathering of about ten gruff men, was already drowning out pretty much everything else with raucous laughter and drunken shouting. I reckoned it wouldn't be too long before they either passed out or were thrown out.

Ignoring the stares from the rough-looking comrades, I walked over to the bar and took one of the two empty stools. The other two were already occupied by a couple: the woman maybe mid-twenties with a cute face and fair hair pulled into a bun; the man a few years older, only the first signs of grey in his receding hair and a gentle, clean-shaven face. They both looked up at me as I sat down. I nodded and smiled. They smiled, then turned their attention away from me.

I ordered a beer from the sole barman, a tired-looking man with a creased face, and was given some local muck that I'd never heard of. I didn't care. It was cold – how could it not be in Siberia? – and it tasted better than any drink I'd had in a long time.

The lengthy sleep hadn't eased any of the tension in my mind. Hadn't de-stressed me. Hadn't helped me to forget or to understand. Maybe alcohol would. I emptied two-thirds of the bottle in just one gulp.

As I put the nearly finished bottle down on the bar, I noticed the woman next to me staring. I looked over at her and she quickly glanced down at her drink, a tumbler of something. It wasn't a surprise that she'd been staring. I probably looked out of place here, wearing what appeared to be military fatigues – big black leather boots, grey combat trousers, a grey pullover. Just as well I'd taken off the jacket and overcoat. Plus I had seen the state of myself in the mirror in my cabin. My hair had been crudely cut short, looking like a toddler had hacked away at it with pinking shears. I only had a few days' stubble but nicks and scratches covered my face from the blunt razors that had been used. My once-sparkling green eyes were bloodshot and dull. I was a mess.

I glanced from the woman to her companion. I caught his eye and looked away childishly, just like she had to me. I stared down at my drink, conscious that the man's eyes were still on me.

'Where are you travelling to?' the man said after a few moments. I couldn't detect any particular accent in his Russian.

'Omsk,' I said, looking up at him.

'What a coincidence; so are we!' the man said, excited. 'Where are you from? You're not Russian. I can tell.'

'England.'

'Whoa, long way from home then.'

'You got that right.'

Someone at the table of raucous men behind hurled a comment in my direction. They must have heard what I said, where I was from. I didn't catch it all, but it was something to do with the English and faeces. The taunt was followed by more rapturous laughter from his companions. I didn't bother to turn around to see which one thought himself a comedian. I didn't need a fight, no matter how much better it might have made me feel.

'Ah, don't worry about them,' the woman said. 'They're just a bunch of loggers. Finished their rotations. Off home for a few weeks. Just ignore them.'

'I wasn't worried,' I said, looking into empty space ahead of me.

'They work for weeks on end away from home in the worst conditions,' the man said, as though needing to justify their behaviour. 'This is like a big celebration for them, being on the way home. They'll be drinking all the way to wherever they're going. You can bet on that. But it's good natured. They're harmless.'

I wasn't sure I agreed with him. Put that much alcohol into a group of any ten men and it's fair to say they won't stay harmless for long. But I knew what he meant.

'You're travelling alone?' the man asked.

'What you see is what you get.'

I took another drag of my beer, emptying the bottle. I had enough cash for three more. Not enough for any food if I did that, though. So what? I needed a bit of relief. I signalled to the barman for another.

'Hey, this one's on me,' the man said, pushing a note over to the barman. 'We'll have the same again as well.'

'That's fine. Honestly,' I said in protest. Though as much as I wanted to be left alone, I wasn't going to protest too much at the offer of a free beer.

'Don't be silly,' the man said. 'You can get the next one.'

'Yeah, of course,' I said, knowing fine well that my cash probably wouldn't stretch that far unless his girlfriend was willing to have the cheap-as-shit beer as well.

The bartender passed the drinks over and I clinked bottles with the man before taking another thirsty gulp.

'I saw you getting on at Taishet,' the man said. 'What brought you there?'

'You saw me?' I said, one eyebrow raised, feeling just a little perturbed now by the questioning.

'Yeah – you know, you're easy to notice, I guess,' he said, then looked down at my clothes. 'You don't exactly blend in. No offence meant.'

I guess he was right on that. With the clothes and what I knew was an unkempt appearance, I must have stuck out like a sore thumb.

'The railway,' I said. 'That's what brought me to Taishet. How else can you get around this place?'

'Yeah, that's about all Taishet is used for. Not much else to see at this time of year.'

'Not unless you like snow, ice and darkness.'

'Hey, this is Siberia!' he said, chuckling. 'If you don't like those things, you're in the wrong place.'

I didn't go as far as smiling back at him, but I did feel some of my tension ease slightly. Just having a normal conversation with a normal person. It felt good after what I'd become used to.

'I was here a few months ago,' I said. 'Not a spot of snow in sight. I was walking around in a t-shirt. I even got sunburn! It's hard to imagine that now.'

'Yeah, that's the funny thing,' the man said. 'You get nice weather here in the summer. Not for long, but while it's here it's just so beautiful. And there's so much to do and see.'

'I agree. And yet so few people get to see it,' I said.

'Tourism isn't quite the pull that it could be, that's for sure. You get your backpackers and trekkers but few holidaymakers. But then you have to take a week off just to get here and back!'

I'm not really sure why I was bothering to engage in the conversation. It wasn't like me at all. But it felt nice to be doing it. For all these two cared, I was just a hardened tourist or businessman. Nothing out of the ordinary except for the strange choice of clothing.

'What are you two going to Omsk for?' I asked.

'Work,' the lady replied. 'We're work colleagues,' she added, as if the clarification was an important point.

Just work colleagues. As I digested her comment I pulled my beer bottle up to my lips. I took a more leisurely sip than I had before. No point in accelerating the embarrassment of not being able to return the favour.

'What's your name?' the lady asked.

'It's John,' I lied. Not for any reason other than I was used to not giving my real name.

'John?' the lady said, snickering. 'Ah yes, of course. John Burrows, right? One of your many covers?'

I froze mid-sip and felt my whole body go tense.

How could I have been so stupid – talking away to these two like they just wanted to be my friends? They were such an obvious plant. A couple at the bar, happy to talk to the odd-looking, out-of-place stranger. Even buying him a drink. Three months out of it had certainly taken its toll on me. At a time when I should have been on high alert I'd let my guard slip so easily. Maybe the drunk loggers were part of the ruse too.

My brain began to race, wondering who these two really were. Planning what I would do next.

'Don't worry,' the man said, speaking in English now, in a calm and reassuring manner as if wanting to alleviate the obvious tension in my face. 'We're from the agency,' he said. 'We're here to help. Mackie sent us to find you.'

But hearing those words, *his* name, didn't help at all. If anything, they made it a whole lot worse.

Chapter 11

My eyelids felt heavy – it took a real effort to pull them open. My head was a mess. Every time I closed my eyes my mind went into a relentless spin. I felt drunk. But I knew that I hadn't had any alcohol. It was the lack of sleep. The lack of nourishment. The abuse. All of those things. They were making me delirious.

Unfortunately the delirium wasn't doing anything for the pain. That was as intense as ever.

I was in the interrogation room. The bright light blinded me so that I couldn't see the face of the man behind the desk. But I knew he was there. I knew there would be questions asked. This time was different, though. This time the questions would be accompanied by something else.

Or rather, my lack of response, if that was the path I chose, would be accompanied by something else.

'I'll make this really simple for you,' the man said, his voice now familiar to me even though I'd never seen his face. I had an image of what I thought he looked like in my head: bald, skinny, with rat-like features and piercing, dark eyes. I wondered how close it was to reality.

As always, he spoke to me in English. I'm not sure why. Maybe to unsettle me, provide me with a false sense of security. There was no way I was in England.

Was there?

'I've got some questions for you. And I want you to think really hard about how you respond to them. Now, you know what those are, don't you? The clips attached to your scrotum?'

I bowed my head to look down. I wasn't sure whether my eyes were actually open or closed. I saw myself, my body, but maybe it was just in my mind. Maybe all of this was just in my mind.

I could see my naked body. Could see that my wrists were tied to the chair arms, as they always were. I tried to move my legs. No, they were secured too. The same each time. But the man was right. Something was different this time. Two crocodile clips, attached to my body, the wires from them trailing off somewhere behind me.

'As you've seen before, we normally attach those to the chest,' the man said. 'But you've been particularly obtuse with us so far. You're way behind where you should be by now. So we thought we'd try a different tactic. Perhaps it will help to change your mind about this silent treatment that you're set on.'

I closed my eyes again, the spinning getting out of control as I did so. But I wanted them closed. I wanted to take myself somewhere else. I knew that was the only way.

In the intensive training period I'd had with the JIA many years ago, I'd been through brutal mock interrogations many times. I'd been trained in subversive techniques, ways to cope with and ultimately ignore pain. I was good it. At least I had been at one time. But here I could feel my resolve weakening by the day. I wasn't the same man I used to be, that was for sure. And their tactics and persistence were starting to weigh me down.

'What is your name?' the man said.

I tried to block out the sound, tried to take my mind to a happier place. But really my life had seen so few. When I thought about it, my many years with the JIA seemed to blur into one. And I had never really lived during those years. I'd been a robot. A by-product of the intense training I'd undertaken. The only happiness I was able to grasp was my brief time with Angela. The only time I had felt true attraction to someone else. But I was finding it harder and harder to remember those good times now.

In the end, all I was left with was a swirling darkness and the echo of the man's voice.

'What is your name?' the man said again. Still cool, calm and collected.

I squeezed my eyes shut. So hard that they began to hurt.

But then it came.

My entire body jolted. My eyes sprang open on a wall of white. Pain ripped through me. And it seemed to go on for an age.

When the electric flow finally stopped, my whole body slumped. If it hadn't been for the shackles, I would have collapsed onto the floor.

My body throbbed. Twitched. The feeling of the electricity rushing through me was still there, even though the power had been cut. But worse than that, by far the worst thing and what I knew then would haunt me most, was the smell.

The burning smell.

Flesh.

'Where were you born?' the man said, his voice unchanged. No emotion. No threat of what might come.

I didn't reply. No matter what they did to me, I wouldn't say a word. I couldn't. For one thing, I knew if I talked, I became expendable. But more than that, I couldn't betray Mackie, the JIA. My talking could very likely put Mackie's and others' lives in danger. I had to do everything I could to prevent that.

I just hoped my brain would eventually take me somewhere else. Because I didn't want be there when the next wave came. And I knew that it would. Many times.

Because I had been here before. In this room. With this man. Listening to these questions.

And I knew that he had only just started.

Chapter 12

I didn't move from my stool. Didn't say anything. The man and the woman were both staring at me. Waiting for a response. But hearing Mackie's name had stopped me in my tracks.

The thing about Mackie was that he was more than just my boss. He was my mentor and the closest thing I had to a friend and father. I was a lost teenager when I first met him. He rescued me from the clutches of a wasted life. As an unruly teenager being passed from foster home to foster home, I was throwing my life away getting involved in tit-for-tat quarrels amongst rival drug gangs. I'd been going nowhere fast, and in all likelihood would have ended up in a body bag before I was out of my teens.

But Mackie came from nowhere and took me under his wing. I don't know what he saw in me. Something no-one else had seen. And even though the rebellious me didn't at first trust him, I quickly came to cherish the fact that someone in the world seemed to give a shit about me.

He brought me into the JIA, gave me something to live for. Turned me into the man I became. Made me indestructible – or so I thought. I'd now spent more than half my life working for him. Carrying out his orders. Unquestioningly. And he'd always been there for me when I needed him.

I thought back to a training exercise, many years ago, where I'd almost lost my life in the wilds of the Scottish Highlands. In conditions not too dissimilar to those I was now experiencing in Siberia. In the aftermath, me with a broken leg and suffering severe hypothermia, it had been Mackie who'd sat by my hospital bed each day. In fact he'd been my only visitor for weeks on end.

He was one of only a handful of people I'd ever truly trusted. Trusted with my life. At least, that's how I'd felt three months ago.

I wasn't sure what I thought anymore.

I'd always known what working for the JIA entailed. I worked special ops. Black ops, you might call them. The stakes were high. My job was ruthless and deadly. And it came with big risks both for the agency and for agents like me. If you got caught on foreign soil, hell, even if you got caught on home soil, they may not bail you out. There had to be a get-out clause for them to deny you ever existed, because everything we did was officially unofficial. Below the radar.

I had always known that and had always been happy to play the risks. I didn't have anything – anyone – to go back to, so what difference did it make? But knowing it and living it were different. Deep down, I'd thought Mackie would come for me if I were caught behind enemy lines.

He had done in the past.

For starters, it was in the JIA's best interests. I was their man. A good agent. Not totally irreplaceable, but why would they want to replace me when they could just come get me? And think of everything that I knew. The agency wouldn't want that falling into the hands of the enemy, would they? But more than that, it felt personal. How could Mackie, the man who'd given me this life, whom I trusted with mine, let me rot in some torture chamber?

Doubt had begun to creep in within days of my capture. It's much easier to prepare yourself, to hold out under interrogation, even torture, when you know it's for a finite period. Two weeks, four weeks, three months, whatever. But as each day passed and no-one came for me, the doubt grew. By the end, I wasn't sure what to think, what to feel.

So to have two strangers sit next to me, on a Trans-Siberian train in the middle of a most barren and desolate part of Russia, telling me that Mackie had sent them for me? Well, what was I supposed to think about that?

'What was with the cheap conversation?' I said, in English now. 'And buying me a beer? You going to put that through expenses?'

I could feel more stares from the group of loggers. But they really were the least of my concerns now.

'We just wanted to test your coherence,' the lady said, responding to me in English, all pretences disposed of. It would make sense if they *were* English, but their Russian had sounded spot on to me – not that I was an expert. 'You can understand our wariness. We don't know what's happened to you in the last three months. We wanted to make sure you were still…you.'

'And what was your verdict?' I said.

'That it was okay to approach. I imagine you've been through a lot, but you're not a bumbling mess. That's good. Now, it's time we got you back home.'

Her voice was smooth and confident. Her neat and tidy appearance together with her mannerisms and stuffy accent suggested she was from a well-to-do family, or had at least been well educated and brought up to appear that way. I don't know why but it made me all the more wary of her.

'You think because I made small talk and accepted a free beer that I'm okay? What, are you trained psychiatrists?'

'No. We're agents,' the man said, his voice quieter than it had been before. 'Just like you.'

'You're *nothing* like me,' I hissed.

'I wouldn't be so sure about that.'

What did I care whether they were or not? I wouldn't have felt any differently toward them either way. Well, maybe I'd feel just a little sorry for them – it's hardly a life full of happiness and rewards. But I wasn't going to be their best pal just because we worked for the same employer.

'How did you find me?' I said.

'We shouldn't talk here,' the woman said. 'Why don't we go to your cabin?'

That sounded like a really bad idea.

'I'm fine here. What are your names?'

'Mary and Chris.'

'Covers?'

'Of course,' Mary said.

'Tell me, Mary, how did you find me?'

'We should do this somewhere else,' Chris whispered, leaning over.

'I said I'm fine here. I'm still drinking my beer.'

'We're going to attract too much attention here,' Chris said, looking behind him.

'What? Those guys?' I blurted, deliberately turning around to the group, whose conversation had died down somewhat.

I said, in my best Russian, 'Oh, they're just loggers, coming home from their rotations. I wouldn't worry about them.'

One or two of the group raised an eyebrow at my comment, not sure whether they should be offended by my words or not. But their heads quickly turned back to one another.

Chris shook his head at me, trying not to rise to the bait. 'Look, Mary and I are supposed to be Russians,' he said. 'We're travelling with our Russian IDs. No point in sitting here talking like this, making anyone suspicious.'

'Why not?' I said. 'Who do you think is watching us, Chris? Do you reckon these guys even understand a word we're saying? I'm not moving anywhere until you tell me what the hell is going on.'

'Okay, okay. We'll do this quickly,' Chris said, nervously looking around. 'And quietly. We need to get you out of sight. They'll still be after you.'

'The FSB, you mean? How do I know you're not *them*?'

'What do you want me to do to prove it to you?' Chris said, exasperated.

'Tell me why Mackie left me to rot for three months.'

Chris sighed. 'It's not like that,' he said. 'We've been searching for you for weeks. It was a lot harder to find you than you think. They moved you to a place we didn't even know existed. We found you about four weeks ago, but we couldn't get to you. It was too well protected.'

'*Four weeks ago?*' I fizzed, unable to hide my anger. 'You could have got me out four weeks ago? What the hell have you been doing?'

'It just wasn't possible. Why would we have left you there if there was another way?'

'Indeed. That's exactly what I want to know.'

'It's not like that, Logan.'

'Was it only the two of you?' I asked. 'Was that it? The entire search party?'

'What's that supposed to mean?' Chris said.

'Nothing.'

'We managed to turn one of the guards,' he said. 'Those guys are low-paid slaves. They'll turn like that if you give them enough in return. He was feeding us back info, telling us about the place. About you. But that was as close as we got. We were making good progress but we needed more time.'

'And what did you hear? That I was enjoying every minute of it? That it was like a beach holiday?'

Chris shook his head. 'We found out that you'd escaped,' he said. 'It was a natural conclusion that you'd head for the railway. It's the best route around this place. Most of the time it's the *only* route.'

'Natural conclusion? *I* didn't even know where I was. Not at first. I stumbled across Taishet through nothing more than luck. I could've been lost out there in the wilds to die. What would you two have done then?'

'We managed to catch up with you. Followed you onto the train.'

The whole explanation made me feel uneasy. They were trying to make me trust them. It wasn't working. How had they followed me here? There hadn't been another car in sight of my Jeep the whole way. It didn't make sense. And if these two had found me so easily then where were the Russians?

Mary leaned over and put her hand onto mine. I didn't appreciate the gesture but didn't move my hand away.

'You've made it this far on your own,' she said. 'You're trained for this. But we're here to help now. We want to help you get back home, Carl. But you've got to be sensible about this. We followed you here and found you on the train easily. Don't think for a minute that the Russians won't have done the same. We just don't know how many or who yet.'

No-one had caught my attention on the station platform or on my way through the train. But then clearly I hadn't really been on the ball. I hadn't spotted Chris and Mary getting on at Taishet for starters. And I'd sat down next to them and chatted away in Russian about nonsense without even an inkling that they'd been following me.

'Where's Mackie?' I said.

'London,' Mary said.

'So this is the extent of my welcome party?'

'For now, yes.'

'What time is it?'

'It's just gone half twelve.'

'Two and a half days more to go,' I said, finishing the last of the beer.

'Something like that.'

'Well, plenty of time to catch up then. I'm going back to my cabin. Alone. I need to rest.'

I got up to leave. Mary and Chris didn't try to stop me. They were obviously wary of creating a scene. I walked off toward the other end of the carriage, not bothering to look back to see whether they were following me or not.

On my way out I scrutinised the other customers. But what the hell was I looking for anyway? They wouldn't have 'FSB' tattooed on their foreheads. I didn't spot anyone else who looked like they might be after me. But that was no guarantee.

I headed to my cabin. As I unlocked the door, I did a quick left and right. I saw Chris and Mary just coming into my view off to the left. I shook my head theatrically, so that they would see, then went into my cabin and locked the door behind me.

I stood looking at the door for a few seconds, watching as the outline of two figures passed across it. They didn't stop, just kept on walking all the way past.

I double-checked that the cabin door was locked, then lay down on one of the bottom bunks, fully clothed. In theory the cabin could sleep four. But with just me in it I had barely enough room to get around.

Having said that, compared with what I'd been used to for the previous three months, it felt like the penthouse of the Ritz.

I felt tired again, even though I hadn't long been awake since my last sleep. But I wasn't about to shut my eyes. The twelve hours I'd had earlier, however disturbed they had been, would be enough to keep me going for a while.

The time wasn't far off one in the morning. Two and a half days until we would reach Omsk. About four hours until the train's next stop. I was going to be wide awake until then.

Because that was where I was getting off.

Chapter 13

I was beginning to lose my mind. I could no longer tell what was real and what was a dream. If I'd been further down the line, at least I'd have been so damaged as to no longer realise there was a reality and a non-reality. Unfortunately I still knew there was a difference – I just could no longer tell them apart.

I thought I was lying in my cell, the faint sensation of cold concrete beneath me. My eyes were shut, but I didn't think I was sleeping.

I heard the key turning in the lock of my cell door.

Two men walked into the cell. I saw their feet moving toward me, those same leather boots as always. I didn't look up at their faces. I didn't have the strength.

One of them bent down, stuffed something in my mouth. Food? No, I wasn't that lucky. It was a linen gag. The other man taped it in place. The sack came next, over my head.

They pulled me to my feet, dragged me out of the cell. My legs were too weak to walk. Instead, I let the men pull me along, my feet and ankles scraping across the cold, hard stone floor. They took me down corridors, a left turn, then a right, then two more lefts. The same pattern as always.

We arrived at the room that I had now been to countless times before. Not the questioning room. An altogether more sinister place. They hauled me up onto the table and secured my ankles and wrists so that I was lying flat.

Suddenly the table was tipped at an angle. My head was pointing downwards. I began to struggle against the restraints. Weak, pathetic attempts. I don't know why I bothered, simply an instinctive reaction to what I knew lay ahead.

Rise of the Enemy

The men carried out their well-rehearsed duties in eerie silence. I imagined them moving around me like doctors and nurses over an operating table – each fully aware of the others' roles, gliding with a rhythmic precision.

Moments later, without a single word spoken, water gushed down onto me, covering my face and soaking the hood, which clung to my nose.

I tried to breathe but my brain was stopping me. An automatic reflex to stop me inhaling the water. I writhed and struggled against the ropes, more power in my body now, my brain calculating and responding to the risk that I faced. The ropes cut into my wrists and ankles, quickly rubbing away the scabs from my previous visits, which had yet to fully form. Blood poured down my legs and arms from the wounds that once again opened up.

But no matter how much I struggled, there was no way out.

The water seemed to go on for an age. My lungs were aching for air. I couldn't hold out much longer. I'd been subjected to water torture countless times before. The instinct is for the brain to believe you're drowning, even though you're not. And I'd already rationalised that they were trying to break me, not kill me.

But it was going on too long this time.

They might not have been trying to kill me, but if they didn't stop and give me a chance to breathe, I was toast.

After holding out for as long as I could, I took a quick breath – I had to. As I did so there was nothing to stop the water pouring into me, filling my nostrils. My throat. My lungs.

And that was when I started to panic. Because I didn't know whether I could stop it. I had to keep breathing. But with the water still pouring, I was drowning.

My body writhed violently against the restraints, desperately trying to break free. No use. I couldn't move.

I gulped, swallowing the water that was pooling in my throat, then inhaled again through my nostrils. More water poured in. Nothing to stop it now.

Then, when it seemed like I was on the brink, the water suddenly stopped.

I immediately took heavy breaths. My nostrils hurt from the force as I tried to replenish my lungs with fresh air.

The soaked bag was taken off my face. I opened my eyes, my vision blurry, my eyes darting around frantically, trying to find something to focus on. But all I could see was the glare of the spotlights.

From somewhere out of view, a hand came toward me. The tape was ripped off my face, the gag pulled out of my mouth.

I breathed even harder, spluttering and retching as I tried to clear the water that I imagined was sloshing around inside me.

After five deep breaths, I opened my mouth to speak. But before I got the chance to say a word, the wet sack was placed back over my face.

And the water began to pour again. Heavier and faster than before.

I pursed my lips, as tight as I could. I tried to resist, tried not to breathe, but after a while I couldn't stop it. I opened my mouth. I swallowed the water once more, gagging and gasping to try to stop it filling my lungs.

I didn't know how much longer I could take it. It went on for even longer than before.

I was dying. I was certain of it. I was drowning and I was helpless to stop it.

They were torturing me. I had seen it done before. I had been on the receiving end before. But it had never lasted this long. Surely I was dying?

Why wouldn't they stop?

I tried to moan. To scream. A signal to let them know it was going too far, that I couldn't take it anymore. That I was on the brink. But I could do nothing to stop them. My lungs were almost filled right up. No room left for air. I struggled some more. One last attempt to stay alive. I kicked and bucked, my bound body worming up and down on the board.

And, as if in answer to my desperate, feeble protests, the water finally stopped and the bag was taken away from my face.

I coughed. I spluttered. Water and vomit came out onto me. I didn't care. I filled my lungs with air. Big gasps. It felt so good to be alive.

I wanted to speak out. To tell them that I could take no more. But I didn't have the strength.

I took in more breaths, my heart pumping so fast it felt like it would explode. I felt the rush of blood in my body. The oxygen diffusing into my brain. I was breathing too fast. Hyperventilating. But I couldn't stop. I had to breathe to stay alive. Had to be fully stocked before they started the water again.

I kept on taking heavy breaths. But the water didn't come, and my frantic breathing was too much, too soon.

Unable to stop myself gasping for more and more air, my terrified brain soon left me and I drifted away from that place.

Chapter 14

The next stop was scheduled at five minutes to four. I hadn't been trying to count it out but my head told me the time was somewhere just before that when I felt the train begin to slow. I knew the next stop must be only a few minutes away.

I got up off the bunk and pulled on the grey insignia jacket and the thick woollen overcoat that stretched down almost to my knees. On the man it was made for it would have gone a few inches past them, but I was a good half-foot taller than him. The sleeves stopped two inches short of my wrists but it fitted just fine around the chest and waist – it was made to be worn over bulky clothing.

I waited until the train had slowed right down before opening my cabin door. As I stepped out I did a double-take at the figure standing a few yards off to my left, down the corridor. Mary. Her head was resting against the side of the carriage. She looked wide awake and alert.

'Good morning, Carl,' she said without looking.

'Good?' I said.

'Figure of speech. You going somewhere?'

'Just stretching my legs.'

'Yeah. Same thing,' she said, looking down at my coat. 'Must be cold in your cabin.'

'I'm going for a breath of fresh air while the train stops.'

'That sounds great. I'll go and get Chris.'

She tootled off down the corridor, away from my cabin. Her jovial mood riled me. I was sure she was doing it just to aggravate me.

I trudged off to the opposite end of the carriage. The train had already pulled to a stop when I reached the door. I stepped down onto the platform. It was still dark outside; probably would be for a few hours yet. The temperature was as cold as it had been the night before in the woods. It gave me a chilling reminder of the feeling of isolation I'd felt out there and a fearful shiver coursed through my body.

I looked over to the right. Mary was already on the platform edge, wearing a bright-red puffer jacket, hat and scarf. She was facing the train, her eyes darting along the open carriage doors. She spotted me, waved, then turned back to the door that she was standing by and ushered Chris out. She obviously didn't trust me, had been waiting to make sure I was really getting off before signalling to Chris.

And she was probably right not to trust me. I had no intention of being babysat all the way to Omsk, whoever the hell these two were.

Chris stepped off the train, lugging a large suitcase. Part of their tourist front, no doubt. I ignored them and walked along the icy platform toward the station building. It was a tiny place, somewhere I had never heard of before. The station had just two tracks; one for eastbound trains, one for westbound. The terminal building was conveniently adjacent to the westbound platform where we'd got off. It was an old structure, ornate even, with a high roof, polished floors and wooden benches. The only amenities were a set of toilets and the ticket booth, which had four windows, only one of which was open. At least it was warm. The heating system was rattling away noisily, taking the temperature up toward the low teens. Certainly bearable compared with outside.

I walked over to one of the wooden benches and sat. The train outside began to pull away. I wasn't bothered. There would be another. I was happy to sit and wait in the warmth for a while. I doubted there would be much outside the station anyway. Probably just a town with a few thousand people. Nothing to do or see. Particularly at four in the morning. And that wasn't why I was there anyway. I hadn't got off to acquaint myself with small-town Siberia. I was there to lose the two goons.

Chris and Mary shuffled over to me on the bench.

'Now what are we supposed to do?' Chris snapped. His pissed-off tone made me feel just a little bit better.

'I guess we either walk to Omsk or we wait for the next train,' I said, trying not to sound smug. 'Which do you fancy, Mary?'

Mary smiled at me, but then quickly stopped when she saw Chris scowling.

'What are we doing here, Logan?' Chris said. 'You trying to lose us or something?'

The use of my real name made me wince. I found it strange to hear it from these people whom I didn't know but who were claiming to know me.

'Well, if I am, I've not done too well so far.'

'Maybe you just didn't think we'd be watching you, and you could get off without us realising.'

'Why *were* you watching me?' I said.

'For this very reason. We're supposed to bring you in. We're not to let you out of our sight.'

'Bring me in? Have I done something wrong?'

'I didn't say that,' Chris snapped. 'You know how this works. You've been away for a long time.'

'Thanks for the reminder. I'll come in. But it'll be on my own terms.'

'That's the point,' Chris said. 'It won't be. It'll be on *our* terms. As well as one hell of a debrief, you need to undergo a full psych evaluation for starters. For your own benefit as much as anyone else's. Isn't that obvious?'

'You make it sound like I'm not trusted anymore.'

'That's not it at all,' Mary sighed, the good cop to Chris's bad. 'We just want to get you back home quickly and safely.'

'I've handled three months of being locked up. I think I can handle a train journey just fine.'

'Then why have you just jumped off?' Chris said.

'I jumped off because of something you said to me at the bar.'

Chris looked at me, waiting for me to finish. When I didn't he shook his head, gesturing that he wasn't there with me yet.

'You said it had been easy for you to find me. And that *they* would've been able to find me easily enough as well.'

'So?'

'So I got off. And when I did, I got a good look at every other passenger who got off with me. There weren't that many. Place like this doesn't get many visitors. Most people get *on* at the westbound side, heading for the big cities. They get off on the eastbound on their way home. From our train, just eight people got off. Including you two and me. And the other five didn't look to be much of a threat to me. Plus they've all headed out of here already.'

'Maybe whoever is after you didn't know you were getting off,' Mary interjected.

'Then they're really stupid, aren't they? They track me from my cell all the way to Taishet without me ever suspecting they're there and then fail to spot me getting off the train in the middle of nowhere?'

'Why are you trying to convince yourself that no-one's after you?' Mary said.

'I'm not. I think there are people after me. I'm just trying to figure out *who* they are. And the way I see it, the only people who got off that train who even remotely looked like they were interested in me is you two.'

'So you think we're with the Russians?' Mary said. 'The FSB?'

'I haven't ruled it out. Otherwise where the hell are they? Why *aren't* they after me?'

'What?' Chris said. 'You've lost it, Logan. We're here to *help* you. When are you going to stop pissing around?'

'What's in the suitcase?' I asked, deliberately changing the subject. I didn't want to dwell on who or what these two were. It really didn't make a difference to me. I didn't trust them and I didn't want to do what they told me.

'Clothes,' Chris said. 'We're tourists.'

'You're a pretty similar size to me, Chris.'

I had noticed that as he followed me over to the bench. But he didn't seem to catch on to my point.

'Do you think you could give me a change of clothes?' I said. 'I'm not loving this mock security guard shit.'

Chris sighed. 'Yeah. There's probably some jeans. A jumper. Haven't got any shoes, though, or coats.'

'This coat's fine. The boots too.'

Though in truth I was disappointed I wouldn't be getting out of the boots. My bleeding, blistered feet could have done with some respite, something more cushioned.

'I've got plenty of socks and underwear as well, if you need it,' Chris said, sounding more accommodating.

'That would be great. I haven't got *any* right now,' I said.

Mary couldn't contain her smile at that and I reciprocated in kind. Chris, though, remained deadpan. He pulled the suitcase over, unzipped it and lifted the lid. He began to root around inside.

'Have you got any cash as well?' I said. 'Or maybe a credit card I can use? I've used up virtually everything I had.'

'No, sorry,' Chris said, without looking up from the luggage. 'If you need anything, food or whatever, you just need to shout and we can get it for you.'

'Trying to keep me on a short leash, are you?'

'Well, we wouldn't want you wandering off from us, would we?'

'So you're not denying it?'

'Denying what?'

'That you're looking to keep me on a leash. You're not the first person to have likened me to a dog, you know.'

'I never said anything about dogs. You mentioned leashes.'

Chris pulled up from the suitcase, dumping a pile of clothes in my lap: a pair of faded blue jeans, a black roll-neck jumper, thick socks and jockey shorts. A tiny part of me felt elation just at the sight of these regular, washed clothes. They felt soft to the touch and I could smell the cleanliness. Such a simple luxury that I had been long deprived of.

'I'll go and get changed,' I said, standing up.

'I'll come with you,' Chris replied, getting to his feet to follow.

I turned to face him. He gave me a smug smile. I didn't bother to protest.

'Okay. But no peeking.'

I walked over to the toilets, Chris in tow. The toilet door led into a single cubicle with a toilet and sink. A small window, head height, was above the toilet. Less than two feet wide and about one foot tall. I turned back to Chris.

'You're not coming in here with me,' I said to him. 'You can wait outside, ear against the door or whatever you want to do, but you're not coming in.'

He craned his neck, looking over my shoulder into the toilet, gauging whether or not he would allow me out of his sight.

'Fine,' he said eventually. 'It's not like I want to see your ugly backside.'

'Liar,' I said, winking.

As I closed the door, I noticed him signal over to Mary. She got up from the bench and started to walk quickly over to the double doors that led to the platform. Going around to stand guard by the window, no doubt.

I shook my head in an over-the-top manner and tutted loudly as I pulled the door closed and locked it.

'It's for your own good!' I heard Chris say. I ignored him.

I sat down on the closed toilet seat and began to take the boots off. The pain was excruciating. It felt like my skin was being peeled off as the leather was pulled across it. Both of my feet were a mess. Blisters, cuts, chafes: they were red-raw all over. I tried my best to ignore the pain. On the train I had already washed and showered in my cabin, but I'd had no option but to return to my dirty clothes and inadequate boots. At least now I had clothes that were clean and would fit.

I got to my feet and plugged the sink and filled it to the brim with lukewarm water – as hot as I could get it. Wetting a wad of paper towels, I dabbed at the wounds on my feet. At first it sent shock waves right through me. But a few seconds after, I enjoyed a more pleasant warming sensation as the blood rushed through my chilled feet, encouraged by the temperate air around them. I pulled off the rest of my clothes, then emptied the sink and washed my face under running water before dressing in what Chris had given me. The new clothes felt good. The socks in particular were a godsend.

I stood for a few moments, looking in the mirror, contemplating my next move. I knew that if I wanted to, I could fit through the narrow window. Mary would doubtless be stationed somewhere on the other side. But what was she going to do? Shoot me? I could bulldoze through her in a second. If I wanted to get away from them, this was a good opportunity. They were split up.

One was on one side of the door, the other outside. Tackling one would be far easier than two.

But where would I go? I would just end up running around a small town in the middle of Russia, being chased by two people who may or may not be there to help me. I didn't want to be stuck in a place I didn't know and had nothing for me. I wanted to be in Omsk. But I wasn't going to go there in tow with Chris and Mary. I needed to leave them behind, to lure them away so I could get on the next train.

I unlocked and pulled open the door. As I stepped out I spotted Chris standing about ten yards away, halfway between the toilet and the doors to the platform. He looked surprised as I emerged. Obviously he had thought the window would have been my route of choice.

'What are you doing all the way over there?' I said, mocking him. 'I thought you would have been keeping guard on the door in case I tried to do a runner.'

He didn't answer. But as I walked back over to the wooden bench, I saw why he was there. It was the nearest he could stand to the toilet and still be able to see Mary outside. That way they both would have been able to signal each other and react the second I tried my escape. Well, it looked like I'd saved them some effort. Not that either of them thanked me.

The three of us sat back down on the bench. Other than the grim-looking teller at the ticket booth, we were the only people in the building.

'Next train's in just under two hours,' I said, looking up at the board.

'Yep,' said Chris.

'Well, let me know when it's here. I'm getting some rest.'

And with that I shut my eyes.

But I had no intention of sleeping. I was already busy planning my next move.

Chapter 15

My head came out of the darkness when I heard the voice. It was like a mist clearing in front of me. I was being spoken to. I thought I recognised the voice. But I wasn't sure why she was asking me my name. How did she not remember me?

'*What is your name?' she said again.*

Her voice was warm, comforting. Welcome. It had been months since I'd heard her speak but it was distinctive and clear to me, as though I still talked to her, heard her voice, every day. I still thought about her all the time after all.

'*Why are you asking me that?' I said.*

My head was foggy. My sight blurred. I could feel odd sensations in my body. I knew it was there, but it felt so detached. I wanted to stand up but it was like I didn't know how. I looked around. I couldn't make out the room because of the bright light dazzling my eyes. I wasn't sure why we were in this place. From what I could make out it was dark, dingy. We were the only people here. Such a strange place to come to.

'*Aren't you hungry?' she said.*

'*I'm starving.'*

'*Well, just a few more questions, then you can eat. Okay?'*

'*Okay.'*

'*What is your name?'*

'*It's Carl,' I said.*

Wasn't it obvious? Was this some sort of test? Should I have given one of my covers?

'*Carl what?'*

Did she really not know?

'*Carl Logan,' I said.*

Past the glare of the bright lights I caught a glimpse of her face. She was leaning forward toward me. Smiling. Such a beautiful face. Just seeing her made me feel more at ease.

And yet it was a face that was unfamiliar to me. Not the face that belonged to the voice. It wasn't Angela's.

Nonetheless the woman seemed pleased by my response to the question. Or maybe just pleased that I had *responded.*

Perhaps this was *a test. Yes, it must be. It all seemed so surreal, though. Not like any test I had done before.*

'That's great, Carl. You're doing great. Now just a few more questions, then we can get you that food.'

Well, that sounded good to me. I really was starving.

Chapter 16

We'd been sitting for about twenty minutes in silence. It'd given me enough time to figure out how to get away from Chris and Mary. But I still had plenty of time to kill before I needed to move.

'You got anything to eat?' I said.

'Nope,' Chris said.

'Drink?'

'No.'

'Didn't plan that too well then, did you?'

'Well, we weren't planning on getting off the train so quickly.'

'You didn't have to,' I said.

'Yes, we did,' Chris said, scowling. 'We're following orders. You might think this is funny, but it isn't a game for us.'

'You think it's a game for me? Just remember, I'm the one who's been locked up in a cell for months.'

Neither of them responded to that. We sat in silence again; Chris looking like a sullen child, Mary beginning to look tired and disinterested.

Glancing over at the departures board, I noticed my train was the second on the list. First was an eastbound train, due just fifteen minutes before the next westbound. The westbound was the train I was going to be on. Chris and Mary wouldn't be.

I waited in the warmth of the station lounge until five minutes before the eastbound was due, not wanting to go out in the cold too early. By that point, none of us had spoken a word for what must have been an hour.

'I'm going outside,' I said. 'I fancy getting some fresh air while we wait for the train. Not long before it's due now.'

As I got up I noticed the distrusting look on both Chris's and Mary's faces. But they didn't protest, just shrugged at each other and then got up to follow me. I walked over to the doors and out onto the icy platform, turning left to head toward the far western end.

It was still dark out but daylight would be arriving within an hour or two. The temperature seemed to have dropped at least another couple of degrees in the time that we'd sat in the terminal building. Not surprisingly, no other people were yet waiting on the westbound platform. And only three people stood on the eastbound, eagerly awaiting the imminent arrival.

I hunkered my head down into the collar of my coat, trying to protect it from the cold as best as I could. I pushed my hands hard into my pockets. But I still had no hat, scarf or gloves and there was nothing I could do to stop the chilling air getting to my extremities. I tried my best to ignore the cold and the shivers that were running through me and carried on walking toward the far end of the long platform.

'Logan, what the hell are you up to?' Mary said, keeping pace two or three yards behind me. 'It's freezing out here.'

I ignored her and carried on walking. When I reached the end of the platform, I stopped, turning to face the lines.

'You're up to something,' Mary said, catching up with me. 'I can tell. Just don't do anything stupid. We've been told to use force if necessary. Lethal force. You know what I mean, right?'

I did. It would have been naive to think they weren't armed, whoever they were working for. But Mary's words still shook me. They weren't meant as friendly advice but as a clear threat. If I did anything stupid, anything to compromise their position, they had been ordered to take me down.

And if they really were from the JIA, that was a patent sign that I wasn't trusted. I was no longer seen as one of them. I was a hostile. My mind had been toying with the idea for some time. But her words had made it seem all the more real.

So much for wanting to bring me in to make sure I was all right. To them, this was just damage limitation.

Probably the only reason they were trying to bring me in quietly rather than just getting rid of me out in the middle of Siberia was because they didn't want to create an unnecessary scene. Plus they didn't want to finish me off before first finding out whether I was now an asset for another agency.

I turned my head and looked at Mary. She had her hat and scarf back on now. Her hands, like mine, were pushed into the pockets of her coat. Chris, who had caught up and was standing next to her, took the same stance. I wondered whether they already had their guns in hand, inside their pockets, in anticipation of what I might do.

'Don't do anything you might regret, Carl,' Mary said.

But I didn't say another word to either of them. I turned my head away and looked up the track. And waited.

After a couple of minutes, the eastbound train came into view in the distance, its bright twin headlights piercing the hazy darkness. Next came the rumbling sound from the guzzling diesel engine and the whine from the friction of the wheels rubbing on the iced-up tracks.

I focused on the lights and the noise, both getting more intense as the slowing train came closer. The brakes were pushed down harder and a screeching sound filled the air. The vibrations resonated in the pit of my stomach as the train slowed for its final approach. It was just a couple of hundred yards away.

I took a step closer to the platform edge, the tips of my boots hanging over.

'Logan,' Chris said, 'whatever you're about to do, don't. Just come back to Omsk with us. That's all we want. Don't make us do something that we'll all regret.'

I ignored him. I got no comfort from his words. Their position had been made clear. I took one more look at the approaching train, just a little over fifty yards away.

And then I jumped down onto the track.

Chapter 17

'Shit!' Chris shouted, the only thing I heard from either of them above the roar of the oncoming train filling my ears.

I jumped the set of westbound tracks, then into the middle of the eastbound, feeling the rush of chilled air as the train ploughed its way toward me. I thrust my hands out to the platform edge, grasped the icy surface, tried to pull myself over.

But my plan hadn't taken account of the difficulty of cold, bare hands clinging on to slippery, frozen concrete.

My grip gave way and I fell back down, the base of my back smacking off one of the raised tracks.

I thought I heard gasps and shouts from the small cluster of bystanders but I couldn't be sure above the din of the train. Its bulk filled my entire peripheral vision. I didn't dare look just how close it was. I knew I must only be seconds away from being crushed to death under its massive weight.

In one last desperate attempt, I jumped up. I put both my forearms over the platform edge, placing my weight right across them from my wrists to my elbows. It gave me more grip than my numb fingers had been able to muster.

And it worked.

I hauled my body up and over the edge. Almost simultaneously, the train swept past as I lay on the ground, panting heavy breaths. More from relief than anything else.

I didn't wait for long, though. I quickly got to my feet. The three passengers on the platform stared at me, aghast. I gave a meek smile and turned my attention to the other side of the station. Looking through the windows of the train as it made its way through, I could see the blinking outline of Chris and Mary, still standing on the westbound platform, confusion fixed on their faces.

They had a simple choice now. To get to this side, they could either take the overhead bridge, which was toward the middle of the platform, or wait for the train to fully move into the station before crossing behind it and over the tracks the same as I had. Whichever route they chose, I probably had at least a minute on them.

I didn't waste any more time: I turned on my heels and ran.

The eastbound side had no station building. Just the overhead walkway for passengers to get onto and off the platform. At the back of the platform was a wire fence, closing the station off from the unknown darkness beyond it. That was where I headed.

The fence was somewhere between seven and eight feet high. I cleared it without too much effort, then trudged across the hard ground that lay beyond on which lay a covering of soft, fresh snow, maybe an inch or two thick. Within a few yards I was into a clump of trees.

The memories of being out in the desolate forest came rushing back to me. I shook my head to clear the depressing thoughts from my mind. Thankfully this wasn't a seemingly never-ending expanse like before. I knew the station was just behind. And as I moved forward, the trees soon opened out again into a dark clearing.

In the dim moonlight, it looked to be a small industrial plant of some sort with numerous low-rise buildings of various shapes and sizes. I headed toward the second nearest, which looked like an outbuilding, maybe holding a generator or something similar. I stopped alongside it.

Only then did I turn to look behind me for the first time. I had no doubt that Chris and Mary would follow me here. The only question was how they would approach. I had to assume they would draw their weapons and I was now a shooting target. I could do nothing about that. But would they stick together or move apart? Would one or more of them use a torch to try to find me? Would they approach slowly with stealth or opt for speed and surprise?

I couldn't yet see or hear anything of them, which suggested some of those possibilities more than others.

But Mary's voice soon broke the silence. Her pitch was raised. She was shouting, but her voice was still distant.

'Please, Logan. Don't do this. You're only making this harder for yourself. Someone could end up getting hurt.'

Her voice was coming from the direction that I had come from. But I couldn't see any sign of her at all. No torch beam. No moving outline.

'That was some crazy shit you pulled back there,' she said. 'I wasn't sure you were going to make it. You only had a second to spare, you know.'

I gazed into the darkness, my eyes squinting as though that would make my night-time vision better. But other than her voice, I had nothing to pinpoint her position.

'I was relieved that you did make it,' she continued. 'But the longer this goes on, you dodging us and running like this, the greater the chance that one of us is going to end up getting hurt.'

Her choice of words was interesting – *us*, rather than them and me. Trying to make me feel like we were still part of the same team. Like I was just having a momentary lapse that would soon pass. But I wouldn't trust that. She'd already made it quite clear that they had orders to take me down if necessary. I wasn't going to give them that chance.

The other, more interesting, thing, though, was that she had spoken at all. Making it obvious where she was positioned, even though I couldn't see her yet. And Chris had been silent. Which I knew could only mean one thing: they had split up.

Chris would be moving around, trying to outflank me. Even if they didn't know exactly where I was, it would still have been a good a tactic, considering their options. They probably assumed I would stop and wait behind one of the buildings. And they were right. I wasn't about to go on the run in a cut-off town in the middle of Siberia, in freezing temperatures, when the station was where I wanted to be.

That was why I saw no point in staying where I was. Because they would corner me eventually. I moved away from the building, walking quickly off at a right angle to where I had approached from.

Depending on which way Chris had gone, I could be heading directly toward him. That didn't matter. In fact, that was the plan.

They thought they had the upper hand. I would take it from them. I would pursue *them*.

If I didn't find Chris as I headed in this direction, well, at least it would give away where he actually was. If that was the case, I would turn around and charge straight for Mary, going back to take him out after.

Either way, I planned to get to them before they got to me.

I had been moving for about a minute when, as if from nowhere, the figure of Chris came into view from around the trunk of a tree, illuminated by the dim moonlight. He was holding his gun outstretched in both hands, pointing off to my right. He was almost within touching distance of me and yet I'd seen nor heard nothing of him until that point. He turned his head toward me, his eyes glinting in the moonlight.

The sudden appearance of him to me and vice versa caught us both by surprise. But I'd had a second longer to process it. And I wasn't going to give him the chance to dwell.

I lunged forward, tackling him just above the waist, hearing the burst of air from his lungs as I knocked the wind out of him. We fell back in a tangle and I heard a loud cracking sound as his head bounced off the tree trunk behind him. We were both on the ground, me straddling him. I was alert and ready for action, fists clenched.

But there was no need.

I soon realised Chris was already out cold. The blow to the head had been enough to subdue him. Nothing more than an accident. Unlucky on his part, lucky on mine.

I felt around the back of his head with my left hand. His hair was wet and sticky. Even in the dark I could see what it was. Blood. But he was still breathing. He probably wouldn't have anything more severe than a cut and a concussion. A relief. I certainly hadn't intended to kill him.

I rummaged in his pockets, looking for a wallet or some loose cash, and found both. I didn't feel good about robbing him, but how else was I going to survive?

I didn't sit in contemplation any longer. I got off Chris and searched the ground around him for his gun. I quickly found it, a pristine-looking Glock, and was back on my feet again, heading in the direction where Mary should be. That was presuming that she hadn't changed course or doubled back.

She hadn't. And it didn't take me long to find her.

She was moving, just as I hoped. I approached her from behind. Creeping as quietly as I could, I got to within a yard of her, then I pulled the Glock up, aiming it at the back of her head.

I was about to announce my presence when, without warning, she whipped around.

Her pose mimicked mine with her gun held out in her right hand, the barrel just inches from my face. Professional moves, for sure. Surprisingly so, in fact. Even though she and Chris claimed to be from the JIA I'd noticed a softness about Mary that had made me assume she might not be up to the challenge. But her actions were certainly slick.

Her face, though, told a different story. She looked scared.

'Stalemate,' I said.

'What the hell are you doing?' she said.

She was shivering violently. Probably a combination of the cold and fear.

'I'm leaving,' I said.

'Not without me, you're not,' she said, her voice still strong and assured in contrast to the evident unease in her face and body.

'I'm going alone. Like you said, the longer this goes on, the more chance there is that one of us gets hurt. I don't want to hurt you, Mary. Not unless I have to.'

'That's why you were sneaking up on me, pointing a gun at my head?'

'If I'd wanted to shoot, do you not think I would have done?'

She didn't answer that. But I could tell from the look of panic on her face that it had finally dawned on her that I was holding her partner's gun.

'Where's Chris?' she said.

'Back there,' I said, indicating over my shoulder 'You should go check on him. He won't last long out here.'

'Jesus, Logan! What have you done to him?'

She was angry. But also quite clearly scared of where this was going.

'Don't forget, you two are the ones who came out here hunting. I'm just protecting myself.'

She shook her head, as though I'd missed the point.

'So are we, Logan. These guns are to protect us from you! And don't you think if we wanted to kill you, we'd have done so by now?'

'No. I don't. I don't know what's going on. But I know that you're not here for my benefit. Just toss your gun, then we'll both step away.'

'Why don't you toss yours?'

'Because you're the one who's got orders to kill. I'm only holding this gun in your face because you won't let me leave. You toss your gun and I'll be gone.'

'They're not orders to kill,' she said. 'Our orders are to bring you in, whatever it takes.'

'Exactly. Bring me in. Even if it's in a body bag, right?'

'Why don't we both toss the guns?'

'You don't trust me?' I said.

'How could I? Look at what you're doing.'

'You really should go check on Chris. The stakes are simple. You toss your gun, probably all three of us live. You don't…well, all three of us might end up dead right here.'

The twitch in her face told me that this registered with her. Orders were orders, but she knew that I could pull the trigger just as quickly as she could. We would both be down and out for good. Chris would probably die of exposure if he didn't come around soon. The collateral damage of the lives of both her and Chris were not worth it. Better to regroup and come back after me later.

'Fine,' she said.

'Go on then. Toss it. Off to the left.'

She did so, hurling the weapon. I heard it smack into the ground well away from where we were standing. That was good enough for me. Even if she wanted to go and find it and fire after me, it gave me plenty of breathing space.

I lowered my weapon, but still kept myself ready for a wave of attack. I slowly began to step away, one small step at a time. She did the same, neither of us breaking eye contact until we both faded away into the darkness.

We were probably still only twenty yards away from each other but I fancied my chances from there. As soon as I could no longer make out her shape, I turned around and ran, heading back to the station platform.

By my reckoning, I only had two minutes until my train arrived.

Chapter 18

The food was good. The best I'd had in weeks. A true gastronomic delight. Fresh bread and some sort of meat and vegetable stew. I had no knife or fork, just used the bread to scoop up the bits and to soak up the gravy. I didn't care. I just wanted, no, I needed, to eat.

But after five big mouthfuls, I could take no more. My belly felt bloated. It gurgled away, unused to the sustenance that was sloshing around inside it. I forced one more piece of meat down, but it seemed to stick in my throat. I knew that if I tried to eat any more, it would only end up back in the bowl in front of me.

I felt disappointed. Defeated. But I knew that even the small amount I'd managed to eat would do me the world of good.

If I could keep it down, that was.

'You're done already?' said a voice – a female voice – with a condescending laugh.

A strange woman. I hadn't even noticed her come into the room. I'd been too engrossed in gorging my way through the food that had been put in front of me. But her voice – it felt familiar. And like the unseen man who had so often been in here with me, her English was perfect.

'Depends how long we're going to be here for,' I said. 'Give me a few minutes, I'm sure I can finish it off.'

I'm not sure whether I'd intended my words to come out as confrontational or playful. She must have thought the latter, because she laughed again as she sat opposite me, behind the desk. I was disappointed with myself for that. For speaking at all. Ever since I'd come here I'd tried not to communicate with them, no matter what they'd thrown at me. Now here I was on the brink of flirting. Maybe it was a direct response to their gesture of giving me some real food.

Maybe it was because of the person who'd asked me the question.

There was no bright light in the room this time. I saw that the room was square with dirty white-painted walls and a smooth concrete floor. It had no furniture other than the desk and two chairs, and only one other occupant aside from me and the two ubiquitous guards at my back: the woman.

She was dressed for the office in a tight black skirt and white shirt. She had dark, silken hair held in a tight bun. Her cheekbones were high, her eyes penetrating, her lips full and rounded. She looked Eastern European – Russian? She looked beautiful.

Yet behind her sparkling eyes I saw a creepy darkness that was so out of place with the rest of her dazzling features. And despite my initial openness, that made me mistrust her all the more. Because I knew at first sight that this woman was a snake. Her looks were her deadly weapon, no doubt about it. I wondered how many men she'd suckered in her short life. She couldn't have been older than thirty.

'I know you've had a rough time in here,' she said. 'But it doesn't have to be like that.'

This time I stayed silent. I didn't want to play her game.

'You can have food like that all the time,' she said. 'If you want.'

I didn't say anything to that either. Whatever reason they had to now be hospitable wasn't for my benefit, however they tried to play it.

'You don't want to go back to how it was before. Do you?'

I pushed the half-eaten bowl of food across the desk, toward her, away from me. A signal to her that I was done here. That I didn't want their hospitality.

'You know that they're not coming for you,' she said, sterner this time. 'Mackie and the others. They've left you here to die, Carl.'

Her words slapped me in the face. How did she know my name? I'd never told them my name. How did they know about Mackie? No matter what they'd done to me, I hadn't given them anything.

But it wasn't just the names she'd used. It was what she'd said. That no-one was coming for me. Because doubt had been creeping into my head more and more. I was having a hard time convincing myself otherwise. Hearing this woman say it made it all the more real.

Why hadn't *they come for me?*

The only other time I had been captured on a mission had been my fateful assignment to bring down Youssef Selim. On that occasion I'd been gone a mere three days before I was rescued.

'Come on, Carl. You like this food, don't you? Don't you want to be eating food like that every day?'

I did, but at what price would it come?

'Come on, don't go shy on me now. We can go back to the way it was before if you like? The interrogation room. The questions. The water. We've talked about this before, remember?'

'What do you mean, remember?*' I spat. 'This is the first time I've seen you.'*

She laughed again. That same condescending laugh, mocking even.

'Oh, Carl, think about it. Put the pieces back together.'

She went silent but her wicked smile remained as she stared at me intently. I got a sickly feeling in the pit of my stomach. From the food or her words, I wasn't sure. It was surreal. My head was a confused mess and yet it was like I knew what was coming. But I wanted to be wrong so badly that I tried to push the thoughts to the very back of my mind, tried to ignore the inevitable.

But I couldn't. I had to know.

'What do you mean?' I said.

'How long have you been here?'

I racked my brain.

'I don't know,' I said, shaking my head.

'Well, how long do you think? Two weeks, three, four?'

I had no way of knowing the answer. But that wasn't the point. I could see where she was taking this conversation. And more than anything, I felt scared.

'Something like that,' I lied.

'It's been nearly nine,' she chuckled. 'You've been here two months now.'

She let it hang there. I knew what she was doing. Disorientating me. Toying with me. Trying to create doubt in my mind. I had no way of knowing how long I'd been there. But nine weeks? Could it really have been that long? And if it had, what the hell had happened to me in that time? I seemed to have so many blanks in my memory.

Nine weeks?

'This isn't the first time we've met,' she said. 'It's not the first time we've had this exact conversation even. Do you really not remember?'

I searched my brain for a memory that made sense, but it was all a scramble. Thoughts were coming and going without taking hold.

'No. This is the first time we've met,' I said again, wanting to believe it, but no longer sure that it was the truth. I certainly couldn't grasp a memory of ever seeing this woman before and yet, in a way, her voice and her pretty face seemed so familiar to me.

'What's the last thing you remember?' she said.

My brain clunked and whirred, cogs turning, trying to figure it out. I felt so useless. What was happening to me? What had they done to me?

'The water,' I said.

It was the last thing I could get to. The water being poured onto my face. The knowledge that I was going to drown. It seemed so distant to me now and yet it was the last thing that was there in my head. I couldn't even remember how I had come to be sitting in front of this woman now.

'The water,' I repeated. 'That's the last thing I remember.'

'They really messed you up, didn't they?'

They? Like she wasn't part of it!

'Carl, this isn't the first time we've met. You've been in here with me every day for almost a month. I've been trying to help you get your head straight. You've been making great progress. The interrogation, the waterboarding, was weeks ago. All of that was weeks ago. Check your wrists if you don't believe me.'

I looked down. The marks were unmistakeable. Each wrist had several rings of lumpy, whitened flesh, blending into one another. After the waterboarding these would have been open wounds. I could still remember the feeling of the blood trickling over my hands, over my feet, as I writhed against the restraints, trying desperately to free myself.

But these wounds had healed. These scars were several weeks old.

'What happened to me?' I asked, trying to hold it together.

'Nothing happened. You've been in here with me. Talking. Recovering. They really went to town on you. We thought we'd lost you at one point.'

I had tried to hold out. I had held out over countless interrogation sessions, countless bouts of torture, all of the disorientation and other mind-screwing techniques. But it looked like it had all been in vain. I squeezed my eyes shut, trying not to think about what had been done to me. But more importantly trying not to think about what could have happened during the lost period.

The period of time, weeks, that my mind was deliberately omitting from my memories.

Because it looked like I had been broken. And I didn't want to think about what that meant.

'But you've been doing great in here, Carl, since all that nastiness stopped. You're well on the road to full recovery, I'd say.'

'Who are you?' I said. Though in my head, I really meant, What?

'Carl,' she said, leaning forward, her pretty face contorting into a look of menace, 'I'm all that you've got.'

Chapter 19

I slept for a good part of the journey to Omsk, only coming out of my cabin when I needed food. Chris's wallet had provided me with enough cash to last me for a number of days.

The train arrived in Omsk at just past ten in the morning. The sun was out, the sky was deep-blue and the cold had lifted to somewhere not too far below zero. Compared with what it had been two days ago, it felt positively balmy.

I remained alert as I left the train and the station, looking out for any sign of people who might be waiting for me – whether other passengers on the train or the people milling about off it. I'd been sure there would be a welcome party for me. Chris and Mary had known where I was going. But I saw nothing. At least no-one who looked like they were there for me. It made me feel uneasy, even though it certainly made my life simpler.

I still had a lingering doubt in my mind about whom Chris and Mary were working for. Their actions told me that in all likelihood they had been sent by my boss at the JIA, Mackie. If the two of them had been with the Russians then they surely would have just taken me back to the same hellhole I'd run from? But if that were true, that they were from the JIA, then just where *were* the Russians? Why weren't they after me?

I headed off on foot toward the safe house I'd been using some months ago when the plan to infiltrate RTK had first begun. It was an apartment in a better-off part of town that Dmitri had rented under an assumed name.

I'm not quite sure why I went there, other than it was somewhere familiar and a place that might hold some answers. Answers as to what had happened to me. And to Dmitri. I hadn't seen him since we'd first been taken. I'd been told by the Russians that he died at RTK, but I had no way of knowing whether or not that was the truth. It seemed plausible. He'd certainly been in a bad way back at RTK, far worse than me.

I'd prepared myself that going to the apartment might simply be walking into a trap. But I wasn't about to run away from my problems. I was ready to face them head on. Now I was back on familiar territory, away from my prison cell, I felt like the home advantage was all mine once more.

Omsk wasn't my home, but it felt good to be back in a place that was familiar. It felt like real civilisation rather than the barren tundra I had travelled through over the last few days. And that fortified bunker that had been my prison for the last three months.

During my confinement I'd always been taken through the same short and narrow corridors to the same worn rooms. I'd only come to appreciate the full expanse of the complex during my escape. It was a simple concrete monstrosity, probably one of the original gulags from the Stalin era. From what I had seen it certainly wasn't being used in the same way that it would have been in that bygone time, and yet its repressive past seemed to ooze from its walls still. It was a place that I knew would haunt me for the rest of my life.

And I would never be taken back there alive.

It took me just over an hour at a brisk pace to get to the apartment. It would have been forty minutes but for the fact that I stopped off at a shoe shop on the way to buy some trainers. Taking off the too-small boots and swapping them for the soft fabric trainers was heavenly. Together with the thick socks from Chris, walking felt like floating on air.

The apartment was on the fourth floor of a six-storey block that lay on the corner of a busy crossroads. A handsome pre-war building with high sash windows and wrought-iron balconies, it wouldn't have looked out of place in any of the hippest and trendiest European cities. A nice building in a nice area that was well kept.

Over the years of travelling to far-flung places I'd come to recognise that many often-overlooked mid-sized cities have rich histories and architecture, often mimicking their nearby, more illustrious neighbours. Omsk was no different.

The apartment building was nice, for sure, but it wasn't top-end luxury. It didn't have a concierge or security, for instance. That would have been counterintuitive for a supposedly safe location where a certain level of discretion was required. It meant that I was able to get into the building without any issues.

Getting into the apartment itself, however, would be a different story. I had no key. The door had two locks: a standard latch and a five-lever mortice deadlock. I couldn't pick them both. I had neither the tools nor the skills.

The latch would be easy enough to kick through. The lever mortice lock, not so. I knew from past experience that it simply wasn't possible to break one of those with only the force of your foot or shoulder. You had to rely on the frame or door itself failing.

Your best bet was usually to kick against the hinges side of the door. People generally pay much less attention to the quality and strength of their hinges than they do their locks. Kick at the hinges side and often the door will snap straight off the frame, with the locks still intact. A small part of me wished that I was still wearing the thick steel-toed boots. They would have come in handy for breaking down a door. But doing so would also create noise. And draw attention. And I didn't want to do that.

In the end it wasn't even an issue. Because it turned out the door was unlocked.

I'd turned the handle while I stood contemplating what to do. I'd only done it because it would have been careless to assume the door was locked and not even try. And to my surprise, it swung open right before my eyes.

As soon as I stepped into the apartment, though, the initial pleasure at my good fortune dissipated when I saw that the place had been ransacked. It had only been partially furnished back when Dmitri and I had been staying here, just basic, necessary furniture, no real fittings or personal touches. But what there was had been completely trashed, turned upside down. Sofa cushions were torn to shreds, their contents strewn across the lounge area. Splinters of wood from the smashed bookcase, dining table and chairs lay everywhere. Holes had been punched through walls, the plaster ripped off in great chunks. In the kitchen, the cabinets had been pulled from the walls, the appliances broken into pieces. Crockery had been smashed and scattered across the floor.

Whoever had been there had gone to town. And it was a short list of candidates. Either one or the other. My own agency knew of this place; they had been paying for it. And the Russians, of course, would have been looking for this place since the day I'd been captured. But whichever party had done the trashing, the main question was: what had they been looking for? And had they found it?

Dmitri and I had been staying at the apartment for a number of months while we put together our plan. We had always been so careful about what evidence of our identities and our work we kept there. That wasn't a procedure just on this mission but on every single one.

Something niggled about the mess and destruction that I looked at. If whoever had done this was after information of some sort – and my own agency would have known we kept nothing there – why had they gone to so much trouble to destroy everything? Turning a place upside down is one thing, but this felt more deliberate. The way I saw it, either this had been done simply to make a point, or because someone was trying to blinker me. Pull the wool over my eyes, send me in the wrong direction.

But about what?

And that was when I noticed something odd. In the kitchen, tins, packets and jars had been burst, broken or torn open and the contents spread across the room. A creamy puddle oozed from a spilled carton of milk. The remnants of meals clung to large shards of broken plates. But I noticed no stench, no sign of mould or rot. The food looked relatively fresh. Which meant that the apartment had been trashed recently. Probably within the last couple of days. Someone had been living here.

I knew then that I had to leave. There was nothing there for me now. No Dmitri, no answers to the questions that remained about what had happened to him, to me, and why.

I had half-wondered whether Mackie might have been sitting in the apartment, waiting for me like a parent waits for a son or daughter to return home from war. In fact, in a way, I felt great disappointment when that had turned out not to be the case. In the end, all the apartment held was more questions. I walked out of the door, not even bothering to close it behind me, then headed down the winding staircase and back out into the cold street.

I walked across to the other side of the road and around the corner to a payphone. It gave me a good view of the apartment block but was also well placed for escape if needed, with a number of side streets nearby. I hadn't yet seen anyone lurking. In fact, I was becoming more and more suspicious and uneasy that I was seemingly alone.

Regardless, it was time to check in. I'd been on the loose, away from the place that had been my prison, for something like three days. Maybe Mackie would have the answers that I was looking for.

Mackie, the father-figure boss who'd left me to torture and abuse.

I dialled the number for Mackie. I didn't need any change for this call. I could call from anywhere in the world and get through. Every field agent like me had a telephone number that was effectively an ID. When I called this number, it would route to Mackie, because he was my commander. The caller ID that came up on his phone would tell him I was calling. It didn't matter what phone I was using, or where I was in the world, as long as I dialled that number.

Mackie answered on the third ring. There was an awkward silence, neither of us willing to break it at first. But then Mackie spoke.

'Logan? Is that you?'

His voice sent a rush of memories through my head. Most of them good. But the memories were tinged with betrayal. I wasn't sure that feeling would ever go away.

'It's me,' I said.

'Thank God you're all right! You are all right, aren't you?'

'What do you think?'

Another silence. I don't know what I expected him to say. 'Sorry' would have been nice, but I knew that it would never come.

'Where are you?' he said.

I didn't answer. If I was on the line long enough, he'd be able to trace the call anyway. And I wasn't sure that I wanted to make it so easy for him. I didn't know whether or not I could trust him anymore. Whether I could trust anyone.

'Logan,' Mackie said, breaking the silence once again, 'you need to come in. Where are you?'

'That's not important. I need to know, Mackie. I need to know: why?'

My question was vague. Why what? It could have meant anything. But it made sense to me. And I knew that it would to Mackie.

Why was I left to torture for months? Why did nobody come for me? Why did *Mackie* not come for me?

'You need to come in,' Mackie said again. 'It's not safe for you out there.'

'Oh, so now you're concerned with my personal safety? Isn't it a bit late for that?'

Mackie sighed. 'We can get you looked at. We can help you.'

'Looked at? Why's that, Mackie?' I said through gritted teeth.

As ever, his choice of words had been telling. This wasn't about me or my wellbeing. This was all about them.

'Why? We need to make sure you're okay. Because you've been gone for so long. We need to know what's happened to you.'

Mackie didn't need to be any more explicit than that. I knew what he meant. They thought I'd been turned. Or at the least that I'd talked.

'And whose fault is that, Mackie? I was there, alone, for three months! Whose fault is that?'

'This isn't the time, Logan. What we've seen so far suggests you're not exactly all there. You know, you didn't have to leave poor Chris for dead.'

So Chris and Mary *were* working for Mackie. At least that was one answer I had. Too bad about Chris. It didn't make me feel sorry for having split his head open, though. He and Mary had brought it on themselves with their underhand tactics.

'Nice of you to send two goons after me.'

'They're not goons. They're agents, just like you.'

'They're *nothing* like me,' I snapped. 'And orders to kill?'

'Come on, man, don't exaggerate. Their orders were to bring you in any way they could. Why would I want them to kill you?'

'Why indeed?'

'I'll say it again: this isn't the time. Look, where are you? We'll send someone to get you right away. Wherever you are, it can't be safe.'

'Tell me about it. Held captive for three months and I get out only to find my own people are after me with orders to kill me.'

'Logan, goddammit!' Mackie blasted. I pulled the receiver away from my ear, expecting a torrent of abuse, but Mackie held it in. 'Where are you?'

'I'm in Omsk.'

Another pause. Even down the phone I could feel Mackie winding himself down from his near explosion.

'You're in Omsk now?'

'Yeah. I'm at the apartment.'

I figured I didn't have anything to lose in telling him. Where else was I going to go now? Who else could I turn to?

'The safe house?' Mackie's voice had gone quieter, like he was being distracted.

'Yes, I'm at the safe house. The trashed safe house, I should say.'

'Trashed? What? Look, you're at the safe house now?'

'Yes, I'm at the bloody safe house. Why's that so hard to understand?'

'Just hold on a minute.'

I heard a clunk as Mackie put the phone down, then whispered voices, too far away from the receiver for me to make out any words. Mackie was gone for a good half-minute and I started to get impatient. I was about to shout down the phone to him to ask what was going on.

But then…

A deafening explosion came from behind me.

The ground shook and swayed. A shockwave of air smacked into the side of me, almost taking me clean off my feet. Car alarms began to blare. People began to scream. Dust and grit clouded the air all around me, filling my mouth and eyes.

I was shaken. My ears were ringing with a high-pitched whine. My eyes were blurred from the grit. My head was dazed and confused.

I stood, shocked, wiping at my eyes to try to remove the grit while people around me screamed and moaned and ran or wandered aimlessly. The cloud of dust began to disperse, leaving behind a dirty haze. Still rubbing at my eyes I turned back to the apartment.

Half of the building was engulfed in a fireball; thick plumes of black smoke towered into the blue sky. Shards of wood and glass were hanging from the stricken structure. Some debris was still falling to the ground where a crumpled heap of bricks and what used to be the kitchen of the safe house lay.

'Logan…Logan? Are you there?'

I'd forgotten that I still had the phone pressed to my ear. Mackie's voice shook me back to reality. I quickly refocused.

'I'm here,' I said.

A pause. Then: 'What the hell's going on?'

'The apartment just exploded.'

'What?'

'It just fucking exploded!'

'The apartment? Are you okay?'

'I think so. I mean…'

'I thought you said you were in the apartment?'

'No, I'm standing outside it. Wait a second…you thought I was *in* the apartment?' I said, my voice raised, not just with growing anger but also so that I could be heard over the din around me.

'You said you were in the apartment.'

'What the hell is happening, Mackie? Why did the apartment just blow up seconds after I tell you that's where I am!'

'Logan, just cool it, okay? It's pretty clear what's happening here. There are obviously people still after you. You're lucky you weren't just killed. You're not safe there. I tried to tell you that already.'

'Lucky? I think I've been anything but lucky.'

'Enough! Chris and Mary are on their way. They'll be with you within a few hours. Wait with them, Logan. They can help you. I'm coming as well. You wait there until I come for you.'

'You? Where are you?'

'I'm in Moscow already. I'll get to you as soon as I can.'

'What are you doing in Moscow?'

'I was on my way to Omsk to meet with you. I heard that was where you were heading.'

I was surprised he was so close. What was he doing in Moscow?

'Where and when?' I said.

'I'll let you know. Just wait for Chris and Mary. Meet them at the station. But keep your head down. You need to stay out of sight.'

'Fine.'

I hung up, confusion sweeping over me. I didn't know what has happening, or why. One thing I did know, though, was that Mackie had been right. There definitely were people after me.

The only question was: *which* people?

Chapter 20

Every night that I lay in my cell, I rummaged in my brain for any recollection of the lost time. But my mind was completely blank. Those memories had been locked away from me. I'd have put it down to an inner defensive mechanism, pushing away those difficult days, except the painful memories of those initial weeks of physical torture were still there, loud and clear.

The worst part was not the evident fact that during those lost days I had talked, but that I didn't know what I had talked about. How much information had I given them about me? The mission that I was on? Previous missions? The agency?

I had no idea except for the snippets of information that would be slipped into conversation by the woman who called herself Lena.

She'd seen me each of the last eight days. It was becoming routine. Just an hour or so each time. More than once I'd refused to talk to her at all, not willing to play her games. But on other days I succumbed: the need for food – and, despite myself, my intrigue at what she had to say – was such that it was worth the co-operation.

Not that I was exactly feeling fully nourished from what I was eating. The food was better than what I'd been given back at the start of my ordeal, but it certainly wasn't enough to maintain my full strength. I didn't know how much weight I'd lost – a lot. My ribs were starting to show through for the first time in my entire life. My muscles were slowly being burned for fuel.

In a regular prison, inmates can keep themselves super-fit exercising in the confines of their own cells. The extreme boredom of up to twenty-three hours a day locked up gives them plenty of time to carry out insanely hard regimens using nothing more than their own body weight. Stories of press-ups a thousand at a time are common.

But those prisoners get three proper meals a day. On the basic foods that I was being given, push-ups would just burn the limited fuel I had and that I needed to survive. I had no choice but to just lie there and take it as my body wasted away before me. Or maybe I had another choice, but it was one I wouldn't even contemplate.

'Where does this sense of loyalty that you have come from?' Lena said.

I'd already eaten the paltry food that had been put before me. Today I felt like talking. If for no other reason than it made me feel human.

'I could ask you the same question,' I said.

'It's simple for me: my country. It's something else for you, though, I think.'

'But you don't do this for your country,' I disagreed. 'You do it for a group of people in the shadows that nobody knows about. Doing it for your country implies that what you do is for the good of all of its people. The people are what make a country.'

'What I do is for the good of the people,' she said, entirely convinced by her own answer.

'According to who?'

'I wouldn't do it otherwise,' she said.

'Would you do anything for them? The people who give you your orders?' I asked.

'Yes.'

'You'd kill for them?'

'Yes.'

'Would you kill anyone they asked you to kill? Anyone at all?'

She took a little longer in answering the question this time. I knew what she was thinking: friends, family, if she had any. Would she kill them if asked to?

'Yes,' she said after only a few moments' hesitation.

'Then we're two very different people,' I said.

'No, I don't think so. I just think our loyalties are in different places. For you, maybe you do love England. But you love Mackie more.'

I felt my face redden slightly at her words. She had touched a nerve there. I'd never thought about it like that, certainly never used that word to describe my feelings for Mackie. But he'd given me this life. No, he'd given me a life. I'd done everything he'd asked of me for more than half of my sorry existence – nearly twenty years. Of course I loved him. Like a dog loves its master.

When I'd first met Mackie I was still in my teens. He moulded me into the man that I'd become. Yes, he'd moulded me into the man he had needed; it hadn't all been for my benefit. But he'd also shown incredible faith, dedication even, toward me. More than once he'd fought my corner when others had wanted to cast me aside.

Five years ago I'd led a bungled mission to Iran. The intention had been to get to the bottom of an illegal arms-trafficking ring, supplying weapons from Western Europe to militants all across the Middle East. We had a source from the Iranian Defence Ministry who'd been an asset for almost two years. I'd been working with him day in, day out for twelve months when I found out he'd been trying to sabotage the whole operation. Feeding us false information, taking information from us to pass back to the terrorist cells, even setting traps to try to ensnare other Western agents.

On finding out, my orders were to return home immediately. The mission had been aborted. But that wasn't good enough for me. Before I left, I shot the asset in the face and dumped his body outside the hideout of one of the militant groups he'd been helping. He didn't deserve anything more. And I wanted the message to get back to his allies.

But I'd underestimated the political machine that was still attached somewhere high up at the JIA – at least when it wanted to be. The Iranian government was outraged that one of their men had been killed by me, a foreign agent, on their own soil. It didn't matter that he'd been working for terrorists; the powers that be were ready to give me up to win some diplomatic favours, expose me as a rogue agent. And I think it would have happened too, if it hadn't been for Mackie. He fought for me. He fought for my life. And not for the first or last time.

My life had never been perfect. In fact, there had been a lot wrong with it. The scars that marked my body were testament to that. And it wasn't just the physical scars, but the emotional ones too. From my horrific experience at the hands of Youssef Selim through to the betrayal of Angela Grainger. But despite those, I still believed my life would have been a whole lot worse without Mackie. It almost certainly would have been shorter.

'I can see it in your eyes,' Lena said. 'The hurt. You can't understand how he's left you in here, can you?'

I wasn't going to talk to her about that. I really didn't want to think about it. As naive as it may have been, some tiny corner of my mind still held out hope that any second they would come for me. Come to my rescue. I was still waiting for the walls to explode and for armed troops to come storming in to take me away.

So far there had been no sign of that happening. But I didn't want that hope taken away from me. Mackie had helped me out before. I had to believe that he would again.

'It's not just Mackie out there,' I said. 'He isn't the boss of all bosses. If they can't get to me, it's not because of Mackie.'

'But he's the one you take your orders from.'

'Yeah.'

'And you trust every order that he gives you?'

'I always have. But that doesn't mean that I always would.'

'And do you trust that Mackie always knows what it is that he asks of you?'

'Of course.'

'So what were you doing in Russia?'

'Every time that question is asked it's in the past tense,' I said.

'You don't think you're in Russia now?'

'I don't know where I am.'

'And that's the way it has to be,' Lena said, shrugging.

It didn't really make much difference to me where we were anymore.

'But you still didn't answer my question,' Lena said. 'What were you doing in Russia? Why did Mackie send you there?'

I was pretty sure that she already knew the answer to the question. Even if I hadn't already told her in previous conversations, my cover had been blown way back on that day at RTK. She wasn't interested in the answer to her question, just with messing with my head.

She didn't wait long before she continued.

'Well, let me remind you. You were brought here from RTK Technologies. You broke into there, killed three people. So what were you doing there?'

I didn't say anything.

'Okay,' she said. 'I can see we're going to be doing this the hard way. Now, based on what you told me before – I know it's a shame that you can't remember it, but we really did have some very open discussions – based on what you told me, you were at RTK to recover files related to something called Project Ruby. Does that ring any bells?'

I remained silent, wondering, as I often did, just how much information I'd given her. She seemed able to read my mind from start to finish.

'Do you even know what Project Ruby is?' she asked.

My lack of response prompted her to carry on.

'So you're sent all the way to Russia, you spend months preparing yourself, and then you raid RTK to kill innocent people and steal information about something called Project Ruby when you don't even know what it is? Why? Because Charles McCabe told you to?'

'No. Not just because Mackie told me to,' I said, not wanting to rise to the bait, but unable to stop myself. 'I never do anything that I don't want to do. I came to RTK because your scientists are developing chemical weapons like nothing we've ever seen before. They're making millions of dollars of profit selling their heinous concoctions to God knows how many of the world's terrorist states. To me, it was a no-brainer.'

Lena laughed. That same mocking laugh that she so often directed at me.

'Wow, and that certainly does sound like something that would need to be stopped,' she said.

I shifted in my seat, feeling increasingly uncomfortable at the way she was toying with me.

'And which countries are we talking about?' she said. 'I hope you weren't including Russia in your list of terrorist states. We're one of your closest allies now, surely?'

'So close that you'd hold me here like this?'

'So close that you'd raid one of our corporations and kill three innocent workers?' she said.

'They weren't innocent. They would've killed me.'

'Are you a scientist, Carl? Wait, you don't even need to answer that. Of course you aren't. Have you actually seen any evidence of what Project Ruby is?...Wait, you don't need to answer that one either. Because I know the answer. The answer is no. The only thing you were given was Mackie's word.'

'I trust him.'

'Well, maybe you shouldn't.'

Lena bent down behind the desk and came back up with a stack of papers in her hand. She threw them over to my side of the desk. The neat pile scattered and some papers fell off, onto the ground.

'Take a look for yourself,' she said.

I didn't pick any of the papers up, but I couldn't stop my eyes wandering over the scattered pile. The words were in Russian but I noticed that the papers were mostly headed up as being from RTK. I could see analysis, charts, graphs. I noticed the words 'Project Ruby' in bold letters at the top of more than one piece of paper.

'These are just some of the files that your friend Dmitri took on his clever little gadget. Before he took one too many rubber bullets to the head, that is.'

I cringed inwardly. It wasn't the first time Lena had mentioned Dmitri's death. An accident, she'd have me believe. If you ask me, it's not much of an accident when you fire a weapon at someone's head. If he was dead, it was no accident. If. I wouldn't have put it past the Russians to have made up the story of his death and to be holding him in similar conditions to mine.

'This is all very interesting,' I said, *'but what am I supposed to do with these?'*

'These papers are the reason you were sent here. Don't you want to take a look? See exactly what Mackie was willing to sacrifice you for?'

'No. I don't second-guess orders.' Though I knew deep down I didn't fully believe my own words. There was a time for sure when orders were the be-all and end-all for me, but not anymore.

'But I thought you said you only do things that you're comfortable with? How do you decide that if you're shown no evidence beforehand?'

'I trust Mackie.'

'Let me fill in the blanks for you then. Project Ruby is biochemical research into vaccines and remedies for a number of common diseases that affect military troops in the field: dysentery, cholera, malaria, legionnaires'. And some of your so-called terrorist states that have funded this research, well, they include France, Germany, Italy, India, and...wait for it...even the mighty UK.'

I tried not to betray any reaction to her words. I didn't want her to know that her tricks were working, that the doubts in my mind were growing larger by the second. But I couldn't help but scan the papers again. Looking for anything that corroborated what she was saying. Nothing jumped out at me. But how the hell was I supposed to know the difference between the chemical formula for a vaccine and a poisonous weapon?

Regardless, I was intrigued. Could what she was saying be true?

'So what do you think about that, Carl?'

'How do I know you haven't just made all of this up?' I said, willing for that to be the truth.

'Well, I guess you don't. You have to just take my word for it. The same way you so often just take the word of your boss.'

'I don't believe any of it. If any of it were true then why would the JIA have sent me here in the first place? There'd be no point. Why would they want me to steal that information?'

'You're right, they wouldn't. They didn't. They had no need for that information. For any of it. But you're wrong about there being no point to your mission. It had a purpose.'

'What possible reason could there be, then?'

Lena laughed. 'Carl, don't you get it yet? Mackie sent you to Russia to die.'

Chapter 21

After ending the call with Mackie I slunk away into the foyer of a nearby building where I waited, nervously watching, for over an hour. It gave me a good view of the apartment block and phone box I had used and felt safer than standing out in the crowd. The whole time I had my hands in my pocket, my right hand tightly coiled around the ice-cold grip of the Glock handgun I'd taken from Chris.

I'm not quite sure why I stayed near the scene. Confusion was sweeping through me. I needed time to think. I was in shock. It was almost as if I could see my life falling apart before my eyes. Everything I had come to know and trust, everything solid that I could grasp, was just not quite there anymore.

I fought hard to banish the melancholic thoughts. I knew they were useless. Knew they wouldn't help the situation and would only make me weaker. For that very reason I'd long ago been taught to control and ignore emotion. At times I wished I still could.

As I stood and waited I watched the other people there, anyone out of place, people just hanging around like I was. Any sign of someone who might be connected to the explosion. Anyone who might be watching or looking for me.

Any sign of Dmitri.

Despite what Lena had told me, was he still alive? I was struggling with the concept. I'd seen nothing of Dmitri in months. The last time I'd seen him he'd had a gaping hole in his shoulder and had taken several rounds of rubber bullets to the head. But someone had certainly been using that apartment. I couldn't get my head around what it would mean if it had been Dmitri.

Why *would* he be alive? He'd been caught with me at RTK. If he'd survived the ambush there, wouldn't he have suffered the same fate as me at the hands of Lena and her cronies? And even getting past those hurdles, if he was still alive then where was he now?

But the question of Dmitri's whereabouts, distracting as it was, didn't matter as much as other questions:

What caused the explosion? A bomb? A rigged gas main?

And why was the apartment destroyed right after my visit there? Had I unknowingly triggered a booby trap? Or was it simply a timer? Had someone seen me go in and set off a remote detonator?

Most importantly, whatever the answer to those questions, just who had laid and detonated the explosives? And that was a question part of me didn't want to think about.

Could it really have been my own people? Mackie?

One thing was clear: the explosion had been intended to kill. And I was pretty sure I had been the intended target.

Finally the local fire service put out the flames but they continued to spray the smoking embers. Most bystanders had moved on. Many of the residents who'd survived the blast had been taken away by the police. I had no idea how many people had died. I'd seen two black body bags being rolled on gurneys into waiting ambulances, to the gasps and cries of bystanders. But there could have been more bodies trapped underneath the rubble or some who'd simply been blown to pieces and whose charred, dismembered body parts would be coming out in many smaller bags.

I could do nothing more there, so I moved on.

I wasn't about to obey Mackie and go back to the station, though. If he or Chris or Mary or whoever else was out there wanted to find me then they'd just have to try for themselves.

I still had some cash left in the wallet that I'd taken from Chris. It would be enough to buy some basic provisions but it wouldn't last forever. I needed more cash funds and my two other main staples: IDs and weapons.

Although I had the Glock that I'd taken from Chris, it only had one magazine. I needed more. I didn't really trust a single person out there anymore and I wanted the security of knowing that I had some firepower at hand. And I had no ID on me at all. Some form of ID would be my only ticket out of Russia unless I could persuade a local to smuggle me over a border somewhere, but I wasn't quite at that stage of desperation yet.

I had never cared much in life for material things. But the most important things to me were money, IDs and weapons. My security. They were the three things that got me through this life, that got me what I needed and to where I needed to be. And they were the things currently stashed in a safety deposit box in the back of a bank in Omsk. Along with IDs locked away there, I had another handgun, a dozen magazines, and enough roubles and dollars to, hopefully, see me through the mess I was in.

The bank was only a couple of miles from where I was. I knew I could take a bus there but I decided to walk. Despite the cold and my blistered feet, I didn't mind the exercise. Whether it be a prison cell or a Jeep or a bunk-bed train carriage, I'd spent far too much time recently in cramped conditions. I enjoyed feeling my muscles working again, the warmth that it generated, even if the cold air froze my face and lungs in the process.

The walk took less than half an hour and I found the bank where the safety deposit box was located – the Omsk branch of a small Russian outfit – without any trouble. The branch took up a small plot on the corner of a terraced row of shops. Two tellers sat at their desks, the only staff present other than the manager, who worked out of view, behind a closed metal door, in front of the walk-in safe that led to the deposit boxes.

Altogether it was a simple operation. The tellers didn't even have glass separating them from the public. A random chancer might think the bank would be ripe for an armed robbery. Except Dmitri had specifically recommended this place due to it being widely accepted that the local mafia used it both for laundering their cash and for depositing their ill-gotten profits. No sensible person was going to rob the safety deposit boxes and prized possessions of the Bratva.

And despite the bank's apparently basic exterior, the safety deposit boxes themselves were state of the art. Gone was the traditional two-key security. Instead, each box was opened by inputting two eight-digit security codes into the inbuilt keypad: the customer's own personal code, plus the bank's code. Handy for me, as it meant that I wasn't required to cart around a conspicuous key.

I'd only been inside the bank once before, the day I'd brought my stuff there. Now, as I walked in, I didn't recognise either of the tellers. I didn't get the sense that they recognised me either. As soon as I mentioned the manager's name, though, I was whisked straight through to the back room, no questions asked.

The manager greeted me with a double handshake, clasping his left hand over our rights like a long-lost friend would.

'And how are you, Mr Burrows?' the manager asked, in broken but serviceable English, ushering me to sit on the wooden chair in front of his desk.

'Fine, thanks,' I said, wanting to keep the pleasantries to a minimum.

John Burrows was one of my regularly used IDs. The passport for Burrows was in box 621. The many fake IDs and cover identities I had came with the job. I had passports in numerous names and from numerous countries, social security cards, driving licences, security badges, police IDs and other such identities. The list went on and on.

A small number of the identities had a full story behind them and had become mainstay regulars. I could assume these identities for months or even years at a time. These were aliases that sometimes became so ingrained into my psyche that they were as much me as Carl Logan was. Most of them, though, had been used for only a short period of time, for a specific purpose. These were the ones that I regularly travelled with. That I used to book visas and flights and cars and hotels.

'You're enjoying the wonderful Omsk winter, yes?' the manager said with a beaming smile. We both sat. 'I think last time you were here was the summer? Quite a difference!'

'It's what we'd call fresh,' I said, smiling back at the man, not wanting to appear rude.

'Ah, yes, you English have a fine way with words. I like the expression "brass monkeys". It doesn't translate too well in Russian but I like it.'

I smiled again but didn't respond. I didn't want to enter into a long and detailed conversation about the weather, even if I was quietly impressed with his knowledge of the English language.

'Which box is it?' the manager asked, perhaps sensing my impatience.

'Six-two-one,' I said.

He typed away at his computer. Then frowned.

'Six-two-one you say? Are you sure?'

I had just a fleeting moment of doubt, my brain rechecking what it knew. No. I was damn sure.

'It's six-two-one. The box was registered in my name when I was here last time. John Burrows.'

'Sir, the name isn't relevant,' the manager said more sternly. 'We don't keep a register of names on the accounts. I remembered your name because I'm the client manager. But the code is the only ID we use. As long as you have the right code for the right box, it doesn't matter what your name is.'

'Then why are you asking me these questions? I know what the code is. I set the account up myself.'

'Well, the problem, sir, is that the box is not currently registered.'

I shifted in my seat.

'Not registered? As in…what are you trying to tell me?'

'As in the account was closed almost four weeks ago. I'm afraid that box is empty.'

Chapter 22

I didn't feel like talking to Lena today. I was sick of her questions and of her toying with me, enjoying seeing me squirm as she played her little games with my mind.

'You told me before that Mackie was like a father figure to you,' she said. We were sitting in the same room, in the same positions. 'I can't understand that. After what he did to you. The killing machine that he turned you into. The man with no feelings.'

I squirmed in my seat at her words. I had no recollection of saying that to her – or anything else in those lost days.

What else had I said?

She relished dropping into our conversations the things that I'd told her, as though it gave her an unseen power over me. She used my words – forgotten words – to try to open me up, to try to get me to tell her more. Sometimes it worked. But not this time.

'Come on, Carl. You've been doing so well. Don't throw it all away now. You don't want your life here to go back to the way it was before, do you?'

I took her words as a threat. Although my treatment at their hands had certainly improved I was under no illusions as to where I was and what they were capable of. But I didn't respond.

And I didn't want to talk about Mackie. About whether or not he'd lied to me. About whether or not he'd really set me up and handed me over to the Russians to do as they pleased with me – a settling of old scores.

Lena and I sat, not speaking, staring at each other. I could see the look on her face changing. Her confidence and her charm slowly faded. She relished the power she got from manipulating me. But this time I wasn't going to give her the satisfaction. And my refusal to play along was getting to her. She was riled.

In tandem with her own mood changing, I started to feel stronger. Like I was sucking the power straight out of her and into me. It was so simple. Without the ability to manipulate me she was helpless, and yet all I'd done was refuse to speak to her.

But what I hadn't reckoned on was the other side of Lena. One I hadn't seen before.

The build-up in tension had been slow. But when it came, the change was dramatically quick. Her whole demeanour, her features, her face transformed, just like that. It reminded me of a fantasy story where the wicked witch suddenly shows her true colours. Lena stood up out of her chair, her teeth clenched, her face like thunder, her eyes like balls of fire.

She strode up to me. I was grabbed from behind suddenly by the two guards behind me, two sets of thick arms coming around me and pinning me to the seat. I tried to move but I was stuck to the chair.

Lena sat down on my lap, straddling me, her face only inches from mine. And then, in an instant, with the balance of power restored, her calmness returned. Back was the absurdly pretty, delicate face that I hated so much.

She looked down at me like I was her long-lost lover, a warm smile creeping up her face. She reached out and placed her hands around my neck. I could feel the softness of her skin, could smell her rich, feminine scent and her sweet perfume. Her touch on me was light, almost caressing.

But it didn't last long.

She pushed down with her thumbs, driving down onto my windpipe. The pressure built up slowly, the smile on her face growing as my air was cut off. I squirmed, tried to wriggle free, but the men holding me were too strong. As my airway was slowly constricted, I tried my best to fill my lungs, but so little was coming in or out that it was almost not worth the expended effort. It only made my heartbeat and stifled breathing more panicked.

She squeezed harder and harder, laughing, the pleasure in her face unmistakeable and growing. Soon, I couldn't breathe at all. My chest heaved. It felt like my lungs would explode. I could feel *my face contorting, my eyes bulging. But Lena just kept on, her thumbs pulsing against my neck.*

My protests were becoming weaker, more futile. Not long after, I could barely resist at all. The room around me was becoming blurry. I started to drift, my brain taking me somewhere else. I thought about Mackie. About the many years we'd spent side by side. How I'd looked up to him, idolised him, like a small child does his father. I wanted it to be a happy thought, to focus away from my ordeal. But it wasn't. All I could think was how everything I'd been through with him had led me to this ghastly place.

My heart was now pounding violently, uncontrollably, in my chest, a response to the oxygen-depleted blood but also through sheer panic. I knew that any second it might shut down altogether. But Lena's grip on my neck seemed to only get tighter still, her long, manicured nails digging into my skin.

She let out a long scream. Somewhere between fury and ecstasy. She panted heavily, staring deeply into my eyes.

My whole world was turning into one big white mess. I was on the brink.

And then she let go.

She stood up off me. I coughed and spluttered, gasping for air. But I didn't get a chance to recover. The men hauled me from the chair, threw me to the floor and pinned me down. My arms were held, a knee placed into the back of my neck. Even if I'd had the strength to resist, I wouldn't have been able to throw them off me.

'You don't want to talk to me?' Lena said, her words slurred she was so out of breath from exertion or the thrill. 'Well, this is what you get, Carl. Just remember where you are. I'm in charge here.'

A loud cracking sound rang out. At first I mistook it for a gunshot. The pain that came searing across my back told me exactly what it was. I gritted my teeth. The knee that was on my neck pushed down harder, my airway becoming restricted once more.

I heard another crack, then another, as a thick leather whip was lashed against my back. I only had on a simple cotton shirt. It didn't offer much protection.

When the fourth crack came I thought that I could actually feel the flesh on my back splitting wide open. I grimaced and shouted out. The pain was immense.

Lena was speaking to me again, but I couldn't focus on her words anymore. It had been weeks since they had hurt me physically. Her viciousness was so out of the blue. I tried to take my mind somewhere else, like I'd done all those weeks before. I tried to think of Angela. Tried to picture her face. Her hazel eyes. Her silky brown hair. Her smile. Her warm, supple body next to mine. But the sound of the whip, the smell of the dank floor, the pain consumed me.

I started to count the lashes to focus my mind. I squeezed my eyes shut on the tenth strike. My body was tense and unmoving, paralysed by the searing pain ripping through me.

I managed to get to eighteen before I lost count. After that my brain finally succumbed and, as it had so many times before, it took me away from that place.

Chapter 23

The missing contents from the safety deposit box held no emotional value for me. Just a few IDs, a wad of cash, a spare handgun and some bullets. Under normal circumstances their loss would have been merely inconvenient. With cash I could have re-acquired the weapon and IDs in a matter of hours. But these weren't normal circumstances. The absence of any of my possessions was disturbing.

'How could my account have been closed?' I said, unable to hide the agitation in my voice.

The manager's face remained steadfast. 'I'm sorry, but that's not for me to answer. Our role is merely security and administration.'

'Security? What about my things! They're not very secure now, are they?'

The manager frowned, looking put-out by my apparent criticism. It was the first emotion he'd shown since revealing to me that my possessions were no longer being safely kept on his premises.

'I hope you're not suggesting that something untoward has happened here.'

'That's exactly what I'm suggesting.'

'I'm sorry, but if you've given your code to a wife or girlfriend then that's nothing to do with us. We can't control that and our clients don't expect us to.'

Nobody else could have known my passcode. Not even Dmitri, who had been here the day that I acquired the box.

'Who has access to the boxes?' I asked.

'Only me,' he said. 'Nobody but me.'

'Do you keep logs of all customer visits?'

'Of course,' he said, his face crinkling, offended that I should ask such an obvious question.

'And the log shows that the box was opened and the account closed four weeks ago? Somebody actually came here to close the account?'

'That is the only way to close the account. They need the code to verify their ID. Then I have to make sure the box is empty so I can re-set it.'

'Do you keep security tapes?' I asked him, standing up and pacing, trying to figure out what was going on.

'Sir, this is getting a little out of hand,' the manager said as he stood up from his seat, holding his ground, trying to even the playing field a little. Though he was still six inches shorter than me. 'I'm afraid that if you don't have a valid code for a box currently in operation then there's nothing more I can do for you.'

I stared at him blankly. I didn't know what else to do or say.

'I'm going to have to ask you to leave now,' the man said.

I knew that I could cause a scene if I wanted to. Grab the little turd by his neck and squeeze what I needed right out of him. But he was right. It wasn't his problem.

'Please,' I said, trying to sound sincere. 'This is very important to me. I think someone may have stolen that code. I just need to find out who it was.'

The manager remained standing, though his shoulders slumped a little as the chances of the fight that he'd readied for faded.

'I'm sorry,' he said. 'Complete customer discretion and privacy is absolutely fundamental to us. There's nothing I can do.'

'Look, at least take a look at the tapes from that day. I don't have to look with you. Maybe my memory's just got the better of me. Just take a look and then tell me whether it was me or someone else who closed the account. If it was me then fine. If not then we can talk about what to do next.'

'Even if it wasn't you, there's really nothing more that can be done. It's just not the way we operate.'

'Please, just look?'

The manager um'd and ah'd but then relented and sighed as he walked off toward the door that led to the main customer area at the front of the bank.

'Please take a seat for a moment,' he said as he opened and went through the door.

I didn't sit.

He was gone for only a minute or so. When he returned, his demeanour had softened somewhat. I didn't like it.

'Just a few more minutes, sir,' he said, sitting down again. 'Then we'll get all of this sorted.'

'What did you do?' I asked.

The manager shook his head, questioning what I could mean.

I walked over to the door and pushed it open just an inch or two. I spotted one of the tellers, a young lady, phone receiver pressed to her ear. She looked over in my direction, then quickly looked away again when we made eye contact. She was speaking quickly into the phone, but I couldn't hear any words from where I was.

'What did you do?' I asked the manager again.

'Please. Just come and take a seat. We're going to get this sorted for you.'

'Who is she calling?' I said, raising my voice.

'Please, just stay calm.'

'The police?'

The manager sighed. 'They can help you solve this,' he said. 'If you think you've been robbed then they can help you more than I can.'

I wasn't going to hang around and argue the pros and cons of that one. I pushed open the door and walked out into the front of the branch.

The manager shot up out of his seat. 'Sir. Please. Wait!'

But I was already halfway to the front door. The two tellers watched me, goggle-eyed, as I stormed through. I got the distinct impression from their faces that the police hadn't been called for my benefit. Maybe it hadn't been the police that they called at all. For all I knew it could be the Bratva enforcers that were about to descend on me.

The manager caught up with me just as I reached the door. I turned to face him, my anger rising at the thought that this weasel of a man might have been trying to dupe me.

'I don't know who you called, or why,' I blasted. I towered over the manager, who seemed to cower away with every irate word that I spoke. For all of my faults, intimidating was something that I excelled at. 'And I don't actually care who you called. But I can assure you that if you do anything to make my life harder, I'm going to come back around here, tear off your balls and feed them to you. Do you understand?'

The manager murmured and nodded.

'So maybe you've got another phone call to make.'

I turned and left. I wasn't sure whether the manager actually would make that call. But if he didn't, I was sure I could handle whatever came of it.

What worried me more was that four weeks ago someone had walked into that branch with a code that only I knew and had taken my things. Had they done it because they thought I was dead, or at the least would never be getting out of the gulag? More importantly, just who the hell had it been?

Regardless, I desperately needed funds and I debated for just a few seconds whether I should go back to the bank and rob it. Perhaps take some of my frustrations out on that smarmy manager. But that would have been a step too far. I didn't have a problem hurting people who deserved it, but I didn't really want to hurt a civilian who was just doing his job. Plus, I saw no point in adding more people to the ever-lengthening list of those who were currently after me.

What I needed was to call my bank back in England and get some money wired over to me in Omsk. Some money transfer shops had specific wire terminals where you could do that. The good thing about modern technology was that I could access my money almost anywhere. I didn't have a debit card or a cheque book because I didn't ever want to carry my real ID. But I could access the cash from almost anywhere using money-transfer companies. Although expensive they're quick and reliable, with locations everywhere that I'd ever needed. Western Union alone has more than four hundred thousand branches worldwide.

And one of those is in Omsk.

So the plan was simple: I would head to the Western Union and get what I needed. At least with cash I could still move around somewhat freely. Given time, I could even re-acquire ID and some more ammunition.

I had been to the Western Union once before and I knew how to get there from where I was. At a brisk pace I could walk there in fifteen minutes. But the weather had turned: a snowstorm had arrived and would make the walk tough going.

After heading east from the bank, I turned left at the next crossroads, feeling the bite of the wind as I came around the corner. The gloomy stone and brick buildings on either side of the road created a wind tunnel effect and the snow-filled air howled past my ears, the large flakes smacking against my skin. Within seconds, my entire face stung and I was covered in white. My clothes flapped against me as I battled against the force of the wind. I had to lean my body forward to avoid toppling over. The temperature had dropped again too and I wished I'd taken the time to acquire some more appropriate clothes – a hat, scarf, gloves at least.

I noticed two other pedestrians on the other side of the road struggling like me, but other than that the street was deserted. For obvious reasons, I guessed. The snow was thick and heavy, the temperature probably ten below zero already with nightfall still two hours away. The couple on the other side turned into a sheltered ally. I carried on regardless, dragging myself along the now abandoned street.

After a few more strained steps I noticed two figures up ahead, emerging around a corner. They were walking toward me on the same side of the street, about a hundred yards away. It looked like a man and a woman, judging by the size difference and the attire; the man wore a long, dark parka, the woman a bright-red puffer jacket with brown boots that went up to her knees. They were still too far away for me to make out any detail through the wall of white that was coming down, but I could see that they were both hunched into their thick coats, even though they, unlike me, had the wind against their backs.

They were ten yards away from me before I could finally make out their faces properly. I wasn't surprised in the slightest. I stopped walking just as they both looked up at me.

'Logan,' said Mary, not a hint of warmth in her greeting.

Chris stood next to her, no emotion on his face. He drew a hand from his parka to reveal a black Walther handgun, the barrel pointed at my chest.

'Just the man we're looking for,' he said.

Chapter 24

Since that first beating at the hands of Lena I'd suffered three more days of abuse from the guards. Then I'd been given a simple choice. It wasn't too hard a decision to make. I would play along with her games. I didn't want to go back to those early days of torture. Once upon a time I'd been trained to withstand such ordeals, but that didn't mean I wanted to. And I didn't want to be that man anymore – the JIA's machine. I wanted to feel like a human. To be treated like one.

And as long as I co-operated with Lena, it seemed that wish would be granted. Plus from what I could gather I'd already talked, I'd already given them so much information about me, so what would I be fighting for? Of course, a big part of me felt like a traitor. A traitor to the JIA and to Mackie and to the life I had led for so many years. But then, Mackie and the JIA had left me to torture and abuse. And if Lena was telling the truth, my being here was the JIA's doing in the first place.

I was sitting in the interrogation room. Lena was opposite me. My neck still ached when I breathed and my body was covered in ugly gashes and sores. But in the last few days my relationship with Lena and her treatment of me seemed to have moved on. My shackles were off. The conversations were becoming relaxed and open.

I knew what they were trying to do. Despite the obvious threat of violence that never went away, they were trying to make me feel like they were the good guys. I found it hard to resist because so much of what I was being told made sense. And because I was developing an unspoken attraction to Lena. Not just physical either, but an attraction to who she was and what she had to say. I knew that was wrong, I hated myself for it. And yet I was struggling to fight it: in many ways, I simply didn't want to fight it anymore. I liked the way Lena and the men who gave me meals and took me to and from my cell were treating me now.

I still didn't know how much information I'd inadvertently given Lena in the dead period. I could glean bits and pieces from the questions she asked and some of her responses to me. But I knew that she only ever let on to me what she wanted to. I still tried to resist talking about myself, about the agency, but it was becoming harder and harder to do so.

And it wasn't just me doing the talking. In turn, Lena was becoming more open. She talked to me about her life and the things she'd seen and done. Like we were comparing notes as to who had the most messed-up existence.

When it all boiled down, I could see a lot of myself in Lena. A lot of the things I'd gone through she had too.

'Aren't you wondering why no-one has come for you?' Lena said.

'Who says they haven't come? For all I know they've been scouring the earth for me.'

'Oh, come on, do you really believe that?' she scoffed. 'Everything happens for a reason. You being here. Your people not being here.'

'What are you trying to say?'

'If you get out of here at all, it's not going to be because of them. It'll be because of you. Remember what I told you before? About the choice you have to make? Well, that's your way out of here.'

'I don't want to talk about it,' I said, steadfast.

We were both silent for a few moments. Usually Lena would continue to push her agenda onto me, twisting and turning the conversation in the direction she wanted. But on this occasion she didn't. And I wasn't sure whether that was good or bad.

'Tell me more about Angela,' Lena said. 'What was it about her that you liked so much?'

It was the first time Lena had ever mentioned Angela – at least that I could recall. It took me by surprise. But then that was the game Lena enjoyed so much.

And it was impossible for me to answer the question. Because I didn't know. My attraction to Angela Grainger had been a natural instinct. No thought or premeditation had gone into it. Perhaps that was why the bond had been so inexplicably strong.

'I barely even knew her,' I said in response, wanting to play down my still burgeoning feelings for the woman who had betrayed me.

'That's right,' Lena said. 'You really didn't. Given the way she used you. Do you really think she felt the same way about you?'

That was the thing. I had separated my relationship with Angela into two. On the one hand, there was the person I fell for. I remembered the way we had talked for hours, the intimate times we spent together, even the lovers' quarrels that we'd had in our brief time together. And then there was the other person. The one who'd used me to get her revenge on the man who'd killed her father. The one who'd shot me and gone on the run. The two sets of memories, the two sides I'd seen of her, didn't go together at all.

'I understand why she did what she did,' I said.

And my words, to some extent, were true. Angela had wanted to avenge her father's death. I could abide by that. But could never agree with the means by which she achieved it: the whole concocted scheme to kidnap Frank Modena, which had seen innocent people killed.

'Ah, yes. And so we return to the subject of revenge once more. It really is such a central part of your life.'

Lena, of course, was right. It had driven me from when I was a teenager trying to get to grips with a cruel world, through to me tracking down Youssef Selim and putting a bullet in his head.

'Why do you want to know about Angela?' I said, deflecting Lena's comment.

'Because it seems so strange to me that a man like yourself could have fallen so deeply for somebody. Not only that, but to have been so blinkered as to her true intentions.'

'And what do you know about her true intentions?' I said, agitated. Lena had hit a nerve. Because I struggled with the concept too. I just couldn't believe that part of Angela hadn't truly fallen for me, even though she'd undoubtedly used me.

'My point is that revenge has been such a central part of your life,' Lena said. 'You've always sought vengeance before. But not with Grainger.'

'Says who?' I said, grimacing at not knowing just how much of my soul I'd spilled to Lena already.

'Says you. You told me yourself.'

I gritted my teeth. As usual, Lena was toying with me – dropping into conversation revelations I'd already made. And I didn't like the personal nature of the questioning. Talking about my life, the JIA, was one thing. But Angela was the sorest subject of them all. And I didn't know what Lena had to gain from my answers, other than satisfaction at seeing me squirm.

'I'm sorry to have to keep doing that to you,' she said. 'I don't intend to offend you, but I find it odd that you still carry such feelings for a woman who betrayed your trust like that.'

'That's the thing I've learned about feelings: as much as you try, you can't always control them.'

'What would you do if you were to see her again?'

'I don't know,' I said, entirely truthfully.

'I'd love to see that. The lovers' reunion. You know, maybe one day you'll get the chance.'

I was done with this conversation. I stood up from the seat and walked toward the locked door where two uniformed men were standing guard.

'Carl, where do you think you're going?' Lena said.

The men moved across the door, blocking my path.

I stayed on my feet, facing away from Lena. As much as I'd felt relaxed before, I couldn't talk to her about Angela.

'Sit back down,' Lena shouted, her voice hard. 'We're not done yet.'

'I'm done talking about her,' I said, fully aware of what the consequences would be if I resisted too strongly. But I wanted to make a point. Some things were just too precious and too painful to open up about.

'Okay, okay, I get it. Let's talk about something else,' Lena said, to my relief.

'Like what?' I said.

'I want to get to the nub of what drives you. Tell me about Selim. Your life-changing experience.'

I squeezed my eyes shut, trying not to let my anger get the better of me. I wanted this conversation to be over. But I knew that I'd suffer if I resisted too hard.

'Have you ever been close to death?' I asked, composing myself and turning to face Lena. 'So close that you could touch it?'

'Yes. More than once,' she said.

'And did it affect you?'

'Of course it did. I don't want to die.'

'But did it change you?'

'It just made me more determined.'

'Determined to do what?'

'To survive. It made me stronger.'

Part of me admired her apparent strength. Maybe it was just bravado, but I admired it all the same. But at what price did all that strength and determination come? I knew only too well how it felt to be close to death. But my experience had only brought me back down to earth and made me question my life. Question whether my life was really a life at all.

I walked back to the chair and sat down.

'You think my experience is different from yours?' she said.

'Yes, I think it is.'

'So you're not stronger now?'

'No, I don't believe I am.'

'You're talking about Selim, aren't you?'

'Yes.'

Youssef Selim had been a terrorist. One of the most wanted men in the world. I'd been sent to help bring down him and a terrorist cell that he was running. But it went wrong. I was caught. I was held captive.

I was tortured.

Sounding familiar? I was on a losing streak, that was for sure.

But my time being held by Selim had been very different from what had happened to me since being captured at RTK. The torture at the hands of Selim and his men had been much more aggressive, rushed, intense even. The difference was that Selim had let it get personal. He was angry and everything he'd done to me and others was tinged with that pent-up anger. He'd wanted to get his revenge, to inflict pain on me. And he hadn't cared whether I lived or died.

My captivity with the Russians had been very different. Their torture had been deliberate. Very deliberate. Planned. Everything had happened for a reason. They'd never had any intention of killing me.

At the hands of Selim, I almost certainly would have died if I hadn't been rescued. They didn't want information from me, didn't want anything from me other than to see me suffer. The sword was pressed against my neck when my rescuers swept through that place. I was alive, just, but Selim got away.

In the aftermath, I'd been a mess. Years of working and thinking like a robot came to an abrupt halt. I didn't know whether I could go on. But Angela had helped me get there. Had helped me turn my life around.

Angela Grainger was a woman I'd been attracted to like no other person before or after. Lena was a beautiful person on the outside, but underneath I knew she was sinister and menacing and evil. I'd seen that side of her first-hand. And I knew it was the real Lena. My attraction to Angela couldn't have been more different. It had been pure and instinctive. And at a point in my life when everything had come tumbling down around me, she'd helped me to pick up the pieces.

Not long after I'd met her, she helped me to track down Selim, and I'd killed him – thus ending what had seemed like the sorriest chapter of my life.

But then came Angela's betrayal.

And I was back to square one again.

My life had never been the same since Selim first touched me. I wasn't the man I used to be. I was weaker. My mind was rational and I thought too much. I wasn't as strong mentally as when I was that machine, carrying out orders at will. The less you think about a job like mine, the better.

'I don't think it's made me stronger,' I said, coming out of my thoughts. *'It changed me, but it didn't make me stronger.'*

'Well, I think you're wrong,' Lena said. *'I think you're stronger now. Stronger because of what Selim did to you.'*

'And why's that?'

'Well, you're here, aren't you? You came close to death before, but you didn't quit. You carried on. And it brought you here. And look at what you've done here. Still going strong, still surviving.

That's where we're the same, you see. We do what we need to do to survive.'

I grimaced at her words. Because what I was doing, talking to her like this, was against everything I'd been trained for, against every loyalty I had. But she was right. When it came down to it, my choice had all been about my own survival. In the end, my own life had trumped everything else.

'It's not always our choice, though,' I said. 'You could've killed me whenever you wanted. I haven't survived here because of my own strength and determination. I've survived because you've decided not to kill me.'

'You're right,' she said. 'It's not always our choice. But you don't get anywhere without trying. You could have given up. You could have given up back then and you could have given up here. But you didn't. Your body and mind have kept you going through all of this. Through everything that your life has thrown at you.'

I disagreed. My mind had left me plenty of times. And I could see clearly that the Russians had worked my capture exactly as they wanted to the whole way along. The abuse. The games. The questions. The way Lena was playing with me. Even the attraction to her that I was fighting was surely part of their ploy.

I was where I was because they wanted me to be.

The only real question left was: why?

Chapter 25

'Fancy meeting you two here.'

'No games this time, Logan,' Mary said. 'You're staying with us until Mackie arrives.'

'Says who?'

'Says me,' Chris said, anger evident in his voice.

'How's the head?' I asked.

'Screw you,' Chris spat. 'You're lucky I'm not putting you down right here. Who the hell do you think you are? You could have killed me out there. And for what?'

I could understand Chris's irritation. But I wasn't going to apologise. I didn't need these two helping me then and I didn't need them now.

Mary walked up to me. She held her hand out. 'Give me the gun,' she said. 'Slowly does it.'

'If you want it, come and get it,' I said.

The Glock was inside the waistband of my trousers. I was cursing myself for having put it in such a useless position. Less conspicuous, yes, but with my overcoat on much too hard to reach for quickly.

'There's no time for games,' Mary said. 'Where is it?'

I undid my coat and opened it out, indicating with my head down toward the butt of the gun. Mary reached over, cautiously, and took it out of my trousers. I smiled at her as she did so and was pleased to see the look of offence on her face.

'Logan, you need to come with us,' Mary said, stepping back and putting the Glock in her coat pocket. She placed her hand on Chris's gun and pushed it down toward the ground. 'Come on,' she said. 'We're on the same side here. Let's get out of the cold.'

'Where to?' I asked.

'We have a new safe house. We can go and wait there until Mackie arrives.'

'And then what?'

'And then the two of you can talk and get this sorted out, once and for all.'

'Yeah? What about the full psych you were harping on about last time? You know, the one where they'll make me do tests to make sure that I'm not some nut job who's now working for the enemy.'

'Jesus, Logan, listen to yourself, man!' Chris said, his anger turning to exasperation. 'It's not a bloody lobotomy. Yes, they're going to make you see a doctor, give you whatever help you need. But what's so bad about that? What makes you so special that normal protocol doesn't apply?'

He had me there. I didn't see myself as special. The problem was the opposite: I saw myself as expendable. I still didn't trust that I wasn't now simply a target of my own country's security service and that this was merely the ploy that would finally lead me to my end. But I wasn't about to stand and debate that point with these two.

'Enough, all right?' Chris said. 'It's bloody freezing out here. We're going to turn into human snowballs if we stand here any longer. Now come on.'

He turned around and trudged off, back the way he and Mary had just come, heading into the biting wind. I looked at Mary. She just shrugged.

I knew that meeting with Mackie was a necessary step. I didn't entirely trust these two, just as I didn't entirely trust anyone, but I was sure I could handle them if I had to. And I needed somewhere warm to stay.

I started off after Chris, aware that Mary was close by my side. We caught up with Chris within twenty paces or so. He didn't react at all, didn't acknowledge me or Mary, just carried on walking.

The three of us lumbered on in silence for about ten minutes, taking turns down streets that I'd never been down before, heading away from the more cosmopolitan areas I was used to and into the bowels of the city. Here the surroundings were all characterless concrete blocks, remnants of the communist era and the flawed ideology of social living that those times had brought. The grey walls of the vast buildings, many of them now derelict and decrepit, blended seamlessly into the overcast sky, creating an endless dull monotony. The heavy snow had passed for now, just wisps of white left in the blustery air. The temperature remained frighteningly low.

'How did you find me?' I asked neither one of them in particular.

'The bank called through to us,' Mary said. 'We had them watching out for you.'

'How did you even know about that place?'

'We're good at what we do.'

Mary's words made me again question Dmitri's fate: no-one other than Dmitri knew I'd been to that bank. But I didn't push any further for an answer I knew I wouldn't get.

'So you took my things?' I said, not sure whether I was pleased or angered at the prospect of it having been them rather than someone else.

'Yes.'

How had they persuaded the bank to grant them access? I could see two links: the FSB and the Bratva. I couldn't fathom how either of those was the answer.

The streets we were now walking down were desolate. It was hard to know whether that was due to the weather or because the giant buildings alongside us were sparsely inhabited.

'Wow, this is really something special,' I said. 'You two lucked out getting to come to a place like this.'

'Out of sight, out of mind,' Chris said.

Unfortunately that was my thought exactly. If this was just a ruse then the area we were now in was an ideal spot for bumping me off, with countless empty buildings to dump a dead body in. Hardly anyone was around to see or hear anything untoward, and even if someone did, in these parts there was a fair chance that they'd just pass on by without a second thought.

I slowed my pace a little so that both Chris and Mary were just slightly edging ahead of me. I wanted to be able to see their hands. See any move. If there was one to be seen at all.

Eventually we turned and headed toward the outer stairwell of one of the concrete blocks. I spotted obvious signs of occupation, not least the fact that only a handful of the building's windows were boarded up. We began climbing the stairs, Chris in front, Mary behind me, the stench of urine and rotting food coming and going as we went.

When we arrived at the third floor, Chris turned into the central corridor that ran the entire length of the building, down to the identical stairwell that lay at the opposite end. Doors for each of the flats were spread symmetrically on either side of the corridor, with just one small square window separating each door. Chris stopped at the fourth door on the left and his hand went to his pocket. I tensed just a little until I saw the key emerging with his hand.

Chris put the key into the lock and opened the door. He gave me an expressionless look and then stepped in. I hesitated for just a second.

'After you,' Mary said.

'No, no. After you,' I said, turning to her and smiling.

Mary looked nonplussed and stepped past me into the apartment. I felt my tension drop just a little as I followed her through the door. At least they were both in front of me now, where I could see them.

As I stepped over the threshold, I saw Mary, just a yard ahead of me, walking through into the room at the back of the apartment. Without turning, I reached behind and pushed the door to shut it. But I could tell from the bang it made that it hadn't shut properly.

I turned. The catch on the door was up. I went to release it, but as I did so I felt movement behind me.

And I knew then that the move was coming.

After everything they had said, they were going to take me down when my back was turned.

But I hadn't been so stupid as to not have been ready for it. I'd been expecting it from the moment we began our walk.

I ducked low, swivelling as I did so, my right arm recoiling, ready to unleash. In the split-second that it took me to turn, my brain half-recognised surprise at the empty space in front of me, where I'd expected Chris or Mary to be standing, ready to take me out. Unable to stop my momentum, my right arm arced through the air, connecting with nothing at all.

As my body reeled, my head turned and I caught a glimpse of the doorway immediately on my left and the shadow of a figure standing in it. Before I'd even fully processed what was happening, I felt a sharp stab in my neck and the strange feeling of cold liquid rushing into my warm veins.

That feeling was the only thing I was aware of as my legs gave way and I fell to the floor.

Chapter 26

It was strange to think it, but I was starting to feel more like myself again.

They had moved me to a larger cell. Still windowless, still a cell. But bigger at least. It had a mattress and a pillow, a stainless-steel basin and toilet. Luxuries after spending weeks on end sleeping on a cold, hard floor with nothing to keep me company other than a rusted metal bedpan.

The food was still bland but I was now receiving much more of it. I ate and ate and ate, and when I'd finished they'd give me another plateful and I'd eat that too. More than once I threw up because my body just wasn't used to the volume. But that didn't put me off. I just kept on going, eating as much as I could, feeling the renewed strength that each mouthful gave me.

'You're looking good, Carl. Fit and healthy. I've never seen someone regain themselves as quickly as you have.'

Lena's words made it sound as though I wasn't the first person she'd broken and then remodelled. And she seemed to take great enjoyment from it. It made me immensely uneasy to think that I was just another plaything to her. But she was right: I was recovering quickly, at least in body. A lot of the time my mind was still a blurred mess, not sure what to believe or whom. Furiously trying to distance myself from becoming close to Lena and her propositions, her propaganda, but at the same time aware that I inevitably was. Her allure was starting to overpower me and I faced a constant battle to remind myself of the snake that she really was.

She was standing in front of me, on the other side of the large wooden desk, her back toward me. She was looking over a map of the world that was pinned to the wall, proudly displayed like in a war room from a bygone era. The room we were in was some sort of office, brighter and nicer than the other rooms I'd become used to.

As usual Lena had on a tight-fitting suit that accentuated the curves of her tall, slender body. I squeezed my eyes shut for just a second, pushing out the thoughts that were forming in my head and annoyed at myself for gawking at her. However you described our bizarre relationship, I certainly didn't want it to go to that.

I was acutely aware that I was suffering on some level from Stockholm Syndrome – the paradoxical phenomenon in which captives show empathy toward and even develop feelings for their captors. It's not real empathy, simply an inbuilt, subconscious survival technique. It was the Russians' exact intention for me to be feeling this way: Lena's presence – her persona and her looks in particular – were intended to exploit it. I knew that and yet I was powerless to stop it.

I loathed Lena. I hated her. I often clenched my fists together when I thought about her in my cell, wanting to crush her neck, crush the life out of her, much like she'd almost done to me. I wanted to kill her. And yet I wanted to please her too – because I liked how they were treating me now. On some level I longed for the time we spent together. I enjoyed her companionship. I needed *that companionship. Without it I was all alone.*

And the more we talked, the more I opened up to Lena and vice versa, the more I saw that we had so many feelings and experiences in common. She'd had a similarly unhappy upbringing to me – no father that she knew of and her mother had died at a young age. The FSB had been a way out for her, a way to have a life, much like the JIA for me.

Sometimes we talked to each other for hours a day. I tried to be guarded, to give away little of my life. But it was clear that she already knew the most intimate details. I didn't resent that anymore. In many ways it felt good that another human being seemed to get me. Seemed to understand my thoughts and what I'd gone through.

'You know we'd be willing to let you go. You do know that, don't you?' she said.

I snapped out of my thoughts. This was typical bullshit from Lena, it had to be. But her words lured me in nonetheless, as they always did.

'Sounds good to me. Let's go.'

Lena laughed, her smile lighting up her whole face but the darkness still remaining somewhere in the back of her eyes.

'Very funny. Not just like that. But think about it. If you help us, we'll help you.'

'So that's what this boils down to. You want me to betray my country. You want me to betray everything I've ever worked for. For you? For the people who've tortured me and held me captive for eleven weeks of my life?'

Despite my protest, I knew I'd already betrayed my people: the JIA, Mackie. But then, hadn't they betrayed me in the first place, as Lena had so vehemently argued?

'I'm not going to apologise for what we've done to you,' Lena said.

'I'm not asking you to.'

'What we did was necessary,' she said. 'But you have to see that there's a way out for you now. I'm offering you a way out of this. A way to be normal again.'

'I'm not sure that I've ever been normal.'

'Logan, this is the only chance you're going to get. Your own people have left you for dead. They don't care what happens to you. You can either rot in here for the rest of your days or you can get out. If you ask me, it's not a hard choice.'

'So you want me to work for Russia. You want me to become another one of your puppets, doing your dirty work.'

'Yes and no.'

'Meaning what?'

'You'd be working for us, but not a puppet. We've got something very specific for you. And then you're done.'

'Just one job.'

'Exactly. Just one job.'

'And then I'm free.'

'Yes.'

'So what is it?'

'There's someone we want you to kill.'

Chapter 27

When I came to, the first thing I saw was Mary's face. I had to open and close my eyes a few times to bring her fully into focus. My head felt heavy and my body distant. Whatever they had shot me full of was still in my system, making me drowsy and docile.

Slowly, I took in the scene. A square room. One window, off to my right. A small cabinet with a TV on top. A brown fabric sofa on which Mary sat. Looking down, I saw I was still fully clothed but had lost my coat. My wrists were cuffed to a radiator.

But I was surprised I was alive at all. When I'd turned around to face them after entering the apartment, I'd felt sure my time was up.

'You're back,' Mary said, appearing jovial as ever.

I ignored her.

'Sorry about that,' she said, pointing to the small wound on my neck where Chris had hastily injected me. 'Really, I am. We just thought it would be easier this way.'

I simply shook and then bowed my head.

'Look, this isn't easy for us either. We've got pretty clear instructions: we need to keep you safe and within sight. You've already shown that you're not prepared to sit tight with us, so what else are we supposed to do? We'll stay here tonight and then head out to see Mackie when he arrives in the morning.'

I let out a long exhale. Avoided any eye contact with her.

A few moments later, Chris walked into the room.

'Ah, you're awake,' he said. 'Sorry about the needle.'

I looked up at Mary, who smiled apologetically.

'Yes. Everyone's very sorry,' I said, my words slurred and slow.

Chris turned away from me to talk to Mary. They spoke to each other just quietly enough to make sure I couldn't hear them. Then Chris turned back around and headed out of the room.

'I'll be back in a bit, yeah?' he called as he headed down the hall and out the front door.

Mary and I sat for a number of minutes in silence.

'Where'd he go?' I said eventually.

'Just to get some food. We all need to eat. It's been a long day.'

'Tell me about it.'

'Please, Logan, I really mean it – don't be like this with us. We're just trying to do the right thing here.'

I could hear sincerity in her voice. And not for the first time. There was something about her manner that seemed genuine enough, even if I didn't trust her. But what did she want me to say? They weren't exactly making things easy for me.

'How about you take these cuffs off? It's not exactly the most comfortable position. Especially if I'm going to be here all night.'

She tutted. 'I'm not going to do that, Carl. Especially when Chris isn't here.'

She got up out of her seat, walked over and kneeled down on the floor just in front of me.

'Look, Logan, I really am here to help,' she said, her voice soft and quiet. 'I'm going to get you to Mackie tomorrow and from there everything will get back to normal for you. You'll be out of Russia and on your way home in no time. We'll be staying on to finish things off here. But your job is done. Just work with me on this, please?'

I didn't respond but I gave her a look of acknowledgement. I wondered what she meant by saying they were staying on to finish the job but didn't ask the question. I was sure she wouldn't give me a truthful answer if she bothered to answer at all.

'You know, I've heard a lot about you,' Mary said, smiling again. 'You've got quite a reputation. That's unusual in our line of business. Most of the time we don't have a clue who else works for the agency and who's on our side.'

'You can say that again.'

'I was glad when I got put on this. Glad for the chance to meet you. I'm just sorry we weren't able to get to you sooner. I really was trying. We all were.'

Again I felt that she was being sincere but found it hard to buy what she was saying.

The expression on her face changed and I could tell she had something on her mind. But she took a few moments to compose herself.

'There's something else,' she said, her head bowed, not looking at me. 'It's about Chris. I only met him a few days ago. I've never worked with him before. I don't know what it is, but…'

I knew she was trying to tell me something but struggling to find the words. I gave her the time to finish and eventually she did.

'I don't trust him,' she said.

Well, this was a turn-up for the books. My interest was immediately piqued. What can I say? I'm a naturally suspicious person.

'Go on,' I said.

She sighed and scratched her neck. The signs of tension were firing here, there and everywhere.

'It's hard to place. Just some of the things he says and does. Like just now. He's gone out to get food. He's always going out on these little errands.'

'That's it? He goes out on errands?' I said, hoping she had more, though already willing to believe that something might not be quite right, given the course of events so far.

'No. That's not it,' she said. She paused again.

'Tell me, Mary.'

'Well, the other day I followed him on one of these trips. He said he was going to the shop for beer. It was actually a rendezvous. With a man. It's not right. I've seen this before. I might be quite new to the job but I know how things work in our field. And I think Chris might be working with someone else.'

I took a moment to digest what she was saying. Could Chris be a double agent, working for another agency, or at the least passing information? I tried to think through the possibilities of what that could mean, but it only seemed to add another layer of complexity.

'Any ideas who the man was?' I said.

'Well, that's the thing. I took a picture of the guy on my phone. I'm a spy, after all.' She smiled, clearly proud of the fact. 'I sent the picture to the lab, to someone I know I can trust. And it's not what I expected at all. The guy is an American agent. CIA. I can't think of any reason for them to be involved here. But somehow they are. And I think Chris is working for them too. Maybe it's nothing. But I don't like it.'

It's fair to say that I was gobsmacked. What she was telling me felt surreal. I had no idea what it all meant. My agency, the JIA, was technically supported by both the UK and US governments. But other than a couple of people in the upper echelons of command, we operated completely independently of the other well-known agencies of those countries. That meant that the JIA's interests weren't necessarily aligned to those of other agencies.

Unless what Mary was describing was a sanctioned relationship, then on the face of it Chris meeting with someone from the CIA was just as unusual and wrong as if he were giving information to an agent from a third country. It was a big deal that potentially changed the playing field considerably. And added to my confusion as to what the hell was happening to me.

'Why are you telling me this?' I said.

Mary turned away from me again. 'There's no-one else to tell,' she said, looking down at the floor.

'You could tell Mackie.'

'Tell him what? And what if it's something he's involved in too? I haven't known him that long. Or what if it's all just legit, something above my pay grade that I'm not supposed to know about? Chances are it probably is.'

'Then why are you so concerned?'

'Wouldn't you be?'

'Yes,' I said. 'You're right. I would be.'

'Just be careful around him,' she said.

'What else do you know?'

'Well, there's one other thing…'

Just then I heard a bang as the front door closed and a second later Chris came striding back into the lounge.

Mary stood up, giving Chris a meek smile.

'What's going on?' he said, frowning.

'Nothing,' Mary said. 'We were just talking about tomorrow. I'll go and make some food, shall I?'

'Yeah, that'd be great,' Chris said, not looking entirely convinced.

Mary took the bags of shopping off Chris and headed out of the room and into the kitchen, which was directly off the lounge. Chris glanced down at me. I stared straight back at him. After a few seconds he shook his head, turned away and walked back up the corridor and through a doorway off to the right that I guessed led to either a bedroom or a bathroom.

I was alone in the dark and dingy room for about half an hour, mulling over what Mary had said. There had to be a way to play what she had told me to my advantage, if I were just given the chance. But what I pondered most was what Mary had been unable to tell me. Was it more dirt on Chris? Or something else?

The smell of cooking drifted through from the kitchen and my stomach began to growl violently in anticipation. I hadn't eaten anything in too long.

Chris came back into the room and kneeled down by me in pretty much the same position as Mary had some time before.

'So what were you two talking about?' he said, his face sullen. 'When I was gone?'

'We were talking about you actually,' I said, looking hard at his face, searching for any kind of reaction. Nothing.

'Well, I'm sure you couldn't have had much to talk about then,' he said with an unconvincing smile. 'You know, Mary and I only met a few days ago.'

'Yeah, she said.'

'Strange in our line of work, isn't it? You can go years working without knowing who your colleagues even are.'

'She said that too. Look, do you think you can take these cuffs off? I can hardly feel my hands.'

Chris looked at me and sighed. 'If I do, I'm doing it as a sign of trust, yeah? We've got off on the wrong foot, I know. But we all just want this to be over with now.'

'I want that more than you do.'

'Perhaps you do. I'll take them off. But you know this is the best place for you to be tonight. Why waste a good opportunity for some decent food and some rest?'

'Just take them off. Please.'

Chris stood up, fished in his pocket and took out a small silver key. He kneeled back down and unlocked the cuffs, and my arms dropped to the floor. It took a few seconds for blood to flow back thorough my tired limbs and for the feeling in my hands to return. When it did, I lifted my hands up and rubbed them together, getting used to having some sensation back. They were icy cold. The radiator hadn't been on at all since we'd arrived. They were also shaking. I couldn't be sure if it was just shivers or my anxiety symptoms returning.

'Thanks,' I said. 'Maybe you can actually put the heating on now.'

Chris chuckled. 'Good idea.'

He wandered out of the room and I got to my feet and headed over to the worn single-panel window. It was dark outside. Most of the snow clouds that had covered the ground in white powder earlier had parted. The shine from the moon was lighting up the near-clear sky and the buildings around outside. The streets seemed deserted; no working streetlights here. The handful of lights on in the windows of the block opposite was the only sign of human life.

I knew Chris and Mary would be wary of me still, and to tell the truth I was surprised Chris had agreed to take the cuffs off at all. I certainly wouldn't have. He may well have had an ulterior motive for doing so but I didn't care. And he was right: I had no intention of running off into the cold tonight. I would stay in the warmth, refuelling and re-energising.

Tomorrow was a new day.

Chris came back into the room and walked over to me. He stood by my side, arms folded, looking out of the window. I could tell he was building up to something.

'I hope we can use this little sign of trust to move forward,' he said.

'We'll see,' I said.

He sighed. 'Logan, look, about before, when I went out. I saw the look on Mary's face when I came back. I know you two were talking about something.'

'And?'

'And just be careful with Mary.'

'What's that supposed to mean?'

Chris looked behind him, to where Mary was still in the kitchen, pots and pans clanking away. He then took a sidestep closer to me.

'I'm not sure we can trust her,' he said, his voice lowered.

Well, this was certainly getting interesting.

'Go on,' I said.

'I only just met her and I know virtually nothing about her, but I really don't get a good vibe. You know how it is? She's a snake in the grass. I can feel it. I wouldn't trust what she says if I were you. Ever since we've been here it's been like there's something else going on with her.'

'But you haven't seen or heard anything to back that up?'

'Not yet I haven't. I can just tell. I might not have been in this job as long as you but I know when something's fishy. I'm trying to help you out here. We're on the same team. We need to look out for each other. Be careful around her, that's all I'm saying.'

He didn't hang around for another response, turning around and heading to the kitchen.

Now I really didn't know what to think. What Mary had said sounded plausible. I'd been intrigued by what she'd told me. It seemed to make some sense and it played to my naturally sceptical mind. I'd intuitively believed her. Her manner was pleasant. The way she'd dithered when deciding to tell me about Chris had been credible. She seemed professional and genuine, if a little out of her depth.

Chris, on the other hand, I just couldn't read. What he'd said to me hadn't carried the same weight. He had no story of an illicit rendezvous or any other evidence of why Mary wasn't to be trusted. But I knew that wasn't necessarily reason to dismiss his warning.

In a way, I was realising that Chris and I were probably more alike than I'd first thought. From what I'd seen, he played a straight game, much like myself. Because we were alike, we were more likely to butt heads, as we already had done. That didn't mean he couldn't be trusted, though, or that he was the bad guy. After all, he'd been willing to show some trust in me by taking the cuffs off.

Mary, though? Maybe Chris was right. She was so very different from me in persona, and so very likeable, that my interest was immediately piqued by her doubting Chris. But maybe that was the whole point. Maybe she was, as Chris said, a snake in the grass. Much like Lena, my captor, who'd used her looks and her allure against me.

I really didn't know which way to go. Maybe both of them were just toying with me. They could have been in on the same scam. In the end what they had each told me really didn't help me one bit. But one or both of them was lying to me, I was sure of that. And I was sure I would find out which one in time.

Without a satisfying conclusion, my thoughts soon moved on: Mackie. My boss. The man who had tutored me and given me this life. The only person in the world who even barely resembled a friend. But also the man who'd sent me to Russia. The man who, according to the Russians, had sent me to die. In the morning I would be meeting with him. And with that playing on my mind, the question of which one of Mary or Chris to trust didn't seem quite so important anymore.

Chapter 28

'We want you to kill Mackie.'

My heart skipped a beat at Lena's words. Killing had, unfortunately, become a common part of my life. Something I was good at. It wasn't that I was being asked to kill that was so shocking to me. There weren't many other things I expected Lena to want me to do. The shock was hearing Mackie's name in that request.

And yet was it the idea of killing Mackie that was so hard to comprehend? Or the fact I hadn't realised this was what Lena had been building up to?

'You want to be a free man, don't you?'

'If I killed Mackie, I'd never be free,' I said.

'You'd be free to leave here,' Lena replied, shrugging.

'That's not the same thing.'

'Well, right now you're not free, whatever way you look at it. Killing Mackie is your only chance of having a life again.'

'Why would I want to kill him?'

'For revenge. Isn't that what drives you?'

'I couldn't do it,' I said. 'Whatever reason you think I may have, I just couldn't do it.'

Mackie meant too much to me – it was that simple. Lena knew that. We'd discussed my relationship with Mackie at length, despite it being such a sore subject that I'd seemingly been abandoned by him. But it didn't matter. Whatever Mackie may or may not have done to put me in the hands of the Russians, I wasn't sure I could ever see him as the enemy.

Could I?

'Mackie put you in here,' Lena said, as if reading my thoughts.

'No, you and your people put me in here.'

'We just brought you here. It was Mackie who sent you on a suicide mission.'

'So you keep saying. But it makes no sense.'

'It makes perfect sense. Tell me about your life,' Lena said.

'What about my life?'

'Tell me how you met Mackie. Tell me what it is that makes you trust him so much.'

I didn't want to be having this conversation. But I had to defend myself. I had to defend being here. I couldn't face the possibility that the person sitting before me really was on my side. And the person I looked up to, whom I'd trusted for so long, was my enemy.

'It's a long story,' I said.

'So start at the beginning. How did you meet him?'

'When I met Mackie,' I said, aware that she probably knew everything that I was about to tell her; knowing that this was all part of her game, part of her enjoyment, 'I was just a teenager. I had nothing going for me. I wasn't some university graduate with a degree in psychology. I was a tearaway, mixed up with the local gangs. Running drugs, carrying out thefts and assaults. Anything they asked, and anything I needed to stay alive.'

'You certainly have that instinct about you. Survival.'

I ignored the mocking compliment. 'When Mackie came along, my world was in a mess. I'd just lost a good friend. He'd been killed in a gang fight. Knifed to death before my eyes.'

I paused, looking for a reaction to my words in Lena's face. I saw none. I wondered again whether she'd heard this story from me before and what went through her mind when I recounted these episodes from my troubled life. Was it empathy? Pity? Guilt? Or did it merely make her feel some sort of cruel pleasure?

'Go on,' she said. 'And what happened?'

'Mackie told me that my friend had been working for him. Undercover. And that he wanted me to carry on that work. Helping to bring down the rival drug gangs.'

'And did you believe him?'

'I was a screwed-up teenager who'd just seen his closest friend killed. I didn't know what to believe.'

'But did you believe him?'

'No,' I said with certainty. 'I didn't even know him. And he was telling me something that just didn't make any sense. I'd known Pete, the guy who was killed, for months. We didn't just work together, we did everything together. So how could I believe that everything I thought I knew about him was a lie?'

'And yet you started working for Mackie? So where's the missing link?'

'He built trust with me.'

'How? From what you told me before, he lied to you. He got you planting the seed for the destruction of the rival gang without you even knowing it.'

I felt the pit of my stomach churn at the realisation that Lena was, as normal, playing me. Of course she'd heard the story before. She'd heard everything. And she revelled in showing that to me.

And she was right, Mackie had lied to me. Or at least not told me the full truth. I was just a teenager doing small errands for someone I thought was in law enforcement. Mackie paid me handsomely. I didn't understand the consequences of what I was being asked to do. But a lot of people got hurt or killed because of my work for Mackie. Granted, they were mostly bad people. But Mackie used me.

That was all years ago, though. Before either of us had even joined the JIA. And when Mackie moved up in the world and was given a position of commander at the JIA, he brought me in with him. Moulded me into the agent he needed.

A lot of time had passed since then. And the trust had been built. Our relationship cemented.

'If you already know all the answers then why bother asking me?'

'Because I want you to see the answers,' Lena said, pointing at me. 'I want you to see that the situation you're in now isn't too dissimilar to that one all those years ago. It takes years to build up the level of trust you have with Mackie. So I'm not expecting you to suddenly trust me like you trust him. But I want you to see the similarities in your situation right now to that one when you first met Mackie.'

'This is nothing like back then. I was a foolish teenager. I needed someone to take me under their wing, to show me right *from wrong. That was Mackie. He changed my life. He saved my life.'*

'Your life may have changed, but can you not see how the situation you're in now is just the same?'

'No. I can't see it at all,' I lied.

Because I could see clearly now where she was taking this.

'The people you trusted lied to you,' Lena said. 'Mackie, Pete – they both did. They let you down by betraying your trust.'

Grainger too, I thought, but I didn't say it.

'It's the worst thing that anyone can do,' Lena continued. 'My position now is not any different from when you first met Mackie. You may see me as the enemy, as the bearer of bad news, but I'm here to set things straight. You're in denial, Carl. You don't want to believe me. Just like you didn't want to believe Mackie about Pete all those years ago. And I can understand that. Because what I'm telling you is turning your world upside down. But that doesn't mean it's not true.'

'It's different,' I said. 'This is nothing like that. I could never trust you. Just look at what you've done to me. Mackie never hurt me. Not like you have.'

Lena shrugged and smiled.

'These are just mind games,' I said. 'You want me to believe that the situation is the same. But you've given me no reason to believe what you're saying is the truth. Without proof, how could I ever listen to you?'

Lena slammed down a fist. 'Logan, who the hell else have you got to listen to?'

It was an unusual show of aggression from her, making the simple gesture all the more pronounced, and I sat back, unable to find any retort. The only other time I'd seen any sign of real anger in Lena had been the day she'd throttled me. I was forever wary around her since that moment, aware that the slightest indiscretion could lead to her revealing that side again.

'They sent you here knowing that you'd be caught,' she carried on, anger evident in her voice. 'That was their whole plan. They were giving you up.'

'No, it's not true,' I said, but my voice was mild and meek. *Lena was in control here.*

'Listen to yourself. Even you don't believe your own words anymore. They gave you up, Logan. Your own agency blew your cover.'

Her words reverberated in my head. I tried to ignore what she was saying, tried to ignore the growing feeling of betrayal. But I just couldn't.

'It still doesn't make sense,' I said, shaking my head, wanting to doubt what she was saying more than I really did. *'Why would they want me to be caught?'*

'It's all politics, Carl,' Lena said, the anger dissipating now that it appeared her words were having their desired effect. *'That's what everything is: politics. A deal was struck between your people and Russia. We got you. In exchange we passed on some very valuable information.'*

'What information?'

'I can show you if you like.'

I clenched my fists together tightly, frustration threatening to boil over inside me. I didn't want to listen to any of this. How could I ever trust anything that she said to me or showed me?

But I had to know. I had to find out whether her claims held any truth at all. I had to know why I was here. And why no-one had come for me.

'Why me?' I said. *'Why would they give me up? Why would Mackie give me up?'*

'We have very good memories in my country. This is nothing to do with me, of course. But we – my people, that is – asked for you. Your people were willing to give you up. You've got history here, remember?'

'I remember,' I said.

I shouldn't have needed to ask the question. I knew exactly what Lena was referring to. The last assignment I'd been on in Russia had been some years ago. But I was well aware of the mark that had been left.

I'd been in charge of leading a plan to capture and extradite a Russian oligarch from under the noses of the Russian authorities. He was a wanted man in the US and numerous countries in Europe for a whole host of serious offences linked to his rapidly expanding business empire, murders included. But the Russians hadn't wanted to play ball. So I'd been sent in to snatch him. And I'd succeeded, *much to the embarrassment of the FSB and the Russian government, who had close ties to the oligarch. Ever since then he'd been held in secret, without acknowledgment, by the Americans.*

So it made sense to me that the Russians would want the person responsible for that coup – me. But that didn't explain why Mackie or the JIA would want to give me up.

'If my own people gave me up because Russia wants to get its revenge, then why are you now sending me back home to kill Mackie? The person who'd have helped broker your deal in the first place?'

'This was always part of our plan,' Lena chuckled. 'Of course, I wouldn't exactly say that all parties signed up to it. The JIA sent you here expecting us to keep you, torture, maybe kill you. This is just our way of taking a bit extra from the deal. The cherry on top.'

'All's fair in love and war,' I said.

'Yes. I love that saying. Never a truer sentence than that.'

'On the other hand, say I don't believe one word you've told me?'

'Then you can stay here. We can keep doing this, hope that maybe you'll see the truth eventually. Or we could just go back to torturing you. But this is your chance to get out.'

'And what then? If I accept your offer, do you just let me leave? Let me walk out of here under the pretence that I'm off to kill Mackie? It all sounds a bit risky from your side. I could just go running straight back home.'

'Yes, of course you could. It's a risk. But we think we have that covered.'

'How?'

'Because we can prove it to you. Everything I've just told you. We can prove it all. Once you know the truth, I've no doubt as to what you'll do. Revenge, Logan, is what drives you. Once you've seen the truth, there'll be only one thing on your mind.'

The carrot had been dangled in front of my face. I was doing what every good donkey does and was following it. But why was I even still playing along? I would never kill Mackie.

Would I?

No. I would rather rot to death in my cell.

And yet I couldn't deny that a part of me was captivated by what had been said. The seeds of doubt were growing. I had to know whether there was any truth in Lena's words.

'Show me what you've got,' I said. 'Then we'll talk.'

Chapter 29

I slept for twelve straight hours on the sofa of the safe house. Together with the meal that Mary had cooked – a warming meat stew – the long rest had done its job. By morning I felt stronger and fresher than I had done in an age.

After a simple breakfast we left the safe house at midday, on foot, headed to the Café Vite to meet Mackie. The rendezvous point was a half-hour's walk but I was happy to be in the fresh air, even though my feet were aching within minutes. It would be at least a few more days until the sores healed properly.

It was a clear and crisp day, but despite the bright sun the temperature was still unbearably low. There hadn't been any new snow overnight so what lay on the ground had become hard and icy and slippery. On the main streets of the city the piles of snow that had been cleared from the roads and pavements were already turning black from the petrol and diesel fumes of passing vehicles and vast swathes of mucky slush were splattered here, there and everywhere.

None of us spoke on the walk. That suited me. It gave me more time to ponder what was about to happen. I was full of nerves – a strange feeling for me. I had no idea what to expect from the meeting. Was it going to be another ambush? Were they going to off me there and then? Or was Mackie really going to be there in conciliatory mode, to offer a helping hand to me like he'd done countless times before?

Lena and the Russians wanted me to kill Mackie. They'd told me that would be my way out, the way to earn my freedom from them. With everything that had been going on around me, I wasn't sure the proposition was so outlandish anymore.

I just hoped it wouldn't come to that.

We arrived at the café, which was fronted by what would probably be a bustling outdoor area during the brief but warm summer, but it was so quiet now, in the mid-winter, that anyone walking by may not even have realised that the place was still open for business. As we walked in, Mary in front, Chris behind me, I noticed only two other patrons in the quaint, French-style interior. Not really surprising given the weather – who comes out for coffee and a slice of cake when it's minus twenty?

The café was compact with just four rows of neatly aligned tables. I took a seat in the far corner at a small round table that had two chairs. Mary and Chris took one of the tables near to the door, about twelve feet away from me. They were here to babysit me, evidently, but not to be party to my conversation with Mackie.

The waitress came over to me straight away and I ordered a sparkling water. She gave me an odd look, probably unused to people coming in from the cold for a chilled drink. I enjoyed coffee but only when I needed a kick. Mostly I tried not to consume caffeine-based drinks. I'd never seen the point in drinking something that just leaves you more dehydrated than when you started. Actually, no, alcohol was an exception to that. I drank alcohol. And like most people, I sometimes drank too much. But then I'd had a rough life and sometimes alcohol can make things seem better, if only for a little while.

No other customers came in as we sat and waited. My nerves were growing by the second. Despite the cool temperature of the interior, my hands were becoming clammy and I couldn't stop fidgeting in my seat, my heart jumping every time I saw a figure walk past the café window.

I finally spotted Mackie across the street. My gaze stayed on him as he crossed the road and approached the door, a rush of memories and emotion flowing through me. Unfortunately most of it was bad. Mackie wore a thick woollen hat, a scarf wrapped tight around his neck and a big black parka. He had what appeared to be genuine concern on his face.

Despite everything going on in my head – the continual doubts about his betrayal, the things Lena had said and shown me, and the bizarre events of the previous day – I almost smiled when he came through the door and our eyes met. But I stopped myself when I saw that he wasn't alone.

Two burly men came into view and followed him in, dressed in similar attire, though each was a good few inches taller than Mackie. With the bulk of their clothing they were almost as wide as the door itself.

I stood up as Mackie made his way over.

'Jesus, Logan, it's good to see you,' Mackie said, coming up close to me. 'I really mean that. I'm glad you're all right.'

There was an awkward moment where neither of us was sure what to do next. No hug, no pat on the back, no handshake. Eventually we both sat down.

Mackie's thick-rimmed glasses had fogged up from the warm air in the café. He took them off and pulled out a handkerchief to wipe them. Mackie looked exactly as he always did; plump, well-groomed, his dyed hair cut short and neatly styled. He looked like a corporate boss.

'Who are the goons?' I said.

The two men sat themselves down at a table by the window, on the opposite side of the door to Chris and Mary. One looking out, one looking in.

'Oh, those two?' Macke said, rather nonchalantly I thought, as he replaced his glasses. 'Just ignore them. Necessary precautions, I'm afraid.'

'They your protection from me or someone else?'

Mackie laughed. 'They're my protection from everyone. We're not entirely sure what's going on here, what with you turning up, the explosion – it's hard to know who's safe from whom.'

'I can't believe you actually just said that.'

And from that point I could see clearly where the meeting would go. There would be no pleasantries. No reminiscing. And yet what more could I have expected? Even if it should have been, this wasn't two old friends meeting for a social drink. It was awkward and clumsy and fraught.

As sad as it made me feel, neither one of us truly trusted the other anymore. And why would we? I'd been left for dead by my own people. Given up in order to settle an old score, if Lena was to be believed. Now the Russians wanted me to kill the very man they claimed had bargained with my life. And whether what Lena had told me was true or not, from Mackie's point of view how could he be anything but sceptical about my sudden reappearance?

The waitress finished with the final customer, who was paying at the counter, and then came over to our table, her face full of smiles.

'Good morning, Mr McCabe,' she beamed.

'Ah, my favourite coffee shop attendant. And how are you?'

The young girl blushed. Mackie ordered himself a double espresso. I said I was fine with my water and the waitress dutifully went to fetch the coffee.

'So you know this place, then,' I said, stating the obvious, hoping that Mackie would fill in the blanks for me. I'd never known him come to Omsk before, but he was clearly a regular here.

'You've got to have safe places to go to, Logan. Whenever I'm in town I like to come here. I've been coming here for a long time.'

'When have you been to Omsk before?'

'I've been everywhere. A lot of times.'

'I didn't know that.'

Mackie gave a meek smile. 'I guess sometimes we don't know people as well as we think.'

The second sly comment from Mackie in less than a minute. I let it go. I was more concerned about the fact that he knew this place so well. Did that add any more credibility to what Lena had told me?

'Look, Logan,' Mackie said, 'we're not going to stay here long, so why not cut to the chase. We need to get you out of Russia. We need to get you home.'

'And then what?'

'And then we can make sure you're okay. Please don't make things harder for yourself than they need to be. You must have been through hell already.'

'And what would you know about that? Yes, I've been through hell. Three months of it. And where were you? What were you doing?'

'It was out of my hands,' Mackie said. He looked genuinely ashamed, but how much of it was an act? 'There was really nothing else I could do. What would you have suggested? I go on a one-man mission to Siberia to break you out? We didn't even know where they were keeping you.'

'And what about those two?' I said, nodding over toward Chris and Mary. They both looked up on cue. 'They were right there, outside, waiting for me, while I was in there being tortured. They knew where I was and they just sat doing nothing. So don't tell me nothing could have been done.'

'It was out of my hands. We found you, but it was deemed too risky to try to break you out. That place was swarming with Russian agents and military. We could've lost two of our agents going after one.'

'That's what we do. That's been my whole life. How many times have you sent me in with odds much worse than that?'

'You're twisting this. That's not how it was.'

'Why are those two worth more than me?'

'They're not. But they're worth just as much. You know, you're lucky Chris is all right. I heard about what you did to him. He's got several stitches in his head from that clash. He should really still be in hospital. That's testament to how much it means to us all to get you out of this.'

'Hospital? Jesus, where do you get these guys from? All he had was a banged head. I've been held captive and tortured for three months! Do you even have the first idea of the things they did to me? So where's my hospital treatment?'

Mackie looked embarrassed and bowed his head. 'I'm so sorry, Logan,' he said. 'But there was nothing I could do. Believe me. We need to get you back now, though. You'll get everything you need.'

'No. What that means is that you'll lock me up while you perform all your tests on me. That's not too far removed from what the Russians have just done to me.'

'Come on, man, it's completely different and you know it.'

The waitress came back over with the coffee for Mackie. He gave her a less jolly smile this time and she walked off looking just a little uncomfortable. Mackie was looking flustered by the conversation, by the mood that was cast over us.

'You know how these things work,' Mackie said. 'No-one is unbreakable, Logan. You're my best man. We need to understand everything that's happened to you, because we want to have you back out there working for us again. But that can't happen until we know, until we understand, what happened to you.'

'Just admit it,' I snapped.

Mackie took a sip of his drink before answering. 'Admit what?'

'Admit that you don't trust me.'

I'd hit on something. I'd known Mackie a long time. When cornered, his forehead creases over, making him look confused, like he's deep in thought. Which he probably was: trying to figure out how he could deflect another question. I knew if I pushed harder he would blow. That was his style. But I wanted to get to the bottom of this.

'It's not that,' was all he could say in the end.

'What is it then?'

'Just think about it. What would you have me do?'

'Grovel to me? Say sorry for what you put me through? Tell me how you're going to make it up to me? How about any of those?'

'This is ridiculous,' Mackie said, shifting in his seat.

'You don't trust me,' I said again.

'It's not like that,' he said, but it wasn't even slightly convincing anymore.

'After everything I've done for you. The countless times I risked my own life. And now you don't trust me.'

My words were forceful, angry. Confrontational. Mackie held his tongue. But I could tell he was getting hot under the collar. Gone were any remaining niceties. I wanted to see the real Mackie.

'You don't trust me,' I said yet again, raising my voice. 'You're the one who left me to rot for three months. And now that I'm back, you want to get rid of me like I'm nothing to you.'

Mackie sat forward in his seat. When he spoke he was baring his teeth like an angry dog.

'Well, Logan, that's exactly it, isn't it? You've been gone for three months. God knows what they've said and done to you in that time. And what about what you've said to them? How much information have you spilled about you, me, the agency? And then, all of a sudden, out of nowhere, you get out.'

'All of a sudden? I was there for three months!'

'You're missing the point. You were held in an area so off our radar and so secure that in three months we were never certain whether you were even alive. And you got out of there all on your own. And after three months of captivity, do you contact us? Do you call me to tell me to come and get you? No, you run off to Omsk, doing your best to evade us and almost killing two of our agents in the process. So do I trust you? Right now? Hell, no. How could I?'

'You think the Russians sent me here? You think they let me go?'

'I haven't ruled it out.'

'And why would they do that?' I said, recalling my conversations with Lena. What she had told me about the deal. The little extra that the Russians had added on top. About how they wanted *me* to kill Mackie.

'Well, tell me, how *did* you escape?' Mackie said.

'You didn't answer my question.'

'Neither did you. And I'm not going to answer yours until you answer mine. So, tell me, how did you escape?'

'Well, it wasn't exactly a spur-of-the-moment thing,' I said sarcastically. 'It took me three months to get the opportunity.'

'And then what? One day they just opened the door for you?'

The energy of the conversation had shifted. Now it was my turn to be on the defensive. Because I didn't want to take my mind back to that place. I didn't want to put myself back in that cell, remember what it had been like.

Since my escape, I'd tried my hardest not to think about it. But your subconscious has ways of planting these thoughts in your head. I closed my eyes, just for a second, squeezing them shut, hoping that the memories, the smells, the pain and aches in my body would go away. But with my eyes shut it only became worse. All of a sudden I found myself back there again. Gone was the smell of coffee and hot milk, replaced by the smell of sour urine, faeces, blood and burning flesh. The darkness, the dank cell and the sounds of the guards' boots on the cold stone floor.

I opened my eyes and it all disappeared. But putting myself back there had knocked me.

'I overpowered the guards,' I said, wanting more than anything to just get off the subject. 'I'd been building up to it for days. I killed two getting out, another two on my way to Taishet. What more do you want me to say?'

'And they just let you do all that, without stopping you?' Mackie said, oblivious to the turmoil inside me. 'I mean, I know you're good, but are you really *that* good?'

'So what do *you* think happened?' I said, though I could understand his doubt. I had myself doubted the means of my escape. How it had all unfolded. Had it been too easy?

'Well, I'm finding it hard to believe they'd be stupid enough to just let you break out of there. So either they just let you go and you're lying to me right now, or they allowed you to escape. Put on a bit of a show for you.'

'And you still wouldn't trust me, even if it was the latter.'

'No. Because either way, they let you go for a reason. Perhaps you don't know the reason, in which case I'll apologise in due course. But whatever that reason is, I can guarantee you it won't be for our benefit.'

And yet I did know the reason: they wanted me to kill Mackie.

'When you say *our* benefit, I presume you're excluding me?' I said.

'Right now, of course I am. Don't you see why?'

'I'm not sure what I see anymore.'

'Just come back home,' Mackie said, his voice softer.

'I can't. I won't be locked up anymore.'

'We're not locking you up. We just need to understand what happened.'

'That's not how it would work. I'm not that naive.'

'Your reluctance to come with me doesn't look good, you know. You being so scared that we're going to lock you away. Why is that, Logan? What did you tell them?'

And therein was a big problem. I didn't *know* what I'd told the Russians. Told Lena. I couldn't remember. But I did know that I'd talked.

I'd talked a lot.

I'd told Lena things that I'd never told another human being. I may not have known that I was doing it, but I did. It happened. And there was no way I could take it back now. But how could I ever tell anyone? I couldn't.

I'd never been broken before. And I was scared. I had given away so much information. If Mackie or others at the agency ever found out, how could I blame them if they wanted to lock me up and throw away the key? Or just get rid of me permanently like they'd had me do to others in the past?

And I was ashamed. I was ashamed because after the lost days, I hadn't stopped talking. Every day that I was in that room with Lena I'd carried on. I talked to Lena. Told her about myself. And deep down I'd enjoyed the conversations. During that period, those conversations gave me something to live for. I knew that had always been Lena's intention. But I hadn't been able to stop myself. In the end I had *wanted* to tell her things. I had wanted to answer her questions.

And, in turn, I had listened to what she had to say. About me. About the agency. About Mackie. About my ill-fated mission and the real reason I'd been sent to Russia.

But I wasn't about to talk to Mackie about any of that. I couldn't even begin to tell the story. Instead, my mind was filled with Lena's words. If what she'd told me was true then it changed everything. They wanted me to kill Mackie. Just one act and then I'd be free; that's what she'd said. At the time it wasn't even imaginable. But the situation had changed. The conversation with Mackie had already told me that much.

And I was no longer sure that we'd both be walking out of that café alive.

Chapter 30

I hadn't seen Lena for three days. Not since she'd tried to persuade me to kill Mackie. My point-blank refusal had hidden the turmoil in my head. I may not have agreed to her request, but that didn't mean I wasn't at least considering the idea. If what she'd told me was true then didn't Mackie have it coming?

No, I couldn't think like that. Mackie was still the same man he'd always been. My friend. About the closest thing to a father I'd ever had. There had to be another explanation for why the raid on RTK had gone wrong. And why no-one had come for me in the three months since my capture.

What I found most puzzling now was the sudden disappearance of Lena. For the last three days I hadn't been out of my cell at all. I'd been brought food three times daily. They were certainly still feeding me well. But where had Lena gone? What were they planning to do with me now they'd finally shown their hand and I'd declined their offer? I didn't know. But the change in routine worried me. If I wasn't going to help them I was expendable. The whole charade over the last three months had been building to this point. Maybe they really thought they'd done enough to persuade me and couldn't understand my continued resistance. And if I continued to refuse then my days were numbered. At the very least, the days of comparatively good treatment would be over.

So I had to take action.

In the initial period of my captivity escape was unthinkable. I'd been so physically weak, so depleted by the lack of nourishment and the physical abuse, that my brain hadn't even been able to process a likely scenario. But I was physically and mentally stronger now. I was in a different cell. And because I was now casually walked from my cell to the interrogation room and other areas of the compound, I'd seen much more of the inner layout of where I was being housed. And I knew that each of those factors increased my chances of escape.

The problem was that I hadn't been out of the cell since the last time I'd seen Lena. And the male guards who watched over me would pass me food through a slit in the locked door. So the door hadn't even been opened during that time. If the situation stayed like this then the only option I had was to either try to attack a guard as he passed me my food or trick them into opening the door, perhaps feigning ill health or some other ploy.

Maybe I could just ask to go and see Lena. Their response to the question would at least be interesting.

I was still contemplating the various less-than-perfect options when without warning I heard the heavy lock of the cell door churning. A few seconds later the thick metal door swung open. Two guards stood in the doorway. One was armed, holding his weapon, an automatic machine gun. The other man was empty handed. Without saying a word to me, he raised his hand and ushered me over.

In the early days they'd shot me with tranquiliser darts each time they wanted to move me. That had not only added to my sense of disorientation but had also made it impossible for me to attack them. Their changing treatment of me had coincided with the start of the sessions with Lena. Just one of numerous small signs of trust that had been put in place to help win me over.

It hadn't worked. I hadn't been won over. Not yet.

I walked out, blinking in the bright light. The man who'd opened the door for me had already turned and was ahead of me. I followed him down the long, narrow corridor. The grey concrete walls were shiny and soulless. We walked past other cells, doors closed as always, no signs of any life beyond them.

The man brandishing the machine gun kept pace two yards behind me. After twelve strides we rounded the corner to the right and another man appeared, also with his weapon drawn, and began to follow alongside the man at my rear.

This was different. I hadn't had three men with me before, normally just two.

And then something else unexpected happened. Where normally we would turn left, we carried straight on, through a doorway that had always in the past been locked with no sign of what lay beyond it.

The unfamiliar routine was making me nervous.

Was this finally the end for me? Were they leading me to my death?

My nerves were shot to pieces. Even though the men had barely spoken I could sense a sinister air about the whole setup. It reminded me of a movie scene of a death row inmate being marched away from his cell one last time.

And yet I carried on, walking with them, because despite the sense of dread I was feeling I was also intrigued as to what was about to happen.

We took more turns down corridors and passed through rooms that I'd never seen before. Finally we came to a stop in a large but almost entirely empty room, probably about twenty-by-twenty-feet square. A simple wooden chair, placed awkwardly in the centre, was the only furniture in the sparse space.

'Please sit down,' one of the guards said.

I didn't.

'Please sit down,' the man said again. 'She'll be here shortly.'

I took 'she' to mean Lena.

The man who'd led stood by the chair. The other two men positioned themselves around me, one by the door, the other off to my right. The one by the door peered out into the corridor, not really paying attention to me. The other pointed his gun toward my chest, but he was holding it casually as though he wasn't really intending to use it. Which could only mean one thing: they weren't planning on killing me yet. But that really didn't make me feel any better. Not when I'd already seen first-hand what else they were capable of.

I looked around, my eyes darting from left to right, my brain whirring, trying to come up with possibilities of how I could get out of what was surely my intended execution.

The man by the chair wasn't carrying a firearm like the other two. Not in plain sight at least. But he did have on a utility belt. And I could see amongst other things he had a sheathed knife in there.

I began to calculate my move. I didn't like the odds, but I had to try something.

Then, as if justifying the sense of anxiety I'd been feeling, the man by the chair reached into his jacket pocket and my body instinctively tensed. His hand came back out, wrapped around what looked like the butt of a handgun. My brain registered surprise. It seemed strange that the man had been concealing a weapon when the other two had been so brazenly brandishing theirs.

But then I realised why. It wasn't a normal gun. It was a dart gun. Not a usual weapon to be carrying around so he'd stashed it awkwardly in his inner pocket. It was the same type they'd used to subdue me in the early days of torture.

And that scared me.

I couldn't go back to those days. I couldn't be their plaything anymore.

'If you're not going to sit down of your own free will then we'll just have to find another way,' the man said.

A smirk was creeping up his face as his eyes lifted to meet mine. He began to raise the gun toward me. He was only three or four paces in front.

I couldn't stand and wait for the inevitable. This was my chance.

I dived forward toward him. He hurriedly tried to adjust his aim but he knew he only had one shot. The gun only held one cartridge at a time. If he missed, he wouldn't have time to reload. That element of doubt in his mind was all I needed.

I bundled into him before he got his shot off and we tumbled awkwardly into a heap on the floor. He was a big man, wider but not as tall as me. His arms were like tree trunks, and I knew that if the tussle went on for long enough, his strength would overpower me. But I'd taken him by surprise, and if I acted quickly, he'd have no chance.

I'd managed to wrap an arm around his neck as we'd fallen to the ground. I was lying with my back to the floor. He was on top, facing away, his massive body weight crushing me. He was pushing and writhing his body and I knew that my one arm around his neck wouldn't hold him for long. I reached down with my free arm, trying to grasp his knife. He still had the dart gun in his hand. But despite his best efforts he had no way of turning it on me.

I heard shouts from the other two men. They couldn't shoot while their friend was on top of me. Or at least I hoped they wouldn't. Either way I had to be quick. I flailed, trying to reach the knife but not quite able to. The distraction of trying to get the knife got the better of me, though, and my grip around the man's neck loosened, allowing him to free himself.

My time was up.

But his movement also meant I could reach further. I grabbed for the knife, got it and swung it back as hard and fast as I could, straight into the man's gut. He screamed in pain and his resistance immediately waned. He finally let go of the dart gun and it clattered to the floor.

Badly wounded, the heavy man was still crushing my chest, screaming and writhing. At least with him on top, he was offering me some protection. I wrapped my left arm around his neck again. I wanted him right where he was. I looked to my side and the saw the other two men, still looking for their chance. I flung the knife out and it caught one of the men in his leg. He fell to the floor. But if he was tough, he wouldn't be down for long.

I reached out and grabbed the dart gun and hastily aimed at the last man. I fired and the dart hit him in the gut. But the effect of the tranquiliser wasn't instantaneous and he looked up and then began to bear down on me.

I cowered behind the man's body, using him like a shield. The guard with the dart in his belly opened fire, a succession of bullets whizzing toward me. The rounds finished off his friend; I could tell by the way his massive body weight slumped onto me. But none of them hit me. And I only had to wait it out for a few more seconds. When I heard the smack on the floor, I knew the final man was down and out.

But I wasn't home and dry yet. I pushed the dead guard off me, scrambled onto my feet and rushed over to the man with the knife in his leg. He was still on the floor, his teeth gritted, snarling. When he saw me he found the strength to turn his focus away from his wounded limb.

I kicked him hard in the face before he had a chance to reach for his weapon. A shooting pain shot up through my bare foot and into my ankle, but I blocked it out. I smashed my heel down onto his nose, which seemed to squash right into his face on impact. His eyes bulged open and his head lolled to the side. I hit him again with my heel and then again. And then once more with my other foot when the pain in the first became too much.

I don't know whether the blows were enough to kill him. But he wasn't going to be fighting again in a hurry.

The three men were all down, if not entirely out. No need to finish them all off. I had to be quick. I didn't know exactly what I was going to do next but I knew there would be more guards out there. And Lena.

But first, if I was going to escape, go on the run, I needed better clothing. I had on a simple cotton shirt and trousers, but the guards wore jackets and boots and I could tell from the ambient temperature in the place that wherever we were it was cold outside. I strode up to the tranquilised man and began to undress him. When I was done, I grabbed his gun and made my way to the open door.

I peered out and looked both ways. No signs of anyone else. But also no signs of which way to go. I certainly hadn't seen any exit the way we had come, so I opted to go in the other direction.

I was moving fast, almost running. The adrenaline was pumping through my body, making it hard to stay calm and focused. I knew I had to be cautious but I found it almost impossible not to just fall into a full sprint to get out of there as quickly as I could.

But as I rounded the next corner, I regretted having been so hasty when I almost bundled right into her. Lena.

The look of surprise on her face was probably much like mine. But she didn't cower or back away when she finally realised what was going on. Instead her expression turned to anger.

'Carl, what the hell are you doing?' she shouted.

I pulled the gun up toward her chest. Only then did I notice that she was pointing a handgun at mine. She really was a sly fox. I hadn't even seen her move.

'I'm getting out of here,' I said.

'Where are my men?' she snapped.

'Where do you think? You lied to me, Lena.'

'About what?'

'What was that back there? What were you planning to do to me?'

'Oh, Carl,' she laughed. 'What do you think we were going to do?'

'Exactly,' I said. 'I'm not sticking around for that.'

'Are you scared, Carl?' she said, giving a wicked smile.

'No.'

'Then why are you running?'

'I'm not going back to how it was.'

'This place was once a prison,' Lena said, looking up and around. 'Political prisoners mostly.'

I knew what that meant. Anybody who had opposed the communist regimes was locked away in purpose-built facilities. The gulag slave labour camps were notorious. I hadn't quite twigged that we were in one of the gulags but it made sense.

'And what do you use it for now?' I said.

'Well, you know we don't execute our political prisoners anymore. We're not animals, Carl. But we do believe in reformation.'

Her last words were emphasised, the grisly meaning behind them evident to me.

'So now what?' I said. 'You're not taking me back to that cell. Either you let me by or we're both going to die right here.'

'They're a hundred more guards in this place,' she said. 'How the hell are you going to get out?'

'You're going to tell me how.'

Lena laughed. 'Really?'

'Yes. Because you don't want to die. You enjoy your sadistic existence too much.'

'You know me too well, Carl,' she said, still smiling, even though I'd meant my words to be offensive.

We stood and stared for a few seconds. A standoff. Neither of us making a move. But eventually, much to my surprise, Lena lowered her weapon.

'There's an exit down the corridor,' she said. 'Take a right, then it's the second door on the left.'

I hesitated for just a second. Was Lena really going to let me go just like that? I know I'd asked it of her, but I'd never really thought she would cave in. Honestly I'd expected to have to use the gun on her. The only question in my mind had been how to do that and avoid being shot myself.

'Well, go on,' Lena said, her tone terse. 'You're right, Carl. I don't want to die. But don't think for a second that as soon as you're around that corner I'm not going to raise the alarm. The men are getting bored out here anyway. The chase will be fun.'

She smiled at me again. An eerie smile. I didn't trust her. I never had. Maybe she was sending me straight toward the other guards. But I wasn't going to stand and debate it with her. If she'd sent me to an ambush, I'd deal with it. If it really was the exit and they came after me, I'd deal with that.

Without another thought, I started to edge past her, my gun trained on her the whole time. I continued to walk backward, one cautious step at a time, keeping my eyes and my weapon on her. When I finally reached the corner, I turned and ran.

I sprinted down the corridor as fast as I could. As I approached the second door on the left, the one Lena had said was the exit, there was a volley of gun fire, coming from behind me. Bullets whizzed past my head, ricocheting off the floor and walls. I instinctively ducked but it was only through sheer luck that I wasn't hit.

A bullet caught the gun I was holding. My surprise at the sudden jolt sent the weapon flying from my grip. I didn't even think about stopping to pick it up.

Without once looking behind to see who was firing on me, I flung myself into the door, pushing down on the security bar.

And then I was out in the cold, dark forest. Running. Where to, I didn't know.

Chapter 31

'What is Project Ruby?' I said.

'What?' Mackie responded, sounding surprised.

'Project Ruby. The reason you sent me here in the first place.'

'I know what it is. I'm just not sure why you're asking me.'

'I'm asking you because you sent me here on a suicide mission to capture information that never existed.'

'Never existed? You've lost me.'

'Project Ruby isn't a weapon. It's a medicine.'

'Is that what they told you?' Mackie said.

'Is it true?'

'Of course not.'

'Then why did the documents they showed me say otherwise?'

'I've no idea what the Russians showed you, but whatever it was, it wasn't real. Why would we have sent you after something that never existed?'

'Exactly.'

'Hang on. You think we set you up?' Mackie said quickly – too quickly?

'Did you?'

'How long have you known me? Why would I ever do that?'

'Politics,' I said, cringing at my own lame answer.

Mackie laughed. 'Politics? That's funny. Politics isn't really my bag. I don't think I'd be in this job if it was. I do what I want, not what some bureaucrat in an office tells me to do.'

'You say that, but that doesn't mean it doesn't happen. We have sponsors. They *are* the government. How can what we do not get political?'

'You're moving off the point. Everything the JIA, everything *I* told you about Project Ruby was real.'

'How can you know that? Even if you believed that you were giving *me* good information, how do you know what *you* were told wasn't a load of bull?'

'I know because of what I've seen. And I can prove it to you.'

'How?'

Mackie smiled. 'Logan, we got the information. From RTK. We got the information you were sent there for. Your mission was a success.'

My heart lurched. With relief.

I'd been struggling so hard to come to terms with what Lena had told me, all of the confusing paperwork she'd thrust before me. I'd never wanted to believe any of it. But in the end, I had. She'd been very convincing. All bases had been covered. Even though my heart wanted so much to refute it, my head just couldn't.

There had always been that small window of hope, though, that everything she'd told me was the lie. I'd had no empirical evidence to back that up. It had been nothing more than pure, desperate hope. But as the days had gone on, that little piece of hope had been pushed further and further back, as my mind was filled with the information that I was being fed. Pushed so far back to the recesses of my mind that there had come a point when I wasn't even sure whether it was still there.

Mackie's words had just brought it back to the fore. I sat, unable to speak. I was desperate for what he'd said to be true even though I had no way knowing. I'd been lied to so many times that I didn't know what was real and what wasn't anymore.

'How?' I said.

'The wireless feed. It worked. Everything Dmitri tapped into came straight to us. We're not sure the Russians even know that yet. But we got it all, Logan. The mission was a complete success.'

I raised an eyebrow and Mackie quickly caught on why. His cheeks blushed a little and he nervously rubbed the back of his neck.

'Well, you know what I mean,' he said. 'A complete success in that we got the information. Obviously you…well –'

'I think you mean me being caught and tortured would be viewed as less than successful.'

'Exactly.'

'And what about Dmitri?'

Mackie simply shook his head. I knew what that meant.

'But the information,' Mackie said, 'we got it all. You don't believe me?'

'I don't know. I really don't know,' I said.

'What did the Russians tell you?'

'Quite a different story to you. What have you got? I want to see it.'

'You can see it,' Mackie said. 'But not here.'

'No. I need to see it. Now.'

'Come on, man, I don't have anything here with me. It's not the sort of information you just lug around. Think about what would happen if we were caught.'

'Then where?'

'Come back with me. Back to England.'

My heart sank. Because we were back to square one. I wanted everything Mackie had said to be true. But going back to England with him would be a massive leap of faith. And I wasn't sure I had any faith left in me.

'No,' I said. 'Not until I've seen something. I need to get my head around this before I do anything else.'

'The information's not here. We need to get you home. That's not a request. It's an order.'

This was all too much. Not just what Mackie was telling me, but the constant changes in mood. The way the conversation kept going off at unexpected angles, pulling my thoughts, my feelings, my loyalties in different directions.

What was I supposed to believe? The Mackie who was telling me what a success I'd been? Or the one who didn't trust me and didn't believe the nature of my escape?

'You have to show me something, or I'm not going anywhere,' I said.

Mackie finished the rest of his coffee, then folded his arms, sitting back against his chair rest.

'No. You're coming back with us, Logan. It's the only way.'

'Or what?'

'There's no "or".'

'What if I refuse?'

Mackie sighed. 'I hope it doesn't come to this, but we're going to get you back to England whether you like it or not. By whatever means necessary.' Mackie looked around at the two goons as he spoke.

I laughed, but I wasn't amused. 'What? Are you going to take me out the back to give me a beating? Your two chums hold my arms while you throw a couple of punches into my gut?'

'Don't antagonise me, Logan. Why do we even need to talk about that route? Just come with me.'

'You really think the three of you could stop me?' I said.

'There's five of us, Logan. Not three.'

'You're going to need more than five. I thought you knew me better than that.'

'I do,' Mackie said.

'Then why the empty threats?'

'Look, let's not carried away. I'm under no illusions as to what you're capable of, Logan. Hell, I trained you. But don't make us take things to that level.'

'Just get me something to prove what you're saying. Then I'll come home.'

Mackie sighed again and shuffled in his seat, making sure I knew that he was struggling with my request but was nonetheless mulling it over. It would be easy for him to get me some proof. The question was why he was so reluctant to do it.

Did it even exist at all?

'I'll see what I can do,' he said eventually.

'So what now?'

'Now we leave. I'll have to make a few calls. Give me a few hours. You go back with Chris and Mary.'

'You're kidding, right? I still need my chaperones?'

'You're just not getting it, are you?' Mackie said, talking down to me like I was being dumb. 'Right now none of us really knows what's going on here. And quite frankly if you really have escaped from the Russians – which I want to believe – then don't you think they're going to be after you? You'll be better off keeping company.'

I didn't respond. I guess I could agree to stick around with Chris and Mary. At least if only for a few more hours.

'Do you need anything?' Mackie asked.

'What are you offering?'

'What do you need?'

'Money. A gun. Passports. The usual.'

'I can't do that.'

'You can't or you won't?'

'I won't.'

'Because you don't trust me,' I said. A statement, not a question.

'Because I want to know that you're not going to turn around and run away. Chris and Mary will sort you out for food and whatever else.'

'I'm not sure why you bothered to ask then.'

Mackie tutted and shook his head. 'I never thought that the two of us would end up like this,' he said. 'Talking to each other in this way.'

'As far as I can see, you're the one who sees me as a threat.'

'Don't be so self-righteous, Logan. You might feel like a victim right now, but I can see that you trust me even less than I trust you. I don't know what they said to you. I just hope we can make it right.'

'Me too,' I said.

And with that Mackie got up to leave.

Dismay coursed through me. The tone of the meeting was as I'd expected, and yet I was feeling abject disappointment that it had been that way. It should have been a reconciliation, a reunion. The end of the whole sordid affair. It had been anything but, and even though I knew I had Mary and Chris to escort me around, the mood of the meeting and the manner in which it had ended made me feel isolated and alone.

Mackie pulled on his coat, scarf and hat and made his way to the door. Chris and Mary stayed seated. The two goons stood up, taking positions by the exit.

As Mackie approached one of them opened the door and stepped out into the street. A rush of sub-zero air shot into the café and sent a chill right through me. Mackie's other man stayed inside, glaring back into the room, alert for any unexpected movement from within the near-empty café. I found the whole masquerade quite amusing. Hardly discreet. Mackie was being treated more like a mafia don than a member of a secretive agency.

The goon out in the street held the door open for Mackie who turned to look at me as he reached the doorway. I think he gave the slightest of smiles, but I wasn't really sure. I didn't reciprocate, and he turned to leave.

But he never made it out into the street.

The bullet hit him square between the eyes before he'd even stepped over the threshold.

Chapter 32

What I did next I would call a gut reaction. I'm not sure whether it was conscious or subconscious; probably somewhere between the two. Certainly it happened without any premeditation. And there was nothing more to it than that.

I ran.

I hadn't heard the shot. Hadn't seen the shooter. From where I was sitting I could see little of what lay outside the café.

That didn't matter.

The noise of the bullet hitting Mackie – a dull, wet thwack; the way that his head snapped back as his body slumped to the ground; the dark spot in the middle of his forehead where the bullet had pierced skin and bone and entered his body – it was all I needed.

I knew that Mackie was dead. No doubt about it.

And I ran.

The two goons were half-crouching to cover themselves, hands fumbling at their sides for their weapons. Mary had hunkered down in her seat. Chris was up, out of his, facing me. His reactions were quick.

I heard shouts from Mackie's men. Or maybe Chris. Perhaps they'd spotted the shooter. Then the blast of a gunshot rang out. Wood splinters filled the air around me.

They weren't just shouting at me. They were shooting at me.

'Stop him!' one of them screamed.

I didn't stop.

I kept on going.

I flung myself at the fire door, pushing down on the security bar that released the lock. The door flew open a full one-eighty degrees, crashing against the adjacent wall. I launched myself outside, ignoring the shock of the ice-cold air filling my lungs.

I was in a narrow alleyway, barely wide enough to fit a vehicle through. The exit out onto the street was some thirty yards off to the left. I ran toward it. As hard and fast as I could. I stumbled as my feet hit unseen potholes, and slipped where my feet failed to get traction on the icy surface.

More shouts rang out from behind me. I risked looking back. Saw the outline of Chris and then one of the other men emerge from the café doorway. Guns drawn. I was already nearing the corner of the alleyway.

I heard another gunshot. The bullet ricocheted nearby. I flinched and ducked down as I rounded the corner into safety, at least for a few seconds.

The alley opened onto a small side street. I instinctively turned right. Left would only have taken me back to the cross-street that the café was on. Not many vehicles were on the road. A handful of pedestrians had stopped to see what the commotion was. They probably hadn't realised yet that they were hearing gunfire. If they had, they'd have been screaming and running.

I knew I couldn't stay out in the open. I had to find cover. Chris and Mackie's man would be coming around the corner any second. The next nearest road turning wasn't for another forty or so yards. I couldn't clear that distance before Chris and the goon came out into the open. As soon as they saw me, I'd be a sitting duck.

I heard the whir of a car engine, heavily revving, coming up behind me. Without breaking stride, I looked back and saw a dark saloon car, approaching fast. Too fast to be some random Russian out for a drive. For a second, I wondered whether it was Mackie's other man coming around from the front of the café.

The car raced toward me. All of sudden I heard pedestrians screaming. Was it because of the car, which was surely going to mow me down? Or had they seen Chris and the goon with their guns drawn, readying to take their next shot?

Either way, it seemed I was out of luck.

Every muscle in my body strained as I tried my best to keep going, to make it to safety.

I took one more look behind. The car's bulky bonnet seemed to fill my entire vision. But then, at the last second, the brakes were thumped on and it came to a screeching halt just a few feet in front of me.

I didn't know what would happen next, or who was in the car. My instincts, though, told me to keep moving toward it. If anything, it was my nearest cover.

The rear passenger door of the car flew open. A long, slender arm came into view. Then a face appeared that stopped me in my tracks.

Lena.

Lena, here!

'Get in,' she said. Her velvety-smooth voice was the essence of calm, as it so often was.

I turned to see Chris emerging from the alleyway. A look of confusion came to his face. He stopped. The goon came around the corner too. He didn't hesitate at all but raised his gun and opened fire, squeezing off two shots. I ducked. But his shots had been too rushed, not even a nearby ricochet to indicate where the bullets had landed.

I heard more screams from the pedestrians. Maybe one of them had been hit by a wayward bullet.

Chris began to raise his gun too. But rather than fire, he backtracked quickly toward the alley. When I turned back to the car, I saw the reason. The other rear passenger door of the car was now open. A man stood half in the car, half out, an assault rifle resting on the roof, pointing toward the alleyway. He fired off a volley of rounds. I flinched as the booming sound coursed through my head and echoed through the street.

I knew that the shots hadn't been aimed at me. The agonising yell followed by a thud from behind told me Mackie's man was down.

But I didn't dare turn around to confirm that.

Because, more worryingly, Lena was now pointing a handgun at my head.

'Get in the car,' she said. 'Now.'

Chapter 33

What choice did I have? I was certain to be killed if I refused. If Lena didn't shoot me then Chris almost certainly would. I moved toward the car. Lena got back in, scooting over to the middle of the back seat to let me in. She kept the gun, a Berretta, pointed toward me until I was in and had shut the door.

The guy with the assault rifle dived in next to Lena and the driver put his foot down. The car lurched forward. The back end fishtailed left and right as the tyres struggled to keep traction on the slippery surface.

As the car began to move away, I looked back. Mackie's man was writhing on the floor. I couldn't tell where he'd been hit, but it didn't look good for him.

Chris stepped back out into the open. He took aim and fired off the rest of his magazine. But the muzzle flare and the distant sound were the only evidence of his having done so. None of the bullets came close to the vehicle. It wasn't a surprise. Handguns are made for short distances and we were already too far away. Anything over fifty yards and even a trained marksmen would struggle, particularly given the limited time that he'd taken to aim. Luck would have been his only hope. But for now, at least, that seemed to be with me.

Or so I hoped.

As I settled back down in the seat, though, I didn't let the feeling of relief at the momentary respite take hold. It was highly unlikely that I could have got away from that café without Lena's help – I was unarmed and had no transport, no money. But I didn't want to feel anything positive about the situation.

For one thing, I wasn't stupid enough to not realise the mess I was in. Mackie hadn't trusted me. That was for sure. He almost certainly would have passed that message on to others. And now look at me: running away from the scene of his demise with the Russians, the very people I'd tried to convince Mackie I'd escaped from. Whatever lingering doubts may have been in the minds of my people would be gone now.

I was well and truly on my own.

Lena held on to her gun, though she placed it casually in her lap. She stared straight ahead, out of the front window, not paying any particular attention to me now that she had what she wanted. The man to her left did the same. He was holding the assault rifle vertically, the butt on the ground next to his feet, the barrel pointed at the roof of the car. I couldn't see the face of the driver, but could tell it was a man from glancing at the back of him. The front passenger seat was empty.

We drove like that, no-one saying a word, for five minutes as the car meandered through the cold, quiet streets of Omsk.

The silence gave me some time to let what had just happened sink in. A few minutes ago I'd been sitting opposite the person to whom, despite everything, I felt closest in the world. And he'd been gunned down in front of me. I'd seen Charles McCabe for the last time. I tried my best to hold back the tears that were welling in my eyes.

I knew the Russians had to be responsible for his murder. They'd wanted Mackie dead. They'd wanted *me* to kill him. And, rightly or wrongly, given that I'd run straight back into their hands, I was almost certain that Mackie's death would now be pinned on me.

I felt more alone than I could imagine. Every time I tried to do something to get my life back on track, another problem seemed to come along to set me back even further. And now, with Mackie gone, I felt so lost.

With the adrenaline of the chase gone, I was struggling to keep my emotions bottled up inside. I tried not to think about Mackie. Tried not to think about the gap that was now left in my life. I tensed my whole body, focusing on that, not the tears that threatened.

I managed to keep it locked up, like I so often did. But that only made me feel like I was betraying Mackie further. Was I so scared of feeling emotion that I wouldn't even let myself grieve for him?

I looked out of the window. I didn't know where we were going but I could tell from the now sparse buildings that we were heading out of town.

'Why did you kill him?' I asked, finally breaking the silence.

'You know why,' Lena said without hesitation, her eyes staring straight ahead.

'The cherry on top,' I said, referring back to one of the conversations we'd shared during my captivity.

Lena laughed. 'Something like that.'

'Who did it?'

'Not important.'

'It is to me.'

Lena turned to me, scowling. 'Why? Do you want your revenge now?'

Yes. I did. In fact, I knew at that moment that I *had* to avenge Mackie's death. If nothing more than to prove that I wasn't to blame.

'You still don't believe that your people turned against you, do you?' Lena said. 'Even after we saved your life just now.'

'I'm not sure what I believe right now. But I do know that I haven't been saved.'

'What makes you say that?'

'Well, am I free to go?' I said, looking down at the gun in Lena's lap.

'That's entirely up to you.'

'Then what do you want from me?'

'I want you to believe me. And we want you to work for us. You're a real asset, Carl.'

'It's never going to happen.'

'I don't think Mackie's bodyguards would be so sure of that. Nor those two who've been babysitting you. They're probably already telling their superiors how you've turned. How you lured Mackie to his death.'

She smiled at her last words and I had to fight back the urge to wipe the smirk off her pretty face. I clenched my fists as hard as I could, trying to channel away the anger.

She was right, of course. Mackie himself had doubted me, never mind Chris and Mary and the two other men I'd run away from after drawing Mackie to his death. Because that's how it would be portrayed, I had no doubt about that. I would be a wanted man.

'Despite your antics over the last few days, you've done exactly what we wanted you to,' Lena said, picking up on my thoughts and loving every second of it.

'However you try to play it,' I said, 'Mackie's death has nothing to do with me.'

I spoke through clenched teeth, angry with myself as much as anyone else. Because even though I desperately wanted her to be wrong, I knew that she wasn't.

'Do you really believe that?' she said. 'Then why did you run from the café?'

I didn't answer but it was self-preservation. Simple as that.

'You took us right to him,' Lena said.

'How?' I asked, immediately thinking through the possibilities.

Was one of Chris or Mary involved? Perhaps that was what they'd been talking about at the safe house the night before, when each had claimed the other couldn't be trusted.

'Ah, Carl, all in good time. Just be sure that if it wasn't for you, we wouldn't have been able to get to him.'

'Yes, you could. You could have got to Mackie if you wanted. It wouldn't have been that hard. You didn't need to drag me into this.'

'I don't think so. Your agency is secretive for a very good reason. Mackie is like a ghost except to those on the inside. You were our way to him.'

'But you still needn't have set me up like that. Why are you trying to make it seem to everyone else like I betrayed him?'

'That's not my intention at all. I just want you to see the truth. Mackie set you up. He's the reason you were with us in the first place. In the end, he got what he deserved.'

'He told me that Project Ruby is real. That my mission was real.'

'And did you believe him? Did he show you any kind of evidence to back up his claim?'

He hadn't. Nothing at all. But I'd wanted to believe him, no doubt about that.

'Didn't think so,' Lena said.

'He said the mission was a success,' I said. 'That they've got the information. If that's true, it'll all come out in the end. It won't matter what you do to me.'

'You're right. The mission *was* a success,' Lena said. 'We got you, Mackie's dead and they got the information they wanted. But the information was nothing to do with Project Ruby.'

'What's that supposed to mean?'

Lena was grinning, enjoying toying with me as usual.

'I told you before that they gave you up for information, remember? But it wasn't Project Ruby that your side wanted. It was something else. To us, though, having you wasn't enough. So we brokered a new deal. You know, the buck didn't always stop with Mackie. He didn't have to know about everything. So we went higher up the chain.'

Lena smiled knowingly. She was playing me as she always did. Leading me on. Only giving away what was required to further her own needs. I had met some snakes in my time, but she came out trumps as the most slippery and sneaky.

I got the gist of what she was talking about, though. Someone *had* betrayed me. And it looked like someone had betrayed Mackie too. Someone had made a deal with the Russians, sold out not only me but Mackie. And it had cost Mackie his life. I had no idea what the deal was. But I had a good feeling for who might.

Chris or Mary.

I didn't trust either of them. They'd both told me the other was dirty. Perhaps they both were. Though Mary had been convinced that Chris was working with the CIA. Maybe they were the missing link in all this. Or maybe Mary was the dirty one. A snake in the grass, Chris had said. Just like Lena.

'What was the deal?'

'All in good time, Carl,' Lena said. 'I'm going to need you to put this over your head for the rest of the journey.'

She took a small sack from the man next to her and placed it onto my lap.

'Why?'

'Because you can't know yet where we're taking you.'

'Even though you want me on your side?'

'It's somewhere safe. That's all you need to know.'

'And what if I refuse?'

'Please don't,' Lena said, tapping her gun again.

Her point was made. She wasn't going to get her wish, though. Not this time. Not any time. It didn't matter to me whether she was telling the truth or not anymore. No benefit would come from my being associated with her. I would never work for the Russians. For her.

Perhaps I should have let them take me to their supposedly safe place. Find their nest and then pass the information back home so the JIA could wipe out the lot of them. But whom would I tell? With Mackie gone, who else was there to listen to me?

I had only one other option. I lifted off my seat and threw my weight into Lena's side, barging and pushing into her. She hadn't expected the move; her body was relaxed. She provided little resistance to my weight, falling into the man next to her.

Lena let out a yelp and began to right herself, to correct her balance, pulling on her gun as she did so. But I didn't give her any time. Still pushing my weight down onto her, I reached around the handle of her Berretta with my right hand. Lena's fingers were wrapped around the grip, a finger on the trigger, but plenty of room for another. With my hand over hers, I forced my finger as far as I could toward the trigger.

The man to her side was trying to push Lena off him, unable to move freely with both her and my weight bearing down on him. I knew that would buy me a few seconds. I pulled the gun up, feeling Lena's resistance but easily able to overpower it. I pointed the barrel toward the driver. I wasn't even sure whether he was aware yet of the brief commotion. I didn't hesitate to find out.

I fired two shots.

Skin and bone and bloody flesh splattered on the windscreen of the car. The driver's body went limp, his hands dropped from the wheel, the engine's revs died down. At least his foot hadn't stuck on the accelerator.

In all likelihood we would still crash to a stop, but we weren't going fast, probably somewhere around forty miles an hour. At worst, we would collide head on with another, bigger vehicle. Potentially we would simply roll to a stop. I was aware of the risk. Now it was just down to fate.

Lena was squirming, using her right elbow as a weapon. Pulling on her hand to try to release my grip on her gun. Clawing at my arms with her free hand. But she had neither the strength nor the room, in the confined space, to manoeuvre.

I jerked the gun around, the barrel edging toward the man the other side of Lena. He'd almost readied himself with the rifle: his finger was on the trigger, the barrel in mid-arc. But the small cabin made its swing toward me difficult and ungainly. And slow.

In the end, the size of the gun cost him his life. I pulled on the trigger of Lena's gun twice more. One bullet hit the man in the neck, the other just above his right eye. More blood sprayed out into the air, some of it hitting me in the face.

Lena murmured and groaned as she tried to wrestle back control. The car swayed to the left then right as it hit the kerb at the side of the road and bounced off it. The movement pulled me away from Lena. For just a second she must have thought it would be her chance. But it was never going to happen. I threw my left elbow into her side, eliciting a shout of pain from her. I did it again. And then once more. With her fight waning, I took the opportunity to prise the gun from her. It didn't take much effort.

I immediately pointed the barrel at Lena's head. We were both panting, our chests heaving. Lena had a look of both shock and anger on her face.

'What are you going to do now?' she hissed.

I hesitated, waiting for the red mist in front of my eyes to clear. I had the upper hand now. No need to act rashly.

'Are you just going to kill me?' Lena said. She tried not to sound fazed by the situation, but her trembling body gave her away. For all her bravado, she was scared. 'In cold blood?'

'You're going to tell me the truth,' I said. 'I want to know the truth.'

Lena managed a laugh. 'Carl, everything I told you was the truth.'

I wanted to pull the trigger. I'm not sure why I didn't. Maybe I would have done, but in the end, the option was taken away from me.

Even though I'd known it would come, it still took me by surprise when the car finally came to an abrupt halt. Whatever we'd hit, I wasn't prepared for the impact. Maybe Lena's words had knocked my concentration. The sincerity in her voice.

At the moment of collision, I was half-turned toward Lena, sitting forward in my seat. My body was thrust forward, the belt not catching in time before my head cracked off the back of the driver's headrest. The gun that I was holding flew from my grip. I don't know where it landed.

My body slumped back into the seat, my head in a daze. I closed my eyes, hoping that the world would stop spinning. But it didn't. It only spun faster.

And within seconds, I was out.

Chapter 34

The first thing I was aware of was the screams. At first, when I opened my eyes, I thought I was back in my cell – I'm not sure why – maybe because of the fog in my head, the disorientation. But as I came around fully, I quickly remembered what had just happened.

My head was throbbing. I pulled my hand up to it. A lump the size of a ping-pong ball protruded from my right temple. Two slight trickles of blood had wormed down my face.

I looked over at the seat next to me. The body of the dead passenger, the man with the rifle, was slumped in the seat, his head dangling forward at an unusual angle. The impact had snapped his neck. Not that it would've caused him any bother – he'd been dead well before the crash.

Only then did I make sense of the empty space next to me.

Lena was gone.

So too were the weapons: Lena's Berretta handgun and the rifle the man next to her had used.

I cursed, reaching down to unbuckle my belt. As I pulled up, I jumped in shock when I saw a face plastered up against the window next to me. A grey-haired man, in his sixties or seventies, stood there. He looked worried. No, more than that: he looked terrified.

He stepped back from the window when our eyes met. I pushed the door open. The man rattled off something to me in Russian, but my brain wasn't able to process any of the words. It all sounded completely alien to me.

I looked over the scene. A few yards off to the side of me was the crumpled wreckage of another car. Two other vehicles had pulled over, their hazard lights flashing.

The man kept on talking to me. He wasn't hysterical, but he wasn't far off. I started to pick up most of his words amid the screaming still piercing the air. He was asking me who I was. What had happened to the people I was travelling with. Looking at the crumpled black mess, I could see why he was so concerned. Blood and lumps of flesh covered the inside of the car and were streaked across the windows. Clearly not the result of the head-on crash.

When I looked over to where the screams were coming from, I realised the woman who was screaming was doing so not because she was hurt but because of the horrors that lay within the car I'd come from. Three other people stood around her. All had blankets wrapped around them. I couldn't tell which ones were the occupants of the car we'd collided with and which had just stopped to help. Each of them had a stunned look on their face. No-one seemed quite sure what to make of me. Or the car that I'd stepped from with the two bloodied dead bodies.

The man was telling me that I should sit down. That I was hurt and my head was bleeding. I wasn't sure that I *was* bleeding anymore. Other than the trickle from high up on my head, much of the blood on me was from the passenger I'd shot in the face. But I didn't say that to the old man. He seemed distressed enough already.

He told me the police would be there any minute. A strange thing to say. Most people would have called for an ambulance after a road crash. But these people had been spooked, and they had every right to be. Mentioning the police to me was his way of letting me know that I shouldn't try anything funny.

'Where did the lady go?' I asked the man.

The concern on the man's face grew. Maybe my tone had been off with him, or he'd heard my foreign accent, which had aroused his suspicions of me further.

'What lady?' he said.

'There was a lady next to me. She's gone. Did you see her?'

The man shook his head. He seemed confused by the question, like he didn't believe what I was saying was true. I asked him to go and ask the other people. The question was better coming from him than from me. He was hesitant, but telling him that the lady was my friend and that I was worried about her seemed to help alleviate some of his tension. He turned, walked over to the others, and put his arm around the lady who'd been screaming. She stopped.

I heard the distant whine of police sirens. I didn't recognise where we were but I guessed somewhere on the outskirts of the city. The sporadic residential units that were interspersed between the mostly commercial units told me that.

From where I stood, I couldn't hear the conversation the old man was having with the others. But I could tell from the shaking heads and the bemused looks on their faces that they didn't know anything about a lady who'd been travelling in the car.

Lena had simply disappeared into thin air.

With the fast-approaching police, I knew I too should make myself scarce. The body count I was leaving behind was mounting and I no longer had any friends to help get me out of a sticky situation.

Already isolated from the group of people that the old man was now with, I could quite easily slip away without much effort and probably without anyone seeing me, heading into the dense foliage that surrounded us. But where would I go? I was miles from anywhere familiar with no mode of transport, barely any cash, and blood on my face and clothes. Lena must have thought the risk was worth taking, but I wasn't so sure I wanted to be out in the cold, on the run.

I did know that I had to get away before the police arrived. And as much as I didn't want to, I knew I had only one option.

I walked over to the group of people. Without a coat I was already shaking violently from the cold. Or maybe it was adrenaline, or anxiety, or a mixture of all three. Either way, even after standing out for only a minute or so, the cold was too much to bear without the extra layer of protection.

Heads immediately turned as I approached the group and their muted conversation and whispers stopped. The old man stepped forward, away from the others. He was small and slight, but he was obviously the plucky one in the mishmash group of people. The one willing to stand up for the rest. To protect them from me.

'I need a coat,' I said to him. 'And a car.'

I was surprised when he simply nodded, took off his thick coat and handed it to me. He then gestured toward a compact hatchback pulled up on the kerb behind me, before fishing for the keys in his trouser pocket and holding them out. I took them from him without saying another word. He walked back over to the group and huddled under the blanket with the woman who'd been screaming.

He wasn't going to try to stop me and neither were any of the others. I admired his handling of the situation. Sure, he and his group would have preferred the police to have been there to cart me off. But the police weren't there. And allowing me to leave was probably a blessing for all of them. The threat gone. That was what he and the others wanted.

I walked over to the car briskly. It was already facing the direction I wanted to head in: away from Omsk. It was an almost dead cert the police would be coming from the city and I didn't want to end up in a face-off with them.

If Lena had escaped on foot, alone, then the chances were she would have headed in the opposite direction, back toward life and civilisation. She would have had no chance heading out into the cold wastelands that surrounded the city. It was different for me. I had a vehicle now. And at that moment, I wanted to get as far away from everything else as I could, Lena included. She could wait. I would get to her eventually. For now I had to get away.

And then I would figure out what the hell I was going to do next.

Chapter 35

It wasn't long before dusk was upon me – Omsk has few daylight hours during winter – and not too long after darkness had descended I left civilisation for good and the last of the streetlights faded away in my rear-view mirror. The headlights of the car were good enough to light up the frosted surface immediately in front of me, but I couldn't make out anything else around. It just seemed like an endless black expanse. Traffic was sparse and becoming sparser.

After two hours of driving, I pulled onto a track off the main road. I crawled a few hundred yards up the frozen surface, into a wooded area, then shut off the engine. The cabin light came on and, without the beam of the headlights, made it seem even darker outside. The last building I'd seen was a farmhouse some five miles away. I presumed the track I'd taken would lead somewhere, maybe to another isolated house. From where I was I could see no streetlights, buildings or any other evidence of life. The place was eerily quiet.

My stop here was only temporary. I wasn't planning on going on the run in the vast wilderness. Not in these temperatures. Not in this country. But I would make do for a few hours at least. I had the shelter of the car, and the blankets that the owner and his companion had brought with them on their journey would protect me further. It was rare, foolish even, for people in conditions like this not to take precautions in case of a breakdown whenever they ventured out. In addition to the blankets, the old man had been sensible enough to have brought a large plastic bottle of water.

I stepped out of the car and used a handful of the water to wet my face, which I then wiped dry with one of the blankets. I wanted rid of the blood. And if nothing else, having a clean face would make me seem more normal should anyone come across me. My trousers and jumper were also covered with blood, and bone and tissue. At least the coat, taken from the man, was clean. Other than wiping off the lumps, I could do little about the clothes. I had nothing else to change into. I would have to just hope the coat covered up the worst of it.

Although I would be warm enough in the car for the night, I wouldn't stay out in this place any longer than was necessary. I wasn't going to be forced on the run. Coming here was simply a means of getting some breathing space to think about what to do next. I still didn't know what was happening to me. I couldn't be sure who my enemy really was. But I would find out.

The problem was, countless people were out there looking for me: the police, the Russians, my own agency. It wasn't going to be easy to evade everyone. What I had to do, I realised, was get back to Omsk. I was going to pursue *them*. Lena, Chris, Mary, whoever else was coming after me. I had to get to the truth.

How to do that was a different question. I couldn't take the car I'd commandeered back to the city. For all I knew there would be police patrols out looking for it. It would be game over before I'd even made it back to civilisation. And I'd already seen there were few others cars on the road so late in the day. So I didn't have many options left to me. I would stay here, in the warmth, and rest for the night. Then head out in the morning and somehow hitch a ride back to Omsk.

Once there, I would head off to find Chris and Mary first. Because they were the only people I knew how to locate. And a small part of me wondered whether – no, hoped – I could trust at least one of them. Which one, I wasn't sure.

I lowered the driver's seat as far back as it would go and placed the dank blanket over me. It smelled of oldness and mould and had obviously been left in the car indefinitely, awaiting its moment. But it would do.

My belly rumbled and grumbled. I hadn't eaten since breakfast. I now regretted not having had anything in the café earlier. Though the very thought of being in that place, of seeing Mackie's final moments of life, made me feel sick.

I didn't want to replay my meeting with Mackie. I didn't want to think about anything at all. But I couldn't stop it.

Those last moments with Mackie had been anything but poignant. They'd been uncomfortable and messy. He'd thought I was working for the enemy. I hadn't been sure whether *he* was the enemy.

Yet he was still the same man I'd once trusted with my life. And during our brief conversation, I'd really wanted to believe what he'd been telling me. I wanted everything to be just like he said. I'd been willing for him to show me the clincher, the one piece of evidence that would have convinced me that everything I'd been told about him was a lie. That every doubt I'd had was misplaced. Despite all my feelings of hurt and abandonment at having been left to torture, I'd wanted so badly for all of it to be washed away as we sat there in that café.

But in the end I hadn't got there. And now Mackie was dead and I'd run away from the scene, straight into the arms of the people who'd murdered him.

I knew the moment of reconciliation that I'd so craved would never come now. Even if everything Mackie had said was the truth, nothing would ever be the same again.

I closed my eyes and tried to shut out the cold and the blackness all around me. But it was impossible. I was tired, cold, hungry, being hunted by the Russians and my own people. And more alone than ever.

Chapter 36

It had been a long and shivery night in the car. I had been wide awake well into the early hours of the morning. When I finally managed to drift off it must only have been for a few minutes at a time.

It wasn't just the cold air and the cramped, confined space that was the problem. I struggled with the ever-changing predicament that I found myself in. Every time I closed my eyes I could do nothing to stop the nightmarish thoughts. Of the torture chamber and Lena's beautiful but evil smile. Of the last moments of Mackie, my friend and mentor. Of the Russians, closing in on me, willing me to join them. And finally, of my own people, hunting me down, bloody revenge on their minds.

By the time dawn broke, I was a groggy mess. Half asleep, the thoughts came and went even with my eyes wide open. At least I thought they were open. More than a few times I'd dreamed I was awake, looking out of the windows into the faint moonlight, only to open my eyes and realise that I'd in fact been asleep.

But morning had finally arrived and the car engine was now up and running. The heat was on, slowly thawing out my ice-cold hands, feet and limbs. I was en-route to Omsk. With the small amount of cash I had left I'd splashed out on sugary drinks, snacks and sweets from a garage that was just opening for the day. I was riding the crest of a sugar rush. It would dwindle quickly, leaving me no better off than before. For a short while at least, though, I was feeling almost human again.

I was heading back to Omsk but I knew I needed to dump the car. Riding back into town on the same stallion I'd stolen to get out was asking for trouble that I really didn't need. But I had no money left, having spent the paltry amount left over on food and drinks. The only other ways to get back to Omsk were hitching or stealing a car from another hapless victim. In the end I opted for the former.

I pulled up to the side of the road, put on my hazards. Then got out of the car. I had my coat on, buttoned to the top. It did a good job of hiding the mess on my clothes. I also had the blanket wrapped around me for extra warmth.

I waited. But for only a few minutes. I guess when the weather is cold enough to kill you in just a few hours you're more likely to stop if you see a stranded motorist. Nobody wants an unnecessary death on their conscience. Even that of a complete stranger.

The very first car to approach rolled to a stop just a few yards past where I was. A beaten-up old compact from the Soviet era. Not many of them were left now. They were notoriously unreliable, uncomfortable and inefficient. They didn't look too good either. But it was still a car and that was all I needed.

I walked up to the passenger door. The driver pushed it open for me as I approached, before I even had a chance to tell him who I was or where I was going. I leaned my head into the car. The warm air hit my face as it escaped through the open door, making me blink.

'My car broke down,' I said to the driver in broken Russian.

The man raised an eyebrow, probably at my accent. He looked to be in his forties and had a thick face with salt-and-pepper stubble that rose high on his cheeks and sank low on his neck. He was wearing jeans, a thick overcoat and a deer-hunter hat.

'Come on, get in,' he said. 'You're letting all the warmth out.'

I did as he said, got into the cramped seat and shut the door. The temperature inside the car was probably only ten degrees or so, but it certainly beat the outside.

'Where are you heading to?' the driver said.

'Omsk.'

'Me too.'

That wasn't a surprise. What else was there within a few hundred miles in that direction?

'I can take you there if you want,' the man said. 'Or do you want me to take you to a garage?'

'Omsk is perfect.'

'Okay, let's go,' he said, crunching the car into first and pulling away from the verge.

We drove on at a steady pace. A dusting of fresh snow lay on the ground but it wasn't thick enough to cause any problems. The cars that had already been down the road since the last snowfall had cleared neat tracks along the way.

'What are you doing in Omsk?' the man asked. I detected just the slightest hint of suspicion in his tone.

'I'm here on vacation,' I replied.

He raised an eyebrow. 'You picked a funny time of year.'

'Yeah. Those damn brochures,' I said. 'It's never quite the same as the pictures.'

The man laughed and I felt the tension in the tin-can car lift a little.

'What were you doing out of the city?' he said, apparently not yet convinced of my situation. Or maybe he was just being nice and wanted to chat.

'Just a curious traveller, that's all.'

'Yeah, well, I wouldn't bother. Not much out here.'

'Apparently not.'

'And you're travelling alone?'

'I usually do.'

'Huh,' was all the man said.

We managed little conversation for the rest of the journey. I sensed the man wasn't quite sure about me. Who could blame him? But I didn't care all that much. Unless I gave him a reason, he wasn't going to go running to the police to report that he'd given a lift to a suspicious foreigner. And even if he did, what was the worst that could happen? In all likelihood the police were already looking for me and I'd be long gone, away from this man, by then.

The man said he was heading to the western part of the city, only a couple of miles from where I wanted to be. I didn't bother to ask to be dropped off any closer. He told me I could take a bus to the centre, but I decided to walk. The exercise would do me good despite the freezing temperature.

I had an errand to run before heading off to find Chris and Mary. I had barely any cash left in my pocket. I needed more money, and other than stealing I had only one choice still left to me. The cash I'd had in the safety deposit box had gone. But I still had my bank account back in England. I could access that cash from the Western Union branch in Omsk.

First I needed to contact my bank to get them to set up the transfer. They would give me a ten-digit money transfer number to take to the teller in order to confirm the transaction. After walking for a few minutes I found a phone booth that was located just around the corner from the branch and put in a small handful of coins. I just had to hope it would be enough for the long-distance call.

Both the number for the bank and my account details were well ingrained in my brain, I had used them so often. I dialled the number and listened to the ring tone.

A woman answered the phone. She had a sweet, high-pitched voice and her accent, I guessed, was North Yorkshire.

'I need to set up an immediate wire transfer, please,' I said.

'Okay, sir. Let me just take some details.'

I rattled off answers to her questions about my name, date of birth, address and account number.

'Okay, yes, I have you on-screen. You said you wanted a new transfer?'

'Yes.'

A moment's silence followed and I heard her typing away at her keyboard.

'Into the account or out?'

'Out,' I said.

A few more moments of silence.

'Is there a problem?' I asked.

'Do you have any other accounts with us?' the lady responded.

'No. That's the only one. Is there a problem?'

'Well, it's just that the account details you gave me...that account has been cleared. It's been closed.'

'When was it closed?' I said, feeling anger boiling up inside me.

'Yesterday afternoon. The money was transferred to an offshore account with a different bank. Sir, you must have closed it? You're the only signatory. Is there something wrong?'

Yes, I thought. There really is.

She was still talking as I smashed the phone back down into its cradle.

Chapter 37

I was more angry than surprised. Taking my possessions from the safety deposit box was one thing. But this? That account was my personal money. Other than the scars on my body it was all I had to show for nineteen years of toil for the JIA.

But on top of the anger, which was hard to suppress, I also felt sorrow. I wasn't sure why. I'd had no emotional attachment to that money. It had sat piling up in that account for years and I'd never had the time or desire to use it to splash out on material items. The feeling of sorrow was more because of the implications of what the missing money meant.

Because it wasn't just my assignment that had been sabotaged – it was my whole life.

And the timing of the account closure was notable. Yesterday afternoon. After Mackie's death. Not really a surprise, but it was clear the agency were holding me responsible. It felt like my own people were now trying to erase my very existence. Was I just an irredeemable problem to them now? An embarrassment that they wanted to get rid of?

I stood doing nothing for a couple of minutes, trying to figure out my next move.

I had another call to make. There was only one number I could dial for which I wouldn't need money.

Mackie's number.

I didn't know who would answer the call, if it was answered at all. Even if it was answered, chances were I wouldn't know the person on the other end of the line. The agency was necessarily secretive. I'd met only a handful of other people who worked there. We had no functions or conferences or Christmas parties.

The people I knew were the ones I needed to: Mackie and a small number of agents I'd worked alongside at various points in time. Probably fewer than one person for every year I'd worked there. And some of those weren't even alive anymore. It had to be that way. Both for the safety of the agency and its agents. The fewer people you knew – and, more importantly, the fewer people who knew you – the more likely you were to survive a life like mine.

After five rings the phone was answered. Silence for a few seconds. Not even the sound of breathing. Then a man's voice.

'Who is this?' he said.

The tone was terse. The voice was gruff and low-pitched. I didn't recognise it.

The phone signal sputtered a couple of times, crackling coming from the earpiece, probably due to the poor weather. I wasn't sure whether the connection would stick.

It did.

'Who is this?' the voice said again. 'Logan, is that you?'

Now that the connection was clear, his voice fell into place. Peter Winter. Mackie's young assistant. Not a PA as such, more a trainee, being groomed to one day be a commander like Mackie had been.

We'd met before. He was young and clever and enthusiastic and inexperienced and a pain in the arse. We hadn't got on particularly well. But I knew Mackie had thought highly of him. And I knew he was loyal to Mackie.

Under different circumstances he might have been an ally. But I got the sense it wasn't going to be that way today.

'You've got a nerve calling this number,' he said. 'After what's happened. What the hell do you want?'

'I don't know,' was my feeble response.

'Where are you?' he said. 'We're going to find you. You'd better believe that. We will find you. You're a wanted man, Logan.'

'You think I killed Mackie?' The words sounded surreal to me.

'You know, you might think you're some kind of superhero, running around taking out the bad guys, but not this time.'

'I didn't kill Mackie,' I said.

'Really? Then how about you come in and we can talk all about it.'

'I don't think so.'

'I always told Mackie you were a loose cannon. That one day you would flip. I always thought you'd only end up hurting yourself, though. Not this. I never thought you'd end up like this.'

'Don't let your misconception of me get in the way here, Winter. I'm the one who's been wronged. I was the one who was left in the hands of the Russians. Left to months of torture.'

Winter laughed sarcastically. 'You're going to long for those days to be back when we're finished with you.'

'I didn't kill Mackie!' I shouted through exasperation rather than anger. 'Don't you get it? Someone is setting me up.'

'I got a call from your bank just now,' Winter said, ignoring me. 'Sorry about that. Just how long do you think you're going to last if you keep on running?'

I gritted my teeth. I'd already assumed the agency had been responsible for clearing my account. But to be taunted with it by this worm was something else.

'You need to give yourself up, Logan. Come in. That's the only way you can move forward now. If you don't, I'm only going to make things worse for you.'

'I'm not coming in. You should know better than that.'

'We're just protecting ourselves. And our other agents. That's all we can ever do.'

'You had no right to take my money.'

'*Your* money? Everything you've ever had in your life has been because of the JIA. It's not your money. And don't think we're going to stop there.'

'Your threats aren't exactly winning me over.'

'These aren't threats. When this is all over, you'll be begging for your life back.'

'Whatever you do to me, I'm going to finish this.'

'Play it like that if you want. You've still got a choice. If you make the wrong one, you can kiss your life goodbye. There will be no Carl Logan. With a few clicks on a mouse I can have your entire life erased. No fancy flat, no bank account, national insurance number, passport, driving licence, birth certificate. It'll be like you never existed.'

'If that happens, you're going to wish I never had.'

I slammed the phone down. This time I was unable to resist the urge to lash out and I thumped the metal panel behind the phone once, twice, as hard as I could. The whole booth shook and my knuckles were immediately throbbing. I didn't care.

They thought I'd turned. That I'd set up Mackie to be killed.

Yes, it had been a setup, that meeting. For the Russians to get access to Mackie. But it wasn't my setup. Someone else had got Mackie killed. And I had to find out who. I wasn't going to go down without a fight. I was going to get whoever had been involved in the whole sorry mess. Whatever it took. And I was going to make them pay.

Chapter 38

Winter said the bank had already put a call in to him. There had only been a matter of minutes between when I'd spoken to the bank and when I'd dialled Mackie's number. The fact the JIA were keeping such close tabs on me meant they would be close by. They'd probably be trying to trace the location of the calls I'd just made. Mary or Chris or whoever else was out there looking for me wouldn't be far away. That was fine with me. I didn't care anymore if they found me. One way or another I was going to finish this.

Strange as it seemed, standing in that phone box I couldn't help but compare my predicament to Grainger's. Sure, her situation was different. There was no sense that she'd been set up by anyone – the mess she'd found herself in was, ultimately, of her own making. But when she'd shot me and gone on the run, she'd condemned herself to a life in the shadows. Running was certainly an option for me too. But I wasn't going to go that way. Not while the people behind my demise were still out there. I had to believe that I could still find a life for myself, if only I could get to the bottom of what was happening.

My next stop was the safe house that Chris and Mary had taken me to previously. If they weren't looking for me already then I'd make it easy for them.

I retraced my steps from the first time I'd been taken there, back along the street of concrete monoliths, quiet and largely uninhabited. I didn't know what I'd be walking into when I reached the safe house. Perhaps Chris and Mary hadn't been back there at all since the incident in the café. Or maybe a full team of people was now there. I would be ready for whatever was thrown at me.

I arrived at the unassuming apartment building, walked up the slippery steps to the third floor and exited onto the corridor. As I approached the safe house I pulled up alongside the door, doing a quick recce of the area around. I saw no signs of life. I pushed my ear close to the door, straining to hear any movement. Nothing. I knocked three times and listened.

The sound of footsteps caught my attention. But they weren't from inside the flat. They were coming from the stairs, down the corridor, ten yards from where I was standing. Before I could react, I saw a figure appear at the top of the stairs.

A woman.

Mary.

She was looking down, fumbling with a set of keys. When she looked up at me, she immediately stopped. A rabbit caught in headlights. Both of us.

'Shit!' she said, turning on her heels.

She ducked back into the stairwell. I could see as she rounded the corner that she was already reaching into her coat. Probably for a weapon. I wasn't armed. I had nothing at all. But I didn't hide, I gave chase. Because of the look in her eyes. It told me three things:

She wasn't prepared.

She was alone.

And she was scared of me.

As I rushed over to the stairwell I could still hear her footsteps, descending. I realised she wasn't positioning for attack. She was running away. I reached the stairwell and leaned over, looking down. I spotted her, already three floors below, rounding the final bend.

I didn't know why she had run. To get back-up? Because she was genuinely afraid of me? Either way, I decided against going after her. Whatever her motives for running, I knew that it had given me a window of opportunity. Whether she was gone for good or just waiting for support, I had a chance to get into the safe house. Alone. For all I knew there would be money, food, even weapons in there. I needed all three.

I turned on my heels and raced back to the safe house door. I tried the door handle, out of habit more than anything else. Locked. But the door was rudimentary with a simple latch lock. Safe houses are deliberately inconspicuous. No heavy security. It only took one barge from my shoulder and the whole door splintered off its hinges.

If Mary had gone to get help, I had at worst a couple of minutes. I rushed into the flat, rifled through drawers, looked under rugs, behind curtains, under cushions. Nothing.

I moved on to the sole bedroom, which had twin beds. I looked under the pillows, under mattresses, in the cupboards. Again, nothing. Just a few clothes and some toiletries.

I rushed back out and through into the kitchen. I opened cupboard doors. I found tins and packets of food still there. I stuffed some crisps and crackers into my overcoat. I didn't have time to eat there and then but I would need to later.

But I found nothing else of interest. I felt slightly deflated, though what had I expected? Mary and Chris would have been careless to have left anything of value, anything useful to me, in plain view. If time had been on my side, I would have turned the place upside down. I was sure there would be something for me. Maybe under floorboards or in hidden drawer compartments. It would be very unusual to have not kept weapons hidden for times of need.

The problem was I didn't have the time to try to find them. I thought about taking one of the knives from the kitchen, so that I'd at least be armed. In the end I didn't. Without a sheath there wasn't really an easy way to carry an eight-inch blade. At least not without drawing unwanted attention or cutting myself.

Before leaving the flat I took the opportunity to quickly change out of the bloodied trousers and jumper that I was wearing, swapping them for a pair of jeans and a black turtleneck that I presumed were Chris's. They fitted me just fine and it felt great to have clean, laundered clothes on again.

I headed back to the open front door and hesitated just for a second, wondering whether I'd be walking out into someone's firing line. I stole a glance and didn't spot anything untoward. Taking big strides, not looking behind me, I moved back to the stairwell and began walking down.

As I approached the ground floor I again slowed, taking in my surroundings, looking for any threats. I could see none but it was impossible to know. I could only assume that Mary had scarpered or was hiding from me. Regardless, the stairwell was my only means of exit and time was not on my side. Moving forward was the only option.

But as I took the last step the question as to where Mary had gone was answered when I heard her voice.

'Don't move,' was all she said.

She needn't have worried. I wasn't going to. I could already feel the cold barrel of her gun pressed against the back of my neck.

Chapter 39

The choices that people make tell you a lot about their intentions. I knew that Mary wasn't going to pull the trigger. If she wanted to kill me, she'd already had two opportunities. But I had no idea why.

'Do you trust me?' she said.

No. I didn't. Not at all. I didn't trust anybody anymore.

'Yes,' I said.

She took the gun away from my neck and I turned to face her.

'Then follow me,' she said. 'We can't stay around here.'

She turned around and began to walk away. I was confused as hell. But I wasn't about to stop and try to figure out what was going on. Without a second's thought, I set off in tow.

We walked away from the safe house, back toward the city.

'Where's Chris?' I said.

'I haven't seen him since yesterday.'

'What about Mackie's bodyguard? From in the café?'

'I don't know where he is either.'

Something wasn't adding up, but I didn't know what. I got the impression, from her worried expression and her fidgety mood, that Mary didn't either. Unless she was leading me on.

She pulled me into a side street and we stopped walking.

'What's going on, Mary?'

Her head was bowed. I could tell she was upset. And scared. I didn't fully trust her. But her manner was certainly intriguing me if nothing else.

'Yesterday, after Mackie was shot,' she said, 'I headed back to the safe house with Bates. He was one of Mackie's security guards.

The other one was killed in the street. But Chris never reappeared. I don't know where he is.'

'So where's this Bates guy now?'

'I don't know,' she said, her voice fraught. 'He got a call last night and then went out. I've not seen him since.'

'Have you called in?' I said.

'Of course I have. I spoke to Winter. He just said to sit tight. It looks like he's been given an early promotion – the commander position he always wanted. But he's not exactly proving to be helpful so far.'

'And what did he say about Chris? And Bates?'

'He didn't tell me anything.'

Not altogether a surprise. Agents were only ever told what the JIA wanted them to know. Whoever was pulling the strings now that Mackie was gone was obviously keeping everyone tight-lipped.

'They're after you, Logan. They think you're with the Russians.'

'By *they* I take it you mean Winter?'

'Not just Winter. Everyone who's involved.'

'And what do you think?'

'They think you killed Mackie,' she said, avoiding the question. 'Or at least had him killed. They're not going to rest till they get you. They're in a panic about what you might have leaked. And about what further damage you could still do.'

I found it hard to believe her words. Not the sincerity of them, but how my whole life had been turned upside down. I never thought I'd see the day when I was wanted by my own people.

'Then why haven't you already killed me?' I said. 'That's what they want, right? That's what they've told you to do?'

'Because I know you didn't do it,' she said, looking up, into my eyes. 'I know you didn't pull the trigger on Mackie and I don't think you set him up either. I saw the look on your face when you ran. It wasn't the look of someone who'd planned that attack. You were really afraid. I've not known you for long, but I've not seen that look on you before.'

Her words hit me hard. I felt such relief to hear them. To hear that someone out there might be on my side. But it also brought home for the first time just how I'd felt the moment that Mackie had been killed. I *had* been afraid. But more than that, I'd been devastated to see a person so close to me gunned down. Even to the bitter end, with everything turning against me, I'd still wanted my relationship with Mackie to be like it always had been. And that would never happen now.

'What about Bates?' I said. 'What did he think?'

'I'm not sure he does think. He's not exactly a sharp tool.'

I smiled at that. Even though I'd never even spoken to him, he hadn't struck me as such.

'Why had you left the safe house?' I said. 'It's pretty early for you to have been out.'

She rubbed her neck nervously. 'I didn't stay there last night. I just didn't feel comfortable there on my own.'

'Then why bother coming back at all?'

'I wanted to see whether Bates or Chris had turned up.'

'I don't buy it,' I said.

It was the way she'd said it. Either an outright lie or at the least she was holding back on me. She definitely wasn't letting me in on something.

She sighed. 'Okay, look, I'm worried, Logan. You know what I said about Chris? Everything that's happening, Mackie's death, it has to be connected.'

'To the CIA?'

She shook her head, confusion on her face. 'Maybe…I dunno. Why did *you* come back to the safe house anyway?'

'It was the only place I knew to come back to. I'm not going on the run. I'm going to get out of this mess one way or another.'

I could tell from the look on her face that she was dubious about my aim.

'I just can't believe how messed up this is,' she said, putting a hand to her head in exasperation. 'Where the hell *is* Chris?'

'The Russians told me Mackie's death was part of a deal,' I said, looking for a reaction.

'You're speaking with the Russians?'

She looked shocked, as though maybe she'd made a mistake in having shown faith in me. Maybe she hadn't known that's how I got away from the café. I wasn't going to get into that with her now, though.

'I'm not working with them,' I said. 'Not after what they did to me. Don't ever forget that.'

'I never thought you were. Otherwise we wouldn't be speaking here, now.'

'Do you have any idea what kind of a deal the Russians could mean?'

'It's not something I've been told about. But then who the hell would have told me? Mackie was my boss, so I hardly think he'd have told me about a deal to kill him!'

'Yeah, figures.'

'But then…'

I got the impression she was trying to find the right words.

'You know something?' I said.

'Maybe. Maybe not. Not directly, but it's about Chris. You know I was trying to tell you before, but didn't get the chance?'

'Go on.'

'It may be a lead at least. He was on the phone the other day. In the safe house. He was asking about train times to Moscow. For today. I didn't think anything of it at the time. I assumed he was just getting info for his next assignment. Before yesterday, I thought we *both* would've been out of here by now. It could be nothing. But it's all I've got. Something is going on with Chris. There are just too many things that seem to be out of place.'

I thought for a minute. I had no way of knowing whether what she'd said was a complete red herring. Or she could have simply been setting me up. I didn't have many other options, though. And I was here to fight back after all.

'Well, I've not got anything better to do,' I said. 'Let's go to the station.'

Mary hesitated for just a second before turning around and we trailed back onto the main road, then headed onwards to the station. We walked at a brisk pace, trying to keep warm in the harsh winter air. But also because of anticipation over what might come next. A nervous cloud hung over both of our heads. I knew that neither of us fully believed the other. But I got the sense that she was struggling to get to grips with the situation almost as much as I was. Until things became clearer, we would both have to turn a blind eye to our suspicious minds. At least I knew that one way or another Mary would lead me to some answers. Even if she was just setting me up for a fall.

When we arrived at the station it was almost ten a.m. The morning commuters had all but dispersed. We found the departures board and noted the times of the remaining trains to Moscow. Only a half-dozen more were scheduled, mostly clustered in the afternoon and evening.

'Any ideas?' I said.

She thought for a moment before responding.

'It was definitely today he was talking about,' she said. 'And it was in the afternoon. He asked for times after one. That's all I can remember.'

There was a train at ten past one and then another after four. Either way, we had a bit of a wait on our hands.

'I guess we've got some time to kill,' I said.

'Yeah. I guess you're right. So what do we do from here?'

'We sit and wait. It's not like I've got anywhere else to go.'

'We can't just stand here, though. It's not exactly inconspicuous.'

'Why do we want to hide?' I said. 'If Chris is coming here, for whatever reason, then I'm not going to just let him get on his way.'

'Why do I not doubt that?' she said.

'Come on, let's go and get something to eat. I'm famished. Even if he does show up, it won't be for a couple of hours at least.'

The station itself was relatively bare. But outside I'd noticed a line of cafés and restaurants. If we got a good spot, we'd be able to keep a lookout for Chris from there.

We headed out and found a Russian café directly opposite the main station entrance. We chose a table back from the window but close enough to get a good view of the outside. We positioned the chairs so that we were both at right angles to the front. That way neither of us had our back to the door. We both wanted to be able to scope the area for anything untoward.

I ordered blini with sour cream and a pot of coffee. Sod the no-caffeine rule. I'd slept the night in the freezing cold on the folded-down seat of a shitty car. I needed a boost. Mary ordered eggs, bacon and a pot of tea. When I smelled the fried meat coming toward me, I wished I'd ordered the same. But the blini were good and I knew they'd line my stomach well and keep me going if I didn't get the chance to eat again in the next few hours.

'What happened to you?' Mary said, looking up from her cup of tea. It was the first time either of us had spoken for a good fifteen minutes or so.

'How do you mean?'

'When they caught you. The Russians. What did they do to you?'

'It's hard to talk about it,' I said. 'I'm sure you can understand why.'

'It's just that I've never been in that situation before. I don't know how I'd cope. I know they train you for it. But to live it – that's something else.'

'After a while, you don't even think about it anymore. It just happens.'

'Did they have you in a cell?'

'Yes,' I said.

'When we first spoke to you, on the train here, I couldn't believe how with it you seemed. And not just mentally but physically as well. I couldn't understand how you could have kept yourself so together that whole time.'

'I didn't. At times I thought I'd never get out of that place. That's not easy to deal with. It messes with your mind. There wasn't an end in sight to it either. There was never any indication that anyone was coming for me. I got out of there on my own account because I didn't want that place to be my grave.'

'I know,' she said, ignoring the jibe at her, at the agency, for leaving me in there. 'That's what I mean. I just can't even imagine what being in there must have been like.'

I couldn't be sure whether Mary was just fishing or if her questions were born out of genuine interest. I got the impression that it was probably a mixture of both. As someone who'd never found herself in such a situation, so she claimed, I could understand why she'd want to know about it.

'Did they break you?' she said, her face deadpan.

I paused from eating and looked her in the eye. A long, hard stare. I certainly didn't want to start getting into the details of what I did and didn't say to the Russians during my time there.

She broke eye contact first. 'Sorry. I didn't mean to put you on the spot. I just want to understand what happened to you. But it was wrong of me to even bring it up.'

'Let's just talk about something else. Okay?'

'Yeah, okay.'

'Tell me a bit about yourself. How did you end up here?'

She smiled. I hadn't seen her do that much recently. It suited her. She had such soft features, but when she wasn't smiling her face took on a look of perpetual angst – though maybe that was just at the situation that she found herself in.

'I've been with the agency for two years,' she said.

I raised my eyebrows. I'd sensed a nervousness about her manner. Much of that was likely down to her inexperience.

'I joined from uni,' she said. 'I'd always wanted to be a psychologist but I wound up with a data analyst role at the JIA. Mackie soon persuaded me to become a field agent.'

If she'd joined straight from university, her two years with the JIA would put her in her early twenties still. I'd thought she was older than that. But I could now see how the age matched both her features and her manner. I was surprised Mackie had let someone so young, so naive, out into the field on a case like this. But then Mackie never did anything without a reason. Whatever Mary's qualities were, Mackie would have been using them to their maximum.

'So how long have you been in the field?' I said to her.

'Just a little over a year.'

I shook my head.

'I know what you're thinking,' she said.

'Yeah?'

'Yes. You think I'm too young, too inexperienced, to be out here with the likes of you.'

She was dead right. I did.

'You're also probably thinking I had some privileged background. That I went to some posh school and then a top university before walking into this job.'

'It had crossed my mind,' I said. It was something I'd presumed when we'd first met on the train.

'But none of that makes me any less qualified to do this than you,' she said with just a hint of anger. 'I might have been picked for this role for very different reasons to you, but that doesn't mean I'm not good.'

'No, but I agree with you one hundred per cent that we're different. In fact, I don't think we could be any more different.'

She huffed and leaned back in her seat.

'Okay, I'm sorry,' I said. 'I was just trying to lighten the mood, but obviously it didn't work. I don't think you're any less qualified to be here than me. You just have to understand that I'm not here because of some career ambition. This has been my life.'

'I know that,' she said. 'And that's why I feel that I can trust you. I know what this all means to you. What Mackie meant to you. I look up to you, Logan. You're one of the agents that everyone aspires to be.'

'Believe me, it's not as glamorous as it might seem.'

'Not to you. But that's what makes you all the more special. Because you don't even realise how good you are.'

I felt myself blush just a little at her comment and I could see from the twinkle in her eye that she noticed. She beamed a smile at me and I felt my cheeks turn redder.

'See?' she said, a wide grin on her face. 'That's what I mean. You're a good man, Carl. I know it.'

Her words hung in my head and I felt butterflies in my stomach. Such a strange feeling, but I knew where it was coming from. Mary was young and she was pretty. And she was flattering me. I was attracted to her, no doubt. And it was a real attraction, however fleeting. Not the captive's empathy that I'd felt toward Lena but the kind of genuine sexual attraction that I hadn't truly felt since I'd met Angela Grainger.

I hadn't been with anyone since then – I hadn't had the time or the chance to even think about it. Not long after Angela disappeared I'd been sent to Russia. In a way it had been the perfect case to take my mind off what had happened between us. The intensity of living in a foreign, alien place had taken up so much of my focus that I'd been able to push thoughts of her to the back of my mind. But now, sitting in the café, it was hard to not feel an attraction to Mary, to someone stuck in the same dire situation as me. It was a nice feeling.

Mary wiped her mouth with her napkin and got to her feet. 'I'm just popping to the ladies',' she said.

I smiled and she walked off to the back of the café. While she was gone I ordered another round of drinks and some bacon and eggs for myself. The temptation was just too much for my neglected belly to pass up on. The waitress was quick and the extra orders arrived before Mary returned. When she did, she sat down and thanked me for the fresh tea.

'We could be here for a while,' I said. 'May as well keep the hot drinks coming.'

'Yeah, it really is bitter out there. I knew it'd be cold here, but living it is something else.'

'Plus you're paying,' I said to her, grinning.

'Ha. So you're just as chivalrous as I'd heard then.'

I shrugged and got stuck into my bacon and eggs. We sat in silence again for a few minutes while I ate. With each mouthful I couldn't help but feel that the lighter mood that had crept in earlier was seeping away. I couldn't place why, but the atmosphere between us was just that little bit uncomfortable again.

I finished my second plate of food and ordered a glass of water. The two rounds of coffee had perked me up all right but they'd also left me feeling parched.

A tinkle came from the bell above the door to the café. Mary and I both instinctively turned our heads to look at the arrivals.

Two thickset men entered, long black coats closed all the way up to their necks. One was a good six inches taller than the other. They each wore jeans and heavy, work-like boots. The taller man had closely cropped greying hair and a flat, wide nose like a boxer. The small man had a shiny bald head and a protruding brow that cast his squinting eyes in shadow.

Not moving away from the doorway, they both gazed over at our table. I glanced back at Mary, saw the apologetic look on her face.

And immediately knew what was happening.

I'd never seen the two men before. But I knew who they were and why they were there.

Mary had set me up.

Chapter 40

'Logan, it's for your own good,' Mary said, getting to her feet, backing away.

I was already on my feet too. My eyes were darting between her and the two men, who were standing cautiously just a few steps from me, near the door. Other than the waitress, who was now nowhere to be seen, we were the only people in the café.

'Just come in with us, Logan,' Mary said. 'We need to get this all sorted out. But it's not going to happen if you keep running.'

'You lied to me,' I said. 'You set this whole thing up.'

'Not everything was a lie.'

From the corner of my eye I saw the taller of the two men take a step forward. I could sense Mary slowly inching away. Her words were calm and reassuring but her bodily actions were giving her away again. She was expecting a confrontation. And she didn't want any part of it.

'Logan. Come with us,' the tall man said. 'Let's just make this easier for us all.'

I turned to face him. He was just three or four strides away from me. He had both of his hands down at his sides and was standing slightly off from square to me. The smaller man, standing behind him, had taken the same pose. Though I noticed in his right hand he was trying to disguise a weapon of some sort underneath the sleeve of his coat.

'Don't make a scene,' Mary said. 'This is for your own good.'

'Mary, I've got to tell you I'm pretty sick of people telling me that. Let me decide what's best for me.'

I turned to face the men. 'You two, I suggest you leave here. Now. Or you won't be leaving here at all.'

The men stood, motionless, no response to my macho ultimatum.

But, not for the first time, I'd underestimated the threat from Mary. And I would have been suckered by her too, if it hadn't been for the reaction of the tall man.

When he should have been eyeballing me, he flicked his gaze over behind my shoulder. It told me enough. I sidestepped, turned my body and grabbed Mary's wrist, which she'd thrust out at me, stun-gun in hand. A split-second later I'd have been on the floor, game over.

With my free arm I reached around and then yanked her forward. She tumbled over, her arm twisting behind her back painfully. She yelped but I let go before the shoulder popped. I don't know why. It just seemed like a step too far to have broken her arm.

I saw the movement as the tall man rushed me. I was already on my feet, the stun-gun now in my hand. I met him head on.

The knife in his hand, which I'd not seen, arced through the air. I'd come in low and it missed me. I curled my arm around the man's neck, locking his head, and pulled downwards. His body twisted around and I fell to my knees, carrying him down with me. With my left arm I pressed the stun-gun into his chest and pushed on the power button. I heard a fizzle and crackle as the electrical current coursed through him. His body bucked and shuddered and I felt the strength go from him.

As his body continued to spasm, I pushed him off me and looked up to see the little man. His eyes wide, he was still in the same position, about five yards from me. He was grappling with the weapon in his hand, pulling it out from his sleeve, trying to get his aim. It was a gun. If I gave him the chance, it would be an easy shot for him to take.

I grabbed the fallen man's knife and leaped to my feet. The small man managed to adjust his aim but I was already on him. He'd been too slow. His decision to conceal his weapon had lost him the fight. A shocked look was plastered on his face as I slashed at his wrist with the knife. He let out a scream. I thrust a balled fist upward onto his chin. His head snapped back and he went down onto the floor without another sound coming from his lips.

When I turned back I saw Mary getting to her feet. She was reaching in her bag, but she was fumbling. She wasn't used to these situations. One year a field agent. I'd bet my life this was the first confrontation she'd been in. And she certainly hadn't received anything like the training I had.

I grabbed the gun, a Glock, out of the bloodied hand of the small man and strode over to Mary. The taller man was groaning on the floor. As I walked past him I took aim without looking and put a slug in his knee. I wasn't going to give him the chance to come after me. He let out a piercing cry.

Mary jumped at the sound of the gun firing and cowered away from me as I approached. She was holding the handgun she'd been so hastily trying to locate. I grabbed her wrist.

'Drop it,' I said.

She did as she was told. Tears were streaming down her face. Her bottom lip was quivering.

'You set me up?' I spat.

'No,' she pleaded. 'I just did what I had to do. You can't go on like this. You can't go running around taking on everything that gets in your way.'

'That's exactly what I have to do. It's what I've always done.'

'Please don't hurt me,' she said.

'Tell me the truth, Mary, and I won't. Will there be more of them?'

'I don't know. I didn't know who would come. I was just told to wait here with you.'

I wanted to know exactly how and why I'd been led to that place, but we couldn't stand and debate it in the café. I had to believe that the lone waitress, who I presumed was cowering away in the kitchen, would surely be onto the police even if no-one else from the JIA was coming.

'Come on, we need to go,' I said, pulling on her wrist.

Mary resisted. 'Go where, Logan? There isn't anywhere left to run. You're just getting yourself into a bigger mess.'

'I'm just surviving,' I said.

I pulled on her arm, harder, and she relented. I dragged her over to the door and out into the open. I eyeballed the scene outside but saw no indication that anyone else was coming for me.

For now at least. I looked at the clock tower of the station. Quarter to one.

'What you said about Chris. Was that true?'

She looked up at me, offended. 'Of course it was. That's why I'm here. I've been told to follow him to Moscow.'

'Then let's go. We're getting on the next train. Even if Chris isn't on it. I'm not staying in this damned city any longer than I need to.'

We hurried over the road and back through the main entrance to the station. She wasn't resisting anymore but I didn't let go of her wrist at all. We headed over to an automated ticket machine; no point in adding more witnesses to the list. I finally let go of Mary and she immediately began to nurse her wrist with her other hand. I could see that I'd left a ring of red flesh where I'd held on to her, but I didn't feel bad. She was lucky I hadn't put a bullet into her. In fact, I wasn't entirely sure why I hadn't.

We booked a private cabin for the journey. It would take us nearly two days. It would have been far quicker to fly but I had no way of getting through security at the airport anymore.

As we made our way through the station, Mary seemed to relax a little, walking with me rather than me having to drag her. But I wasn't going to take off the leash yet. I needed to find out more from her. First, though, I wanted to be on that train and out of Omsk for good.

We headed down the ramp to the platform. I noticed that the train was already there, waiting. Two policeman patrolled the area, strolling along the side of the train. I slowed down, my eyes fixed on them, willing them to not turn around. I didn't think they'd be there looking for me, but I couldn't be sure and I'd rather not have to test it out. We scuttled across the platform toward an open carriage door, my gaze on the two policemen the whole way. But when the policemen moved past two waiting passengers who had been blocked from my view, there was the briefest flash of recognition in my mind. I did a double-take.

Chris.

He was standing, waiting, at the far end of the platform.

And he wasn't alone.

Chapter 41

I didn't recognise the man Chris was with. I guessed it may have been the man from the rendezvous that Mary had told me about. Assuming she'd been telling me the truth. A big assumption to make given form.

For the next two seconds, as we moved across the platform toward the train, my world seemed to go into slow motion. In silence. As though everything and everyone was now focused on me. I wanted to be on the train, away from the gawping faces. But I just couldn't get there quickly enough. Like in a dream when you're trying to run away from a monster but your legs are like lead and for no explicable reason you just can't move them.

As if on cue, Chris began to turn in my direction.

The next second we were safely through the train door and normality suddenly returned.

I looked over at Mary. She was breathing heavily. I could tell from the stare in her eyes that she'd seen Chris and the other man too.

'Do you think they saw us?' she said.

'I hope not,' I said. 'Was that him? The man you saw Chris meeting with?'

'No,' Mary said, shaking her head. 'I've never seen him before.'

I believed her. But I was also surprised by her response: her expression told me that she knew I didn't quite trust her answer. Which only made me more determined to find out what was going on.

The journey to Moscow would be long. I was glad Chris would be on the train. But confronting him straight away wouldn't help. I wanted to be out of Omsk. I wanted to know what was taking Chris to Moscow.

'We should get to our cabin,' I said. 'Lie low for a while. We've got a lot to talk about.'

Mary looked apprehensive. About which part of what I'd said I wasn't sure. But she only hesitated for a second or two. I could tell that she didn't want to be out in the open any more than I did. She equally probably didn't want to be stuck in a confined space with me. But apparently it was the lesser of two evils.

'I think it's this way,' she said, turning back and heading in the opposite direction to where Chris had been standing on the platform. That was a welcome relief.

We entered the cabin and I slid the door closed behind me and locked it. Along one side of the pokey room was a static bed with another fold-down one above. On the other side was a single chair and a doorway into the tiny bathroom. The conditions were cramped but would be comfortable enough.

Mary sat down on the bed and I took the chair. She stared into space and I could tell that she was mulling over what had just happened in the café.

'I can't believe you attacked them like that,' she said eventually, her voice trembling, looking down at her feet.

'They didn't give me much choice,' I said. '*You* didn't give me much choice.'

'Choice? I wasn't going to hurt you, Logan. I had a stun-gun. We were going to take you in.'

'And then what?' I said. 'Don't be so naive. I've been locked away and tortured for the last three months. You don't know what the agency would do to me. How could you? What I do know is that nobody is taking me anywhere against my will. Not again.'

'Why didn't you shoot me too?' she said.

'Because I didn't need to. I didn't see you as a threat.'

'Oh, you really think you know me, don't you?' she spat.

'I didn't mean it like that. I didn't see you as an imminent threat. Plus I need some answers. And I think you have them.'

'I've already told you what I know.'

'About Chris? Yeah, well, that's not good enough. How did those two in the café even find us?'

'I'd been following you,' she said. 'I was telling the truth. I really hadn't been staying at the safe house. But I'd been on the lookout for you returning. When you did, I followed you up there.'

'And then you lured me to that café?'

'Yeah,' she said, sounding and looking proud of the fact. 'I had to be at the station anyway to check on Chris too. So it was the ideal spot.'

'The phone call you overhead Chris having never happened, did it?'

'No. Winter told me Chris would be on this train. I don't know how he found out or what is going on but I've been told to keep on Chris's tail.'

'When you went to the toilet in the café, you confirmed the hit on me.'

'It wasn't a hit,' she sighed. 'I'd already confirmed I had you when I saw you heading to the safe house. I made a call in the café, but only to set the timer.'

I felt a little foolish for having been so easily snared. But it had worked out in my favour in the end. Based on everything I'd seen and heard, much of what Mary had already told me about Chris, about the situation, seemed to be true. She'd lied to me, had tried to snatch me, but I still sensed that her intentions were good. And that she'd seen some good in me.

'Did you know them?' I asked. 'The two men in the café, I mean.'

'No,' she said.

I heard a whistle from the platform edge and a moment later the train began to slowly crawl out of the station. We passed the two policemen, who were now strolling back down the platform, toward where we'd boarded the train. They didn't look up at all as we passed. Clearly they hadn't been on the lookout for me or anyone else in particular after all.

In any case I knew the real threat was on the train. Time was on my side, though. I had forty hours to decide whether or not to confront Chris and his companion on the train, or wait for Moscow. That was unless they came to me first.

'So what do we do now?' Mary said.

'We wait,' I said.

'They'll be expecting to hear from me, back at the ranch. It won't take them long to figure that something's gone wrong.'

'Yeah well, how are you going to call them now?'

I'd already taken Mary's phone to pieces and dumped it at the station. No point in giving the JIA the chance of tracing our position. Though I had to assume they would guess we were headed to Moscow – they had told Mary to follow Chris onto the train after all.

'So you're kidnapping me now? Is that what this is?'

'Why do you feel so threatened by me?' I said.

She laughed sarcastically. 'Oh, I don't know. Maybe it's because you just felled two people who were trying to help you and dragged me onto this train against my will.'

'I'm not kidnapping you. And it's not against your will. You said yourself you were going to be on this train anyway, spying on Chris. I'm just trying to find out what the hell is going on. You were the one who spoke out to me about Chris. I know you have your orders, but I think deep down you want my help. And I could do with yours.'

'You really do think you know a lot about me,' she scoffed.

'Let's just drop it for a bit,' I sighed.

'No, Logan, I don't want to drop it.'

I was tiring of the barbed conversation. The to and fro. I sat up in the chair, leaned over to her.

'You just don't get it, do you?' I snarled. 'This is my life we're dealing with. It's not just a fun assignment, spending a few months all expenses paid, acting out my childhood fantasies from watching too much TV. You can't even begin to understand what I went through while you sat in your hotel room eating room service. And look how it's turned out. My own people don't trust me, have sent people to kill me. The Russians have set me up for murder. Meanwhile one of our agents has gone rogue and I'd bet my life that fits into this somehow. So you'll pardon me if I don't empathise with your position right now.'

She didn't have a response to that. She looked out the window. I sat back in my chair.

Neither of us spoke for the next couple of hours. The initial anxiety I'd felt at spotting Chris subsided. It looked like he hadn't spotted us on the platform after all.

I watched out of the window as we sped through endless frozen forests and steppes. Once darkness descended, though, I couldn't see a thing. No lights outside, no roads or towns or villages to break up the black. The sky had also clouded over, a sign that snow was probably on the way, and so there was little by way of moonlight even. A feeling of isolation began to creep back around me. Even though in contrast to the previous night I would tonight be warm and in company, it seemed that my predicament hadn't really eased much.

Mary was now lying down, but she was still awake. She had been staring at the ceiling above her, barely blinking.

'I've been thinking,' Mary said. 'About what Chris is doing on here.'

'And?'

'Well, there must be some sort of rendezvous taking place in Moscow, don't you think?'

'Could be. Or he could just be heading home or into hiding. We don't really know what damage he's done yet. If anything at all.'

'True. But the plan's to follow them, right? When we get to Moscow.'

'I guess so,' I said, though I hadn't ruled out just confronting him on the train and being done with it. It would be one less thing to worry about.

'I think we should follow them.'

'I think we should take it in turns to get some sleep,' I said to her, changing the subject. 'May as well take the chance to rest.'

'I'm not tired,' she said.

'Suit yourself.'

I closed my eyes and was off within seconds.

Chapter 42

I'd been dreaming about Angela. We were staying together in a hotel in Paris. On an assignment of some sort, but that wasn't important. We were both tired out from an exhausting day, lying fully clothed in each other's arms on the soft quilt of the oversized bed. Gazing longingly into each other's eyes.

It was definitely Angela I was with, no doubt about it. The way she moved, acted, spoke. Just the way we were with each other – so natural.

But it wasn't her face.

It was Mary's.

And when I woke up out of the dream with a start, I immediately felt guilty. Felt betrayal. Mary was attractive, but I simply didn't want to have those kinds of feelings for her. And yet, in my dream, it had been her face that I'd kissed and cherished.

'Bad dream?' Mary said.

Her voice shook me from my thoughts. I realised then that I was panting and sweating.

'Kind of,' I said.

I was still in the chair, Mary on the bed. She was in the same position as when I'd shut my eyes. We'd each been sleeping on and off for a good few hours. I wondered whether Mary had been sitting there like that the whole time I'd been asleep, just watching me, not sure what to do next. I didn't bother to ask.

Many years ago I'd become accustomed to sleeping in unusual places, unusual positions. And I'd also become used to sleeping with a gun. I'd had my hand in my pocket, feeling the hard steel, the whole time I'd slept on the train – almost like a child uses a comforter.

I hadn't worried about whether Mary might try to grasp it from me while I slept. Not only did I not think she had it in her, but I trusted myself to have woken up if she'd even moved off the bed. What can I say? I'm a light sleeper.

Morning had broken some hours before. The sun shone in through the cabin window. The clouds had cleared, leaving a bright-blue sky once more, but not before they'd despatched a heavy covering of new snow.

Neither of us had eaten since coming onto the train and now that I was awake my belly was starting to grumble incessantly. As I stood up to stretch it let out a long growl.

'You sound as hungry as I feel,' Mary said, laughing.

'Tell me about it,' I said.

'Why doesn't one of us just go down to the restaurant and grab something?' she said. 'There's a restaurant car at each end of the train so I can't see us bumping into Chris, presuming he's at the other end to us, if that's what you're worried about.'

'I'm not worried about Chris,' I said. 'But there's no point in drawing attention to ourselves. Let's just sit and wait.'

I took the crackers and crisps out of my coat, the ones I'd taken from the safe house the day before, and tossed them down onto the bed. They were crushed to pieces but they were still food.

'We can eat these,' I said.

Mary flapped her arms and huffed but I didn't care. As much as I wanted to eat a full meal, the risk was too high. We were in a good position. No point in jeopardising it.

We ate the paltry food then sat for a good while longer, not much left to say to each other. I nodded off a couple more times from boredom as much as anything else. It wasn't until well into the following evening, when darkness had once again returned, that I finally felt the urge to move.

'I'm going to take a shower,' I said.

I got up and walked into the shoebox bathroom and shut the door. The room was freezing compared with the main cabin and I shivered and my skin goose-pimpled as I stripped off my clothing. The shower cubicle was so small that I barely fitted inside and I found it almost impossible to turn around. But the hot water soothed my sore skin and aching bones, and after a couple of minutes I was feeling revitalised. I washed with the soap from the wall-hung dispenser and then just stood, enjoying the water for a few minutes more.

When I was done I stepped out of the shower and dried off with the threadbare and too-small towel. I looked at myself in the mirror. I had a large bruise on the side of my forehead from the car accident the previous day. It was visibly raised and a deep-purple colour, the edges yellowing. Other marks covered my torso and arms, both from the crash and the various other scrapes I'd been in recently.

The sores on my feet were healing well. I had no open wounds there now. They were still painful to the touch but in another couple of days the sores would be gone.

All in all, I felt in good shape again. Certainly better than I had been a few weeks before, during that initial period in captivity.

I was just getting my clothes back on when I heard a knock on the door to the cabin. I stopped what I was doing and listened.

'Who is it?' Mary said in Russian.

I heard a man's voice in response but the sound was too muffled to make out the words. I willed Mary to sit tight and do nothing, but I heard her get up off the bed. And then came the sound of the door unlocking.

I knew that it could easily be a ticket inspector or something else entirely innocent, but I'm a born sceptic. I quickly threw on the rest of my clothes and picked up the Glock, which I'd placed on the floor. I heard the door close and the lock click again.

'Mary?' I said. 'Who was that?'

'Just checking tickets again,' she said.

Sometimes you get a feeling that something isn't quite right. Was it the way Mary had spoken? I kept the gun held in my hand, close to my chest, as I opened the door, not wanting to take any chances.

As I took a half-step out of the bathroom, I noticed the gleaming metal first. The overhead light caught on it, shining a bright beam into my eyes. Only when the metal object was turned slightly could my eyes focus properly. And then I knew what it was. The blade of a hunting knife.

Held up against Mary's throat.

Chapter 43

Mary was across the cabin, almost within touching distance in the confined space. A man stood behind her. One of his arms was wrapped around her body, holding down her arms. The other was across her right shoulder, an oversized hand with thick fingers holding the knife in place.

I looked into Mary's pleading eyes. A trickle of blood ran down her neck, onto her clothes, where the knife had nicked her. The man rose tall behind her. She looked entirely helpless. And the sorry look on her face only confirmed it.

I didn't know the man. A different man from the one I'd seen Chris with on the station platform. But I wasn't overly surprised when I knew the voice that I heard next. It came just as the cold metal of a gun barrel was pushed against my temple.

'Drop it,' Chris said.

I didn't look to where the voice had come from. I didn't need to. Out of the corner of my eye I could easily make out the figure of a man standing off to my right, toward the cabin door. His arm was outstretched, pushing the handgun into my head.

'Or what?' I said.

'What do you think?' Chris replied.

'I think you haven't got the balls,' I said, directing my words to the man holding Mary.

His eyes flicked over to where Chris was standing.

Did he really have the appetite to cut Mary's throat? I doubted it. The nervous glance over to his leader suggested he didn't. But it didn't matter to me either way. He was already a dead man. He'd signed his own death warrant the second he'd walked over the threshold into my space.

I caressed the grip of the Glock in my left hand. Relaxed my shoulders. Exhaled slowly, then inhaled deeply. Readied myself for action.

In an instant I swung my right hand up and grabbed Chris's gun. I pushed it away from my face, behind me. At the same time, I swung my left arm up and fired a single shot, the sound heavily cushioned by the deep rumble of the train. The bullet hit the man behind Mary in his right eye, jolting his head backward. Blood, bone and lumpy brain matter spattered out behind him and streaked down the wall of the cabin as his body dropped to the floor. Mary cupped her face with both hands, whimpering.

Chris was reeling, trying to free his arm. He hadn't fired in haste as I thought he might. As I tried to reposition to take him on, he threw a fist into my side. The power of his punch surprised me and I winced in pain, letting go of his gun. Before I knew it he'd crashed the butt into the side of my head and I felt a searing pain in my ear. I fell to my knees, my vision blurry. The blow to the head had disorientated me.

'Chris, no!' Mary screamed.

I heard a shot fired. But I'd sensed what was coming and had already begun to move. I jumped forward, into his legs, taking him down to the ground in a heap with me. His head smacked off the cabin door.

I'd already dropped my gun and so now had both of my hands free. I arced a fist into his jaw with my right hand. Then went for a left. But he shifted his head in time and grabbed hold of my wrist with his right hand. He was much stronger than I'd anticipated and I writhed, trying to free my arm.

He hit me with his gun again, right across the side of my face. I felt my cheek open up, both on the inside and outside of my mouth. Blood began to pour, filling my throat. But the force of the shot had also taken the gun out of Chris's hand and it clattered to the floor off to my left.

His hands and arms were grappling at my torso, jabbing, scraping, trying to get me off him. I reached out to get his gun. I couldn't. It lay just too far out of my reach. My head was thick and everything spinning. The two blows to the head had taken their toll on me.

But I couldn't let him get the upper hand. I thrust my head down, aiming for the crown of his nose. I heard a crack and knew that I'd made good contact, probably breaking his nose. But the impact had also shaken me, sending a shudder right through my body. The last thing my already concussed brain needed.

Chris managed to manoeuvre a leg free and bent his knee up into his chest, then kicked out, pushing me off him. I lurched backward, and got back to my feet. But before I could react Chris was already up, rushing at me. He crushed me up against the cabin's window, knocking the wind out of me. The window seemed to bend outwards as I made contact with it as though it were made of elastic. It cushioned some of the blow. I was still on my feet at least, but Chris was driving into me, his arms wrapped around my waist.

I raised and threw down my right elbow, catching him just below his neck. Then I used all my weight and the strength in my legs to push him back, away from me. He released his grip and stood off from me, just half a yard away. His face was snarling like an angry dog. We faced each other off. Hands out and ready, like oversized wrestlers in a miniature ring.

He came for me again, but this time I was ready. I ducked to my right. He tried to shift his feet to follow my move but couldn't. I reached out to him and used the strength in my arms to further his momentum, slamming him into the window. Before he made contact he managed to get one arm up in front of him but his head still took most of the impact as he crashed into the glass. The window bent and cracked but didn't shatter.

Chris fell into a heap on the ground.

I got to my knees and used my right arm to scoop him up. He was still conscious, still alert, but much of his strength had now gone. I wrapped my thick right arm around his neck, pulling on my right hand with my left to squeeze the vice tight. Chris began to rake at my arm and my hands with his nails. But I didn't relax the grip, I squeezed tighter.

'Logan,' I heard Mary say. 'Logan?'

I looked up at her. She was cowering away on the bed, the pleading look still in her eyes.

'You can't kill him,' she said.

After what he'd just done to her? I kept on pulling on my right arm, squeezing as hard as I could. Chris was becoming frantic, clawing away to try to get me to release him.

But I'd misunderstood Mary's words.

'You can't kill him,' she said again. 'We have to know what's going on.'

I closed my eyes in frustration, her words resonating in my head. I knew she was right. As much as I wanted to squeeze the life out of Chris, we had to figure out what was happening. The chances were Chris would tell us nothing. I knew, though, that we had to at least try.

'Get the gun,' I said to Mary, nodding over to Chris's weapon, which lay by the cabin door. I hadn't seen where mine had landed.

Mary did as she was told and sat back on the bed, toying with the weapon. After a few seconds she lifted it up, pointing it at Chris's head. I relaxed the grip around his neck enough to let him breathe, but didn't let go. He coughed and spluttered, his flailing arms becoming calm as he filled his starved lungs with air.

'What did you do, Chris?' Mary said. 'Just tell us what you did.'

Chris was breathing deeply, panting. He didn't say a word.

'Who are you working for?' I shouted.

Chris just huffed and coughed out a mouthful of phlegm.

'Chris, what have you done?' Mary said again, her voice calm and sincere, willing him to speak. 'I know you've been meeting with the CIA.'

'You don't know anything,' he said, sounding pleased with himself. 'You're nothing, Mary. Just another puppet.'

'I'm not a puppet,' Mary refuted. 'I just can't help but feel loyalty to the people I work for. I would never betray my own people like you have.'

Chris spat and laughed. 'And neither have I,' he said.

'Then tell us why you're working with the CIA. What have you given them?'

Chris laughed again. A detached and unfeeling laugh. 'I'm not working *with* the CIA, you stupid girl. I *am* CIA. I always have been.'

I didn't like the way he'd spoken to Mary and I tugged on my right arm again until he began to squirm, reminding him of the situation he was in. His words had caught me by surprise, though, and my mind got busy trying to process the consequences.

Mary looked angry. I thought for her it would probably be more at the personal betrayal of someone she'd been paired up with than anything else.

'You tricked us?' she said.

I relaxed the grip on Chris's neck again, affording him an opportunity to respond.

'No. You're just not big enough to have known,' Chris said. 'Mackie knew. Mackie brought me into this knowing I was CIA. Everyone knew.'

'But why?' Mary said. 'Why are the CIA involved here at all?'

'Why wouldn't we be?' he said.

'And why are you trying to kill us?' Mary added.

Her questions were heartfelt and carried a personal weight to them. But it was hardly an interrogation. Mary's questions were born of frustration and hurt and were personal. Chris wasn't going to tell us anything more than he had to. He'd only spoken at all to add confusion to the situation and to rub salt into open wounds. Chris understood the predicament he was in. No matter what talking he did, only two of us were going to be walking away from the cabin alive. He'd come into the cabin to kill me and Mary. And nothing he could say would change that fact.

And knowing that, I was ready for his move when it came.

His arms were down by his sides. He used his legs to push back on me and with his right arm reached down to his boots, trying to recover a stashed pocket knife. But he wasn't going to get the upper hand over me again. I pulled up on his neck, fast and hard. He desperately tried to grab for the sheathed blade but the jarring of his head had brought his shoulders up, away from his legs, and he couldn't reach.

I kept him in the hold, pulling the grip as tightly as I could. He tried desperately to reach his knife. I gave him no chance. When he finally realised his predicament he began to claw away at my arms and wrists once more.

'Logan, no!' Mary shouted. 'We have to find out what's going on!'

She was right. But we weren't going to find out from Chris. I kept the grip firm, pumping away with my arms to squeeze it as tight as I could. Chris scraped and scrabbled frantically. His nails tore at the skin on my arms and dug deep into my flesh. But I couldn't feel the pain at all. I was focused entirely on the grip, on pulling as hard as I could.

My eyes were fixed on Mary. She was speaking, shouting at me, but I couldn't hear the words. I just carried on pulling, squeezing the life out of Chris.

His attempts became weaker, more futile. Eventually they stopped altogether and his arms flopped to the ground.

Tears rolled down Mary's cheeks. But she should have been thanking me. I'd just saved her life.

I finally released the grip from around Chris's neck and threw him off me. Mary jumped at the sight as Chris's head rolled, his bulging but lifeless eyes staring up at her.

I got to my feet and retrieved the Glock I'd dropped, which lay back by the bathroom entrance. I placed it into the waistband of my trousers.

'You just don't know when to stop,' Mary said, sobbing, looking away from Chris, turning her head as far away as she could.

'You need to start to get real on this,' I said. 'People are trying to kill me. To kill you too. You'll pardon the lack of apology but hopefully you can see now why I didn't react too kindly to your friends before in the café.'

'It doesn't mean you have to try to kill everyone who comes your way! And I'm not just saying that because I'm some soft bimbo, which is clearly what you think of me. Just stop and think for a minute before you do things. Chris was talking. We had him, and now what use is he to anyone?'

I fished through Chris's pockets and found what I was looking for.

'He was only telling us what he wanted to,' I said.

'You don't know that. You didn't give him a chance.'

'I gave him more of a chance than he deserved.'

'But what are you left with now? Just more unanswered questions.'

'Maybe. But things are starting to fall into place.'

I opened up the phone I'd taken from Chris's pocket and quickly confirmed what I suspected.

I stood up and strode over to Mary who cowered away from me. I held the phone out to her, showing her the screen.

'What?' she said, her voice small and meek.

'GPS tracking. Chris was following *you,*'

Mary took the phone out of my hand and stared at the blinking dot on the screen. I hauled Mary to her feet, grabbed the phone back off her and began to pat her down, feeling across the material of her clothes, along the creases and seams. Mary was sobbing, I ignored her.

'Here,' I said, holding up the tail of her coat. 'It's in here.'

I ripped the seam and carefully took out the receiver. It was smaller than a penny. Nothing more than a microchip with a sticky coating. A simple app on the phone was all that was needed to show the receiver's precise location.

'He knew where we were,' Mary said.

I wasn't sure if her words were a statement or a question. She took the chip from my hand and inspected it as though she couldn't quite believe what she was seeing.

'Why?' Mary said. 'Why was he tracking me?'

'I don't know. But I'm not sitting here waiting any longer.'

I picked up my coat and strode over to the cabin door.

'Where are you going?' Mary shouted, jumping up off the bed.

I turned to face her. 'I'm going to find out why the CIA had Mackie killed,' I said.

Chapter 44

I didn't look behind me as I marched off through the train. I knew that Mary would follow me out of the cabin. If nothing else, I knew she wouldn't want to be stuck in that space with two dead bodies.

Chris hadn't given much away but I could only presume more agents from the CIA were on the train; for starters, the other man Chris had been with on the platform. I had no way of knowing where on the train they were, or exactly how many more of them there were, but I had to find them. Chris had come to confront us. To kill us. His unseen friend, the one Mary had spied him meeting, had taken on a more sedentary role so far. In the shadows. Away from watchful eyes. There was a reason. And I wanted to know it.

I was still a long way from understanding what was happening. But some things at least were clicking into place. Mackie had brought Chris into this mess knowing he was with the CIA. When I'd been held by the Russians, the CIA had teamed up with Mackie to come and find me. I don't know how they'd sold it to Mackie, but it had obviously worked. Perhaps the CIA had helped muddy the waters and fuelled Mackie's distrust for me. That might have been enough for him to have agreed to bring them into the fold.

But why would the CIA have become involved at all?

I could think of one very good reason. I'd been earmarked. They wanted me dead. I couldn't be sure why. Though I had an inkling.

Whatever the reason, I got the sense that something bigger was at play too. It wasn't just about me. There were too many twists and intricacies and people involved for that to be the case.

Lena had told me the Russians had brokered a new deal. Whatever the deal was, it had cost Mackie his life. The cherry on top. The CIA had okayed Mackie's death to get what they wanted. They'd intended to use me as the fall guy, or maybe I was just their means to get what they wanted and now they were out to kill me.

I needed to find out why.

Eight carriages came and went without me once breaking stride. I hadn't known what I was looking for, but when I saw it I knew I was in the right place.

When I entered the next carriage, I spotted a man standing at the near end. He was trying hard to make himself look inconspicuous but he was way too obvious. His eyes practically lit up when he saw me coming. No doubt he knew who I was but I chose not to confront him. As I hoped, he stayed in character and didn't try to stop me as I walked past.

Further up the carriage was another man, similarly stationed, trying to make himself fit into the unusual surroundings. It didn't work. The problem was, I had seen him before. On the station platform, standing next to Chris. I guessed that the cabin door he was guarding was the one I was looking for.

As I approached him he did a double-take, almost identical to the look his colleague had just given me when I entered the carriage. I knew as soon as I saw his hand move toward his jacket that he wasn't going to just let me past like his friend had. But his surprise at seeing me and the time it took him to process the situation unfolding before him were all I needed.

He was just five yards away from me and I increased my pace, aware that any second he'd probably be pulling a weapon on me. He never got the chance. I sprinted the last two steps, ghosting across the ground. Coming in low, my knees bent, I pounced, throwing my right fist up under his chin. The connection was as good as I could have hoped for. A loud crack sounded out and his head snapped back violently. His whole body lifted off the ground and he was dumped on the floor a yard away from where he'd been standing. With the momentum of my body behind the strike, his jaw would be smashed at the very least. If he was unlucky, it may even have snapped his neck. Either way I didn't fancy his chances of fighting back anytime soon.

As his body hit the deck, I spun around, pulling the Glock from my waistband. Crouching low, I pointed the gun out, back down to the other end of the carriage, where the first agent had been standing. I'd presumed that by now he'd be making a move on me. But what I saw wasn't what I'd expected. Not at all.

The man was on his knees, facing me. His hands were behind his back. Mary was standing over the agent, his service revolver in her hand. She looked up at me and gave a wry smile, then swung the gun down against the back of the man's neck. He crumpled to the ground.

'See? There are other options,' Mary said casually, rifling through the pockets of the grounded man.

I couldn't help but smile at that. Somehow she'd managed to get the better of the man and disarm him, almost silently. I continued to underestimate her, it seemed.

'Give me a hand, will you,' she said, standing up. 'We can't leave these two lying here.'

'We don't have anywhere to put them yet,' I said.

Though she was right. We couldn't leave the two men out in the open. I turned around and got down onto my knees next to the man I'd just felled. I could see from glancing at him that he wasn't going to be getting up in a hurry. I wondered whether he was even still breathing.

I found what I was looking for, stood up, and looked over at Mary. She was holding the other man underneath her armpits, dragging him over to where I was standing.

'Hurry up, will you,' she said.

The look I gave her made her face crease up.

'What?' she said angrily.

'Nothing,' I said. 'Good job.'

'You really didn't think I had it in me, did you?'

I just smiled and shook my head. She was right. I didn't.

'Could you just put him down for a minute?' I said. 'I need you and that gun for this. We don't know what we're walking into here.'

She dropped the man and took out her newly acquired gun again, another Glock.

Holding the key I'd just pilfered, I turned around to face the cabin door that the agent had been covering. The door was wooden with a small window, the blind on the inside drawn so that I couldn't see in. I could tell from the door's shiny finish and embellished decoration that what lay beyond was not your average cabin.

I placed the key in the lock and began to turn it. My other hand gripped the gun tightly. The lock clicked open. I didn't hesitate but flung the door open and rolled into the room.

The cabin was at least twice the size of the one Mary and I had. My eyes immediately fell to the man inside. He was sitting at a coffee table by the window, dressed smartly in light-coloured linen trousers and a collared shirt with a V-neck pullover. He jumped up out of his seat at the unexpected entrance.

'What the hell are you doing?' he said in a thick American drawl.

He didn't make any attempt to make for cover or to go for a weapon. Despite his surprise at seeing me, his voice and his face were steadfast.

'Where's Chris?' he said.

'Where do you think?' I said.

I looked at him for a reaction to my words. He'd know exactly what I meant. But I saw no reaction. Nothing. His face was deadpan.

He looked to be about in his early fifties. He had thinning grey hair cut short but his bushy eyebrows were jet-black. His face was pockmarked and saggy, his features oversized in comparison with his head. Despite his aging face, his deep eyes were alert and full of life.

Mary came up from behind me and walked over to him. She held on to her gun with one hand while she patted him down with the other, going all the way down and into his socks and boots.

'He's clean,' she said, standing up.

'Sit down,' I said to him.

'What about the others?' he said, indicating the two bodies on the other side of the open doorway. 'You've not just bulldozed your way through half my team, I hope.'

'Those two are fine,' I said. 'Probably.'

'Well, don't just leave them there!' he snapped.

His tone was as though he were the one in charge of the situation. It riled me but I knew he was right. We couldn't leave the two men out in the corridor. Not if we wanted to stay on the train.

'I'll get them,' Mary said, and headed back to the corridor.

She dragged each of the men into the cabin. The one she'd hit moaned and groaned. Once on the inside, she gave him another crack with the gun.

I looked at her with raised eyebrows. She just shrugged and got up to close the cabin door.

My eyes had been quickly glancing around the room. Assessing the layout but also any possible threats. I could see just one static bed – much larger than we'd had – and there was a full-sized sofa plus the coffee table and chairs, where the man had been sitting.

'You know, it's nice to finally meet you,' the man said, taking a seat on the sofa and sitting back with both of his arms outstretched across the sofa's back. 'It's strange when you spend so much time watching and learning about someone but never actually meet them.'

'Okay, less of the small talk,' Mary snapped. 'We're not here to play games.'

'Oh, I'm under no illusions about that. The two men lying down next to your feet are testament to that. And I'd guess Chris hasn't been so lucky.'

'You'd be right,' I said.

The man shook his head. 'Shame about that,' he said. 'He was a good agent. Very useful. Very resourceful. In many ways he was similar to you, Logan.'

The use of my name made me wince. This man knew so much about me, and me so little about him. But his words resonated with me. Chris had certainly been more resilient than I'd expected. A tough fighter. But that was really where the similarities between the two of us ended.

'In the end, that was probably his downfall,' the man continued. 'What can you really expect from someone like that? All brawn, no brains.'

I took a seat on one of the chairs. The gun was still in my hand but I wasn't pointing it at the man anymore. He didn't seem to be a threat. Not yet at least. It felt as though this was all part of whatever plan had been concocted.

'Is this him?' I said to Mary, knowing that Mary would realise I was referring to the man she'd seen Chris meet.

'Yeah. It is.'

'Who are you?' I said, turning my attention back to the man. 'We should at least know who we're dealing with. You seem to know so much about me.'

'Yes, well, what harm can it do now? I'm presuming you've already connected the dots to who I work for.'

'Yes.'

'The name's Greg Schuster. I lead the Russian office.'

'Well, Schuster,' I said, 'we've got quite a few hours until we get to Moscow. Plenty of time. So why don't you start at the beginning. What's happening here? To me? To Mackie?'

'And why should I tell you anything?'

'It's going to be a long time for you to hold out. You seem to think that you know me. I'm sure you can use your imagination.'

'Your cheap threats and intimidation are lost on me, I'm afraid.'

'And why's that?'

'Because I'm not going to tell you anything I don't want to. I'll talk to you, sure. We can talk like real human beings. Like adults. I'll tell you what I can. But no amount of duress or torture over the next few hours is going to change what I'm willing to say.'

'You might be right. But it's worth a try,' I said.

I got up off my chair and strode up to him and enjoyed seeing him cower away from me as I approached. His bravado was one thing, but clearly his words weren't as strong as his will.

I grabbed his right arm and twisted my body around so I was almost sitting on him. I gripped his arm tightly between my left arm and torso.

'You've got a choice, Schuster,' I said. 'You've got four limbs. Twenty fingers and toes. Which shall we start with?'

Schuster struggled against my grip but he wasn't anywhere near strong enough to get me off him. My back was to him and I was using my body weight to push down on him. I thrust my left elbow into him, which seemed to calm down his protests.

'Fingers it is,' I said.

I grabbed the little finger on his right hand and pulled it outwards to bursting point. Schuster squirmed some more but my crushing body weight gave him little room to manoeuvre.

'You wouldn't!' he shouted.

He should have kept his mouth shut. I don't like to be tested. I yanked on his finger; it didn't take much effort. I heard it pop as the base dislocated from the knuckle. Schuster screamed out and his body writhed and coiled. His strength all of a sudden was doubled and it took me a moment to get him back under control.

'Nine more to go,' I said.

'Do what you want!' Schuster spat, panting heavily. 'It won't make any difference!'

'Well, let's just see about that,' I said.

I took his next finger in my grip, trying my hardest to block out the thoughts that were creeping into my head. Of my own recent experience of being on the receiving end of torture. It was an uncomfortable feeling. But I pushed it away – maintained my focus as best I could.

'Go on then!' Schuster shouted. 'You think you can manipulate me like this? I've already decided what's off-limits and what's not. If you continue to torture me, you'll only be getting the same information out of me! That seems pretty pointless to me, unless you're just looking to be a sadist.'

His continued confidence and brashness surprised me. Part of me admired him for it. I rarely came across such supreme detachment from what should have been a harrowing situation. His coldness in the face of adversity told me a lot.

I also knew I was struggling to keep a lid on the ever-growing red mist that was descending. Way back I'd been taught to suppress such urges. To act rationally and be in control at all times. I no longer had strong powers of restraint. In truth I wanted to tear the man limb from limb. And I wasn't sure I could stop myself.

But I understood his point. Before long the train would be arriving in Moscow. I had only a small window of opportunity. I could hurt him and hurt him badly in that time. But would I get anything more from him that way? It would be impossible for me to know. It might even just make him too delirious to talk. And I certainly wasn't a sadist. Even though this man had very probably just tried to have me killed, torturing was not something that I could undertake lightly. Not having been at the other end of it so horrifically on more than one occasion.

I didn't relax my grip. But I wasn't going to continue dislocating his fingers. Yet.

'Project Ruby,' I said. 'Tell me about it. That's what started all of this off. Tell me why my life has been ruined for that.'

'Logan, you can't seriously be listening to this guy,' Mary interjected. 'We can't just sit around and chat. This guy wants us dead! We very nearly were. He doesn't deserve anything more than the others got.'

She certainly seemed to have changed her tune. Now her life was at stake she was seeing the world through a very different lens. But she was half-right. Schuster didn't deserve any better than the others. No doubt about that. And I wasn't going to let him off that fact. But everything he'd said rang true. Chris was a doer. He'd had his orders and he'd been trying to carry them out. This guy was something else. He was a decision-maker. I had to give him a shot. He'd get what was coming to him sooner or later. But I had to at least hear what he had to say.

'Go on then,' I said to Schuster, standing up off him. 'Talk.'

As I got off him he immediately grabbed hold of his stricken finger. His face was creased, sweat droplets covering his brow. But he didn't moan or scream or otherwise make a fuss. He may not have been physically up to much but he was a tough cookie all right.

After composing himself for a few moments Schuster gave a smug smile and Mary tutted loudly. I sat back down on one of the chairs by the table and Mary took a seat next to me.

'Project Ruby,' Schuster said, a smirk on his face. 'Well, I guess it does seem like the best place to begin.'

Chapter 45

'I can let you in on a little secret,' Schuster said, loving every minute. Despite the pain he must have been in he obviously couldn't wait to further rub my face in the mess that he'd created. 'The thing is, everything you were told about Project Ruby by Mackie and the JIA was true.'

Schuster paused as if waiting for a response from me. He would have to wait a long time. I wanted to hear what he had to say but I wasn't going to join in with his games.

'You see, you really did manage to steal that information from RTK. That was quite a coup. The Russians had even known you were coming and you still managed to get away with it.'

His words were sinking in. I felt relief – it hadn't been a setup from the start; Mackie hadn't sent me there to die – but also pain. Because it confirmed that somewhere along the line we'd both been betrayed. And Mackie had wound up dead.

'We'd been keeping a close eye on you and that Russian agent friend of yours. We were rooting for you and you didn't disappoint. Chris had already been brought into the fold by then and was relaying information back to me about your progress. When we realised you'd been snatched, we all felt for you. We really did.'

'Oh, I'm sure it hit you really hard,' I said.

'Logan, we don't have to listen to this,' Mary said, getting more agitated. 'How can you listen to a word this man has to say? He's a liar. He tried to have you killed!'

'Carry on,' I said to Schuster, ignoring Mary's protests.

She huffed again, stood up and paced across the cabin.

'The Russians were quite understandably pissed about what you'd done,' Schuster said, looking at me with something akin to admiration. 'That Lena, I've heard all about her. She's quite a piece of work. Not the sort of person you want to get on the wrong side of. She can be quite vengeful, as I'm sure you've already learned for yourself.'

You don't know the half of it, I thought, but said nothing.

'But it wasn't long before the playing field changed.'

Schuster paused, as if for dramatic effect. This time I couldn't help myself.

'Changed how?' I said.

'Logan. Don't let him do this to you,' Mary pleaded.

She was still walking back and forth between the window and the door. I looked up at her but ignored her plea.

'Changed how?' I said again to Schuster.

'Well, we found out that the Russians had something we wanted. "We" being my country. Something that changed the landscape so to speak. Once we knew that, we had to figure out a plan of how to *get* what we wanted.'

'You're going to have to just spit it out, Schuster. Enough of the games now.'

'Oh. Did Mary not fill you in on the rest, then?' Schuster said, the grin on his face widening as he looked over at Mary.

She stopped pacing and turned to him. Her face was contorted and angry. She turned her gaze to me.

'Really? So Carl didn't know, then?' Schuster said.

'I didn't know what? Mary?'

'You bastard!' Mary said to Schuster through clenched teeth. 'Don't you dare turn this onto me!'

She strode up to him and slapped him in the face, hard. The ferocity of the slap took both Schuster and me by surprise and Schuster needed a few moments to compose himself.

'Don't you *ever* do that again,' Schuster spat. 'You stupid bitch.'

Mary screamed and threw herself toward him. I was up and out of my seat, grabbing hold of her from behind, before she got the chance to reach Schuster again. She wriggled and writhed, her arms flailing. She was screaming with rage. But I held her firmly and dragged her away from Schuster, who had sunk low into his seat, trying to get away from her.

Mary stopped fighting and I let her go. She shrugged me off and stormed back over to the window. She was shaking all over with fury.

'Tell me,' I said to Schuster, who was looking just a little less brave than he had before.

'We made contact with the Russians not long after you were taken,' Schuster said, quickly falling back into his role of story-teller. 'Chris and Mary were brought together to negotiate with them.'

I looked over at Mary. She was turned away from me, her head bowed. I didn't like where this was going. And I could see now why she didn't want this brought up.

'I didn't know Chris was CIA, Logan,' Mary said, meek as a mouse. 'Everything I've told you was the truth.'

'Ah, but you clearly haven't told him *everything*?' Schuster said. 'Like I said, the Russians had something we wanted. We went in to negotiate.'

'You tried to sell me out?' I said, directing my question at Mary. 'You tried to give me up? For what?'

My thoughts took me back to that room. Lena and the conversations we'd had. She'd told me that Mackie had sent me to Russia to die. She'd played with words to suit her own needs. But in the end she'd been right. Nobody had been sent to save me. They'd been sent there to negotiate with my life.

'It wasn't like that,' Mary said, turning to face me.

'Then how was it?'

'It's hard to explain. I know you think I'm too new to this to really understand, but I knew Mackie. He didn't want to give you up. You have to believe that.'

'But sometimes we don't get what we want,' Schuster said. 'Mackie was reluctant, sure. But in the end he didn't have an option. He doesn't get the final say in these things.'

'So if it wasn't Mackie then who sold me out? You?'

'Does it matter?'

'Damn right it does.'

'Maybe you'll figure that one out yourself. I'm not going to lay a death trap for someone else.'

I was finding it hard to process all of the information being thrown at me. My mind was a blur. Clearly I'd been lied to. By Mackie. By Mary. For three months I thought I'd been left for dead. I didn't know why. They'd told me they couldn't find me. Then they'd acted like I'd been turned. But all the while they'd been negotiating with the Russians.

Schuster didn't need to name the person who'd decided to sell me out. I already had a pretty good idea whom it might have been. The link between the CIA and the JIA. Jay Lindegaard. He was a member of the JIA committee overseeing all of our operations. A long-time CIA agent. We'd crossed paths in the past. And it had never been friendly. On my last mission, to rescue Frank Modena, he'd tried to get me thrown off the case. When Mackie had refused, he'd sent a couple of heavies out after me, and it was only through a bit of luck that I got away unscathed. I could well imagine that given a chance he'd be all too happy to give me up for good.

But that didn't answer the whole question. What was worth bargaining my life for?

'So what was the deal?'

Schuster shrugged. 'Mary and Chris offered to leave you to the Russians in exchange for what we wanted.'

'You've got to believe that Mackie didn't want it,' Mary said. 'He would have carried on trying to get you out. And when we knew you'd escaped, everything changed. He really did want you back. We just didn't know why the Russians had let you go.'

'No, Mary,' Schuster said. '*You* didn't know why. But I did. They let you escape, Logan, because we'd brokered a new deal.'

'Mackie,' I said.

'Exactly. Offering you to the Russians was like trying to sell a watch to a watchmaker. It was a non-starter. They already had you and what we wanted was just too valuable. They knew it and we knew it.'

I could feel the anger boiling up inside me. So many lies, so many betrayals. I found it hard to fathom out what was real and what wasn't. What I did know was that I was nothing more than a pawn in all this. And in the end, Mackie had been too.

'So you sold out Mackie instead,' I said.

'It was what they wanted,' Schuster said, shrugging as though it was nothing to have set up a man's death. 'There was a lot of history between him and the Russians. They have very long memories it seems.'

The words were playing around in my head as I tried to make sense of what was happening. But I could find no way to look at the mess that didn't simply leave a bad taste. In the end, everyone had deserted me. Even Mackie. Who'd then been betrayed himself.

Maybe he'd had it coming.

Yet I still felt for him. And, in a way, felt responsible for his death. I had, after all, been used by the Russians to ensnare him.

'What was it?' I said to Schuster. 'What did the Russians have that was so valuable to you that you bargained with my life? With Mackie's?'

And it was abundantly clear Schuster had been waiting for this part. Despite the situation, that smile returned. A smirk that spoke a thousand words.

'They know where Angela Grainger is,' he said. 'We negotiated Mackie's death because the Russians have been hiding Angela Grainger. And now that Mackie is dead, they're going to give her up. Very soon, she'll be dead too.'

Chapter 46

People talk about being dumbstruck. About something happening that literally takes your breath away. Knocks you off your feet. When I heard Angela's name coming from Schuster's lips, my legs suddenly turned to jelly. I couldn't stay standing. I back-stepped away from Schuster and slouched down on one of the chairs, his words reverberating in my mind.

When Grainger had gone on the run, I'd vowed that I would find her. I'd always been torn in my mind, though, as to what I'd do when I eventually achieved that aim. Our affair had been fleeting but it had been strong. Unlike anything else I'd ever experienced. I loved her. At least I had no doubt in my mind that I could have loved her. But she'd also brought death and destruction to innocent people through her scheme of revenge. I wasn't sure I could ever let that go. She'd betrayed my trust, like so many others now had. And yet I still clung on to the good that I'd seen in her.

There had been so little time for me to devote to finding her since her escape. I'd been placed on the assignment to infiltrate RTK not long after she'd disappeared. That had soon become all-consuming. I'd kept my ears close to the ground, had people keeping me abreast of anything at all that could help locate her. But she'd simply vanished.

The Americans had immediately placed her on their public most-wanted list. She was a fugitive, right up there with the biggest terrorists and murderers. I'd felt sorry for her, seeing her name being tarnished and dragged through the mud like that. She'd been wrong to do what she'd done, of course. But she was a good person who'd got herself mixed up in something she couldn't control. After everything, I still couldn't help but believe that.

To hear that the Russians had been hiding her was both a blessing and a curse. On the one hand, I felt relief to finally know where she was. But I also knew exactly why the Russians would have been keeping her safe. The enemy of my enemy is my friend. It's an ancient Chinese proverb. Never has a truer word been spoken.

I doubted the Russians' intentions toward Grainger had ever been noble. They'd simply seen her as a bargaining chip. They knew sooner or later they'd be able to use her to their advantage. In the end that's what she'd become. Nothing more than a means to allow them to get what they wanted. They knew the Americans would come looking for her and they'd exploited it. I was a little surprised that Angela hadn't seen that coming. Maybe she had but felt she had no other option.

Now here I was with the CIA. They were ready to close out their deal. They'd come to Russia to kill Grainger. And in the process they'd had Mackie killed and had been more than happy to leave me to my death.

Something inside me snapped. I jumped out of my seat and launched myself at Schuster. Whatever he had to say, Mary was right. He didn't deserve any better. I balled my right fist and slammed it into his side, trying to punch right through him. He doubled over in pain, breathless. I pulled back my fist and hit him again in the same spot, not giving him a chance to recover.

My mind felt foggy. I wasn't in control. An inner rage was trying to get out. I wasn't sure that I could control it anymore. I wanted to hit him. I wanted to hurt him.

I wanted to kill him.

I couldn't let it end like this. He had more to say. And I needed to hear it. But I hit him again and again and again. He wasn't putting up a fight. He couldn't. The beating was too ferocious, too quick. Too severe.

In the end I somehow found the strength to stop. Standing off him, I looked down at Schuster's crumpled figure and then over at Mary. I was huffing, my chest heaving.

'You shouldn't have stopped,' she said. 'He doesn't deserve anything better.'

Schuster somehow managed to pull himself upright. He looked at me. His face was contorted and creased from the pain he was in. He was cradling his midriff. Much of the bravado and confidence had been wiped from his face. The attack had at least shown him who really had control of the situation, even if he did still hold the answers I craved.

'Where is Angela?' I said.

'Moscow,' Schuster wheezed. 'That's why I'm on this train.'

No shit, Sherlock.

'Where in Moscow?' I said.

'Do you really think I'd tell you that, even if I knew?'

'So you still don't know,' I said, a statement rather than a question.

'Everything's in place for us to find her,' Schuster said. 'It's only a matter of time. There really isn't anything you can do to stop us now.'

'I wouldn't be so sure about that.'

'Confidence will only get you so far, Logan. You need to learn when to walk away. You had a chance. I don't know why you didn't take it.'

'I've got nowhere left to go. Why did you try to have me killed? Mary too?'

'We were tracking Mary, hoping she'd lead us to you. When we realised you were both on the train, we thought you'd figured out what was happening. You're a threat to this, no doubt. But we were wrong. You two really didn't have the foggiest what was going on. You only know now because I decided to tell you.'

'Then *why* did you tell us?' I said.

'Why not? Like I said, there's nothing you can do now. If you'd already known what was going on then maybe things would have gone down differently. We thought you might have been a few steps ahead. But you weren't. You didn't know anything. And it's too late for you now. Everyone wants you dead, Logan. The CIA, the JIA, the FSB. You've got nowhere left to turn. It's only a matter of time before someone catches up with you.'

Schuster was still relishing every second of tormenting me. I felt the urge to go at him again. To wipe the smirk off his face permanently. But that would leave me with nothing. As long as Schuster was alive and I was with him, there was a chance I could still get to the end of this and find Grainger. I had to. I'd vowed to myself after the last time I'd seen her, when she'd shot me and gone on the run, that I'd never stop looking for her. And I wanted to be the one to find her. I couldn't let the CIA or anyone else get to her before me. It had to be me.

I had to save her.

We waited in near silence after that. Schuster had done his talking. And I had nothing left to say to him. Mary sat, staring out of the window. I felt betrayal at her having not revealed to me everything she'd known. But in the end I knew one thing – she'd been loyal to Mackie. To the JIA. I didn't fully trust her but I believed that she was more on my side than anyone else. And she could still help me.

It was light outside again when an announcement came across on the tannoy. We would be arriving at Yaroslavsky station in Moscow in five minutes.

Not long after, the train jolted as the brakes were applied and we started to slow down.

'Who's meeting you here?' I said to Schuster. I wanted to know what we'd be walking into when we got off the train.

'No-one,' Schuster said. 'I had company but you've already taken care of them.'

He indicated the two men who lay heaped on the floor by the door. I didn't believe him. We'd have to remain alert as we got off the train, that was for sure.

'You've come here for a reason,' I said. 'I don't think you know where Grainger is yet. Otherwise you'd have just sent a single person in to finish her off. You brought a whole team with you. So who are you meeting and where?'

'I told you there were some things I would tell you and other things I wouldn't. Well, I'm sorry but I'm standing by that.'

Mary took out the gun that she'd stashed in her jacket and jabbed it toward Schuster.

'Then I guess you'll just have to come with us,' she said. 'You're on your own now. If you want this finished then sooner or later you'll have to make the move you came to Moscow for. Stand up.'

Schuster stood awkwardly, still holding his arms around his midriff. He was in a lot of pain. I'd probably broken some ribs, maybe even damaged a kidney. But he was doing his best to fight through it. He had something at stake here too after all. Mary stepped over to him and prodded the gun into his lower back, ushering him toward the door.

'Can I at least get my coat?' he said.

I picked it up off the hook on the wall next to the door and checked through the pockets. I found a phone but no weapons. There wasn't the time to sit and look through what was on the phone. I placed it on the coffee table, then flung the coat at him.

'Thanks,' he said. 'What about those two?'

'We leave them there,' I said, looking down at the two men. One of them had come around and Mary had gagged him and tied him to the bed. The other, the one I'd hit, was still in a crumpled heap on the floor. He was breathing, though. 'Someone will find them sooner or later.'

I opened the door and stepped back to allow Schuster and Mary out. She walked close to him, shielding the view of the gun that stayed pressed up against his back. The train was just pulling to a stop when we reached the carriage exit. I waited for the lock to release, then opened the door.

Built in the early 1900s in a neo-Russian style, the grand terminal building of Yaroslavsky station was still considered to be one of the most distinguished architectural monuments in Russia with its Kremlin-esque towers. Unusually for a station of its size, though, the fifteen parallel platforms were all completely open to the elements. The cold air immediately hit me as I stepped off the train onto the platform and I huddled my head down into the collar of my coat. Two days in the warmth of the train had softened me.

I took a few moments to eyeball the area. I saw no sign of any welcome party for Schuster but I knew we'd have to keep on the lookout. Someone out there would be waiting for him. Looking back up to the train, I signalled to Mary and she nudged Schuster in the back. They both stepped out onto the platform. Mary couldn't stop herself shivering as the cold air hit her.

'You lead the way,' I said to Schuster.

'To where?' he said, feigning bemusement.

'To wherever your planned rendezvous is,' I said. 'It's quite clear that's what's happening here. You had your chums to keep you company, keep you safe. Now you've got us. Take us to wherever you're supposed to be and there might still be a chance for you to walk away from this alive.'

'I'm not going to do that,' Schuster said.

'Then you're not going to get to Grainger, are you?' I said.

'How could I trust you to let me go?' Schuster said. 'After everything I've already told you. How can you even possibly expect me to believe that you'd let me live?'

'It's the only chance you've got.'

'And then what?'

'I haven't got that far yet.'

'You might think you can take on the world, Logan. But you're wrong.'

'You let me worry about that. Off you go now.'

Mary jabbed the gun again at Schuster.

'Will you stop doing that!' he shouted, pulling away from her and turning around. 'I know you're both armed. It doesn't really make a difference if you keep sticking it in me!'

I stood and stared at Schuster. He stared back. I'm not sure what changed in his mind but eventually he relented.

'Come on, it's this way,' he said. 'Let's go.'

He turned and started to march off, a renewed show of strength coming over him. We followed two yards behind him toward the terminal building. I noticed that Mary still held her gun but had folded her arms, placing the weapon just inside her coat to hide it from view. My gun was in my right hand, inside my coat pocket. We had to be ready and alert should things turn bad.

And I knew that inevitably they would.

As we walked through the busy terminal I nervously glanced over to a group of three policemen standing watching the station. Had a search party been organised for me following the multiple incidents in Omsk? I willed them not to look at me, and sighed in relief as we walked out of the station without a single glance in my direction as we passed.

Komsomolskaya Square, which we walked out into, is one of the busiest intersections in Moscow, home to three of Moscow's nine main railway stations. We bustled past tourists, business people and townsfolk, through the square and into the inner hub of Moscow. As we carried on, none of us speaking, the wide streets and grand buildings soon petered out into narrower, windier alleys with low-rise apartments and offices.

The throngs of people also died down as we walked, and before long the streets around us were more or less deserted. I'd spent time in Moscow before, and although I was sure I could retrace my steps to familiar ground, I didn't know the grimy back alleys that we were walking down at all. More than once Mary and I glanced at each other, each of us becoming increasingly anxious over where we were being led.

'Where are we going?' Mary asked, the nerves in her voice unmistakable.

'Not far now,' Schuster said, not turning as he carried on his march.

I looked over and noticed that Mary had taken her gun out from under her coat. She held it down by her side, in open view. She looked up at me and gave me a questioning look, but I didn't say anything and turned my attention back to Schuster. I didn't trust him. Not at all. But at least he was taking us somewhere. Possibly straight into an ambush, but at least we were still moving forward.

Decrepit buildings were tightly packed on both sides of us. As we approached an opening on the left, I got myself ready to peer down it. Not just to look for trouble, but to try to find anything to confirm my bearings. But at the last second, Schuster darted to his left and headed into the opening at pace.

Mary and I both instinctively reached up with our weapons. I had to hold my arm out to stop Mary bounding ahead after Schuster. We had to keep our heads.

We rounded the corner slowly, guns drawn. Schuster was standing five yards off from us. He'd stopped and was turned, facing us. His face placid, no sign of emotion. No sign of that devilish grin.

We walked out into a small square. Four exits were arranged in a neat crossroads configuration. But the square was just a cross-section of the back ends of grotty buildings. In front of us the alley carried on into the distance, ending abruptly a good couple of hundred yards away where an apartment tower block stood. Industrial-sized bins lined three of the four sides of the square, their contents over-spilling. The stench of rotten food and chemicals was overpowering even in the sub-zero air.

I glanced around, up and down, left and right, taking in the surroundings. Nothing seemed untoward. Except for the fact that we'd stopped in this place at all.

'What the hell are you playing at, Schuster?' Mary said.

He didn't answer.

'Is this the place?' I said.

'This is it,' Schuster said.

The smile began to creep up his face.

I heard a thudding sound to my left and I jumped. A small cloud of concrete dust burst in front of me. I heard a distant crack a second later.

I knew immediately what it was.

The bullets of most rifles travel at almost twice the speed of sound. It's disconcerting to experience being fired upon from distance because the bullet reaches you before you've even heard the gun fire. I'd seen this before.

A silent assassin. A sniper.

'Get back!' I shouted, pushing into Mary, shoving her backward, toward the side street we'd just come from. Given the tightly packed buildings on all sides, I could see only one place the sniper could be. The distant tower block. I couldn't help but notice the look on Schuster's face before I turned and bundled into Mary. Such a knowing look. He was already spinning on his heels to flee as we neared the corner.

I heard another crack of gunfire.

The way I had to scoop Mary up as I headed for cover told me she hadn't reacted as quickly as I had. Maybe she hadn't understood what was happening. I more or less carried her around the corner, my momentum easily pushing her slight body weight.

We landed in a heap on the cold ground.

Only then did I realise there had been no pre-emption to the noise of the second shot. No sign of where the bullet had landed before I'd heard the delayed sound from the muzzle.

I soon realised why.

As I looked down, I saw exactly where the bullet had hit. The soft tissue it had struck had made its impact more or less silent.

Mary had been shot.

She had a gaping wound in her neck. Blood was gushing out of it. She had her hand held up to it and I pressed mine against hers. The look on her face said it all. We both knew what this meant.

Her face was already as white as a ghost as the blood rushed out of her.

'Mary, stay with me,' I said. 'Just keep that hand held up there.'

I knew she was dying but I couldn't help but try to reassure her.

'I...I'm sorry,' she blubbered, blood spilling out of her mouth as she spoke.

I pressed harder onto her hand, squeezing it tightly. A tear escaped from her right eye and rolled down and onto the pool of blood on the ground.

'You need to go,' she said, her words slurred. 'Use the phone...I planted the tracker. It's not over...yet.'

I didn't move. I wasn't going to leave her there on her own.

'Go!' she said, louder, more assured, finding an unexpected strength from somewhere.

But I didn't move. I stayed there. Holding her hand. Looking into her pretty eyes as the life slowly faded from her.

And then she was gone.

Chapter 47

I knew where the sniper had been positioned. Both the trajectory of the bullets and the layout of the streets had been a giveaway. Around the corner from the small square, I was at least in cover, though I guessed the sniper would probably have scarpered already. I saw no point in trying to track him down. Either way I knew I couldn't stay in the secluded alleyway for long. Schuster had very deliberately lured us there. I had to assume there were other agents nearby.

Aware that time wasn't on my side, I quickly went through Mary's pockets and found two magazines of ammo. She also had a handful of roubles bank notes and I took those too, stuffing them into my trouser pockets. I didn't feel good about looting her body but I knew I might need those supplies further down the line.

I looked once more at Mary's contorted and lifeless face. I struggled to not feel grief at witnessing the death of someone so young, with so much life still ahead of her. She'd lied to me, or at least not let on the truth, but I felt she'd always been loyal to Mackie and to the agency. With everything else that had been going on around her, I had to admire her for that.

There was no more time for sentiment. I wiped my bloodied hands on her coat and got to my feet. I took the phone out of my pocket and opened up the app that linked with the tracker. It had been cunning of her to have planted the receiver on Schuster. She'd got close to him on multiple occasions, but each time I'd thought she was reacting genuinely to the situation. Instead, she'd been cleverly trying to craft the right moment. I'd not noticed the move at all.

The chip wouldn't be concealed in a seam like it had been in her coat – there'd been no time. She must have planted it in a pocket or a sleeve or somewhere else where the receiver would stick but without being noticeable. I just had to hope Schuster didn't find it.

The app finished opening and I felt a wave of relief when I saw the map with the blinking red light. It was moving. My own position was shown on the centre of the map, a solid blue arrow. The map on the phone was orientated north and the red light was above my position, toward the top of the screen. So I knew Schuster had headed north.

I hurried down the alleyway, retracing my steps, looking for any other route that would allow me to head in the direction that Schuster had gone. I didn't want to follow him up the alley to where the sniper had been.

It wasn't long before I came across another side street and I turned there. The map gave an indication of the prominence of the streets through the thickness of the lines that represented them. I could see that Schuster had moved onto a main road, and as soon as the opportunity came I too veered onto more well-trodden ground. The back streets we'd been ushered down by Schuster were creepy and dangerous. That had already been proven, and I wanted to be as far away from them as possible.

I couldn't see him, but from what I could tell on the map Schuster was only a few hundred yards in front of me. He was moving at a steady pace but I kept up easily enough. He was injured after all. Although I was back on the main streets rather than the cramped alleys, the area I walked through was becoming less residential and more industrial.

Soon, following the red dot closely, I turned into a long, straight road that housed several large warehouses, strewn along either side of the road. Each of them was a basic corrugated steel structure with small office blocks either attached or detached from the main unit. They were of various shapes and size. Some of them were clearly empty – the barren car parks and weeds a dead giveaway. Some were shinier, newer.

Then, all of a sudden, the red dot on the phone stopped. And I paused too. I'd closed the gap somewhat and Schuster had stopped only about a hundred yards in front of me, off to the right.

Looking around me for any signs of life, and satisfied there were none, I continued to walk, closing the distance to the building ahead: a small warehouse, one of the more dilapidated. Weeds grew out of the gutters and up from the sides of the structure. The wire fence that ran around the perimeter had fallen down in places and tall weeds on the grounds surrounding the building came straight up out of the pockmarked tarmac.

As I got nearer I noticed that three large four-by-fours were parked in the otherwise empty car park. No sign of any people, but the lights were on in the building – the dirtied green windows were tinged yellow from the light within.

I carried on walking along the opposite side of the road to where Schuster was, heading right past the warehouse. I spotted large sliding doors at the front of the building. They were ajar, the light from inside seeping out. But I couldn't see what was happening within.

Satisfied from my brief recce that no threats lay on the outside, I hurried across the street and entered the complex through the open security gates. A metal staircase rose up at the side of the building, sweeping up to the very top of the structure to a fire-escape door. I assumed there must have been a mezzanine office level or something to warrant an escape in that position. Given the real risk of walking into a gun fight if I entered through the open main doors, I decided the stairs were the better option. With the dilapidated state of the building, the security up there surely wouldn't be tight.

I sneaked around the side of the cars, keeping an eye on the main doors of the warehouse for any signs of danger. The sounds of muffled voices came and went but I didn't see anybody at all. I came to a stop at the side of the building and took a moment to compose myself. My heart was thumping in my chest from the anticipation of what was to come. And I could feel my arms and my legs twitching. Nerves, but also the adrenaline that was coursing through my body but was so far not being utilised.

Taking two big, deep breaths, I began a slow ascent of the staircase. The steps were icy and slippery and more than once I lost my footing and had to grab hold of the frozen handrail to keep my balance. But the staircase was sturdy at least and didn't creak or crack under my weight. When I reached the top I looked back down to the bottom but still saw no sign of life down there. Hopefully my awkward walk up to the top hadn't alerted anyone.

The fire-escape door looked to be a simple metal structure. Not reinforced. Not particularly secure. It opened outwards, which meant it would be much too difficult to crash through it. The simple lock embedded on the door knob would be easily blown off by my gun, but I couldn't afford to make that much noise. I reached out and tried the knob, just to be sure. Locked. Just as I'd expected it would be.

Other than trying to pick the lock, for which I had no tools, I couldn't think of a way to open the door that wouldn't make noise. Breaking the lock was my only option. I just had to hope that whoever was inside the warehouse wasn't up at this level. If they were at the bottom then the distance alone would, hopefully, give me some cover. If not then I'd simply have to be ready for whatever came.

I took the barrel of the Glock in my right hand and thrust the butt down onto the door knob. A loud crack sounded out at contact and a shower of frost and ice flew into the air. But the knob hadn't budged. Probably because I'd been too cautious, not wanting to make too much sound. If anything, I'd probably made it worse, as having to strike it again would only increase the chance of being heard.

I had little choice, though.

I swung the gun up and crashed it down onto the knob again, this time with more venom. The knob snapped off and dropped to the ground. The noise from the impact and the breaking was one thing, but I cursed my bad luck when the severed knob began to clank and clunk down the metal stairs, all the way to the bottom. I cringed and readied myself for an onslaught. But after a few moments, I realised it wasn't coming. Perhaps I'd got away with it after all.

The door had come ajar, creaking open on its rusty hinges, no longer secured by the now failed lock. I edged it further open and stepped inside. The room I walked into was an office space, dusty, dank – and, to my relief, empty. It was only about fifteen feet wide, twenty long. Along one side windows looked out onto the warehouse below. A closed door stood at the far end. I couldn't see what lay beyond that but guessed either another, similar, room or a corridor. Luckily for me, the fact that I'd entered a closed room was probably the reason they hadn't heard me breaking the lock – at least I hoped they hadn't heard.

I crouched low, crept up to the windows and peeked over the top. The main warehouse below was similarly sparse of fixtures, save for some simple metal shelving that lay strewn around the floor. And amid the metal, a meeting, the participants clustered in the centre of the warehouse floor.

Schuster was in the middle, facing toward me, flanked by two other smartly dressed men. They were standing opposite four other people, their backs to me. I couldn't see their faces but I could tell from their physiques and clothes that three of them were men. The fourth was a woman. She was tall and slender, with silky dark hair. She had on flat knee-length boots over tight trousers and a bomber jacket on top. Even from behind, confidence emanated from her. I didn't need to see her face to know who it was.

Lena.

Chapter 48

The two men flanking the Russian group were holding large automatic weapons, strapped across their shoulders. No-one else was brandishing a weapon but I knew everyone would be armed.

The two groups were standing about ten feet from each other. Schuster's men were scouring the room, on the lookout for anything untoward.

The conversation between the two groups was barely audible and I wasn't able to make out any of the words. Schuster was looking his confident self again, no signs of the pain he must have been in from the beating. His right hand was down at his side, his stricken finger not bandaged. He was a resilient old fox.

As they were scanning the room, one of Schuster's men looked up in my direction. I froze. He quickly looked away again, his eyes still scanning. Somehow, he hadn't spotted me – maybe glare from the warehouse lighting on the office window had kept me hidden. But I didn't want to give him another chance.

I sank lower and moved toward the internal door. This one was unlocked and I turned the handle slowly, then inched the door open until the gap was wide enough to peer out. The door opened out onto a narrow corridor. Off to the right was a toilet. Opposite was another door that led, I presumed, to another office space. To the left the corridor led to a metal walkway that ran along the front of the office level.

The head of the stairs that led down to the warehouse floor was off from the walkway, starting in between the two office spaces and snaking down to the right. From where I was, looking toward staircase, I had a good view of the gathering below.

Schuster took a step forward and then the man to the right of Lena did the same. They carried on moving cautiously, one small step at a time, until they met in the middle. A brief conversation ensued and then an exchange. I couldn't make out what had changed hands. Something small. Schuster stuffed his left hand inside his coat pocket and then began to retreat, still facing Lena and her men.

When he reached his flankers there was a final trade of words and then Schuster turned around and walked toward the exit. His two men initially stayed in position, but then the one on the left turned and began to follow Schuster. Finally, the third man began to move, creeping backward.

I had to follow Schuster. Seeing Lena again had reminded me just how much I loathed her. She may have helped me to escape from the scene of Mackie's demise, but nothing she'd ever done had really been for my benefit. I wanted to kill her. But as much as I wanted to stay and finish off Lena and her cronies, I couldn't let Schuster get away again. I had to believe that Schuster now had all he needed to locate Angela. Her life was very probably going to be over soon if I didn't act. I couldn't allow that to happen. I had to be the one to find her. I still didn't know exactly what I'd do when I did, but I couldn't let her be killed.

Lena would just have to wait.

I went to move backward. But my shoe slipped on the dusty floor and my elbow smacked off the part-opened door. Schuster's man, still edging toward the exit, looked up toward me again. I knew this time he'd not only heard but also seen me.

Lena and her men spun around too, the two on the outside of her already pulling up their weapons. Schuster had exited the warehouse already and his first man didn't stop to turn around but carried on out of the door. I wanted to go after them. But my chance had been blown. If I went back out of the fire escape now, they'd all be waiting for me by the time I got to the bottom.

I had no choice but to stand and fight.

I got to my feet and lunged forward to the top of the stairs. Schuster's second man was already turning around to head to the exit, following after Schuster and his colleague, clearly not wanting to get caught up in the melee that was about to ensue. That was fine by me. One less target only increased my chances.

By the time I reached the stairs, I'd already set myself for firing. The two men holding the automatic weapons were ready to pull on their triggers, but Lena and the other man were still processing their next move.

I fired two shots in quick succession. One of the bullets hit the man on the left in the chest, the other in his neck. He went down before he'd had the chance to pull on his trigger.

But I wasn't going to get to them all that easily.

I heard a crack as the man on the right opened fire with his machine gun. He wasn't holding back. A succession of shots blasted from his automatic weapon and the bullets whizzed and ricocheted nearby. I ducked and rolled forward, hoping my quick movement would make me a harder target.

As I came up against the guardrail at the top of the stairs, I'd already positioned myself for the next shot. I fired off four times, not wanting to take any risks. Only one of the four hit the target. That was enough. The man went down, a randomly aimed spray of automatic fire coming from his gun as he fell to the ground.

Lena and her last man were both rushing for cover, heading under the mezzanine level where I was located. I adjusted my aim as best as I could and fired off the rest of my magazine. I hadn't the time to measure up properly for the shots. I'd wanted to get to them before they found cover. I heard Lena cry out and I knew that I must have hit her. Her shouting and moaning, though, told me that she wasn't yet down for good.

But they were both now out of sight underneath me.

I began to reload but heard a bang and a clank from below that made me jump. One of them was firing up at me from underneath. The walkway I was on and the stairs were a metal mesh. The holes weren't big enough to let through a bullet but I didn't want to stick around to find out exactly how good they were at cushioning automatic rifle fire.

Looking down through the mesh, I couldn't spot the shooter at all. But I could make out Lena's crumpled body, a streak of blood behind her from where she'd crawled from the open space to shelter. The shooter, her last man, must have already been in cover. From my position, I could see nothing of him at all.

Another shot rang out, and this time the clank as the bullet hit the metal walkway came right next to my foot, the vibrations shooting up into my body. The floor had buckled upward, a neat outline visible where the bullet was lodged. If I stayed where I was, it would only be a matter of time before he got me.

I moved quickly across the walkway that ran right along the front of the office area. The two extra magazines I'd taken from Mary were in my pocket. I took one of them and reloaded the gun as I moved, heading for the far end of the walkway.

And Lena's man leaped out in front me.

Only then did I spot a second staircase at that far end. He'd slunk up there, hoping to come at me from behind. The look of surprise on his face at seeing me running toward him must have matched my own.

I began to raise my gun. But he'd already set his position before he'd come out into the open. I instinctively ducked and twisted to my right, hoping to get the chance to retreat.

As I did so he fired.

My quick manoeuvre saved me and I managed to get three shots off without even looking. But my quick change of direction threw my balance off. I tried to steady myself. My body thumped against the guardrail that ran alongside the walkway. I reached out with my free hand, trying to grab the rail, but my fingers slipped. With the bulk of my weight still in motion, I could do nothing to stop my momentum. I toppled over the edge, my arms flailing uselessly as I fell toward the ground ten feet below.

I had no time to prepare myself for the landing. I slammed into the floor, shoulder and hip first. The short distance was the only thing that saved my life. But the shock of the landing was enough to leave me on the deck dazed, unable to move.

From the lack of further fire from the man on the stairs I could only assume I'd been lucky and hit him, otherwise he'd have had no problem finishing me off.

Lying on the ground, I looked around the warehouse floor, my vision blurred. As I started to regain myself, I spotted Lena over in the near corner, underneath the mezzanine level. She was sitting upright against a bare shelving unit, breathing heavily, her right arm slung across her body, cradling the wound in her left shoulder.

I tried to sit up but it was too much too soon. I shouted out from the pain that tore through me. The whole right side of my body was throbbing. The gun I'd been carrying had been thrown from my grip and was lying two yards in front of me, toward where Lena was sitting.

I concentrated and picked myself up, gritting my teeth. Crouching low, more because of the pain and stiffness than anything else, I crept forward toward my gun, my body awkward and unwilling.

Lena's right hand came away from her stricken shoulder. With all the layers she had on I couldn't see down to the wound. But the way her dark jacket was glistening in the dim light told me she was soaked in blood. Her hand moved down toward her side.

Toward the gun that lay by her.

She wasn't going to get the chance to use it.

From somewhere within, I suddenly found clarity of movement and thought. I leap into action. Ignoring the fallen gun I'd been heading for, I rushed straight at Lena. She was trying to ready herself as I reached her. I grabbed hold of her right hand and slammed it against the metal shelves that lay behind her. She cried out and let go of the weapon.

Without giving her a chance to recover, I punched her left shoulder twice in quick succession. She screamed in pain. But I wasn't about to start playing nice. Months of pent-up anger, hatred, vengeance had built up in me. And she was one of the biggest causes. Whatever sordid attraction I'd felt for her in my time of despair was long gone now. She'd used me. She'd had Mackie killed. I wanted to hurt her.

I sat on top of her and dug my knuckle into her stricken shoulder. She cried out again but I held my hand there, grinding into the wound that lay beneath her clothes.

'Where's Grainger?' I shouted.

Despite her position and the obvious pain, her steely resolve didn't waiver. She stared at me coldly, only blinking each time the pain got too much.

'I'm going to make this real easy for you,' I said. 'You gave Schuster something. I'm guessing you've given up where Grainger is. Tell me where she is and I'll make the pain stop.'

Her hard glare didn't shift. Her mouth stayed firmly shut.

I grabbed the collar of her coat with my right hand and pulled her close to me.

'Where is she!' I screamed.

But she didn't respond at all. Didn't react.

I slapped her hard in the face with the back of my left hand. Then I pulled back my arm, balled my fist. Ready to strike. I wanted to punch her. Wipe that look off her face. I wanted to punch her again and again and again until there was nothing left of her.

I knew that if I started, I wouldn't be able to stop. Not like I had with Schuster. I didn't lose it often. But I didn't think I could control myself around her. I could do nothing to Lena that I'd feel bad about. But then nothing I could do would bring satisfaction. Beating her to death wasn't going to make all the bad things she'd done go away. As hard as it was, I had to rise above it.

Some of the steel that had been in her eyes before had gone. Maybe she finally understood that she wasn't going to win this time.

But I also understood something. I understood that she was never going to tell me where Grainger was.

'Just tell me one thing,' I said. 'Why Mackie? Why did you kill Mackie? Of all the things you could have traded, why that?'

Lena began to laugh. Actually more of a cackle.

'You still don't understand anything about me, do you?' she said with pride.

Somehow, despite everything, she'd once again managed to trump me. I hated her for it. I hated her more than anything.

'We didn't kill Mackie,' she said, enjoying her moment. 'We didn't have to. The Americans were more than willing to do it themselves when they found out what we were offering. It's so much more fun watching you take each other out, fighting over something, somebody that we don't even care about.'

And in that moment I finally realised what drove Lena. We'd discussed ourselves many times during my captivity but I hadn't truly known her then. I did now. She didn't do what she did out of duty to her country or her superiors or her family or anything as seemingly noble as that. What drove her was destruction, chaos and other people's pain. It was as simple as that. She thrived on the pain of others.

I pushed her away from me, pressing hard on her left shoulder, eliciting another cry. This had gone on too long. There would never be a satisfactory conclusion. I stood up and strode back to my gun, picked it up, turned around and aimed at her head.

She began to laugh again.

'You can't save Grainger now,' she said. 'You'll never be able to save her.'

I ignored her jibes and walked back up to her. I crouched down by her side and pushed the barrel of the gun onto her forehead.

'Even if you get to her before the Americans do, she's dead,' Lena said. 'You're all dead. You don't think we'd just let those CIA pigs walk away from this, do you?'

Despite myself, I just couldn't help but be sucked in.

'What did you do?' I said.

'The cherry on top,' she said, a beaming smile on her face. 'We don't do deals. You should know that by now.'

This time I couldn't help myself. I threw a punch into the side of her head. I got to my feet and unleashed a kick into her ribs, then another. She doubled over and coughed and spluttered.

'She's dead!' Lena screamed, not lifting her head. 'You can't save her now. You can't save anyone!'

I pulled the gun up, aiming for the spot between her eyes.

'This is it, Carl,' she said, looking up. 'This is your chance. Do it!'

I lowered my aim and fired a single shot. The bullet hit Lena in the gut. She winced and her body creased over onto the floor. She began to cry and moan. I walked up to her, kneeled down and put my face to her ear.

'I'm not letting you off that easily,' I said, my voice calm and quiet.

Both of her hands were up against the wound on her gut. She was writhing on the floor.

'They say it's one of the most painful ways to die,' I said. 'But I'm sure a woman of your experience knows that.'

I rummaged around inside her coat and found what I was looking for. Car keys.

'The bullet has penetrated your stomach. That's what I was aiming for. You'll bleed to death. You're going to die, Lena. And it's going to be slow and very, very painful.'

I got back to my feet and walked away.

As I reached the door, I heard her call out to me. But I didn't take any notice. I was done with her. I carried on out without once looking back.

Chapter 49

When I got outside I noticed that only one of the three cars had gone. Two of them must have belonged to the Russians. I pressed the open button on the remote fob and saw the lights blink on the vehicle to the left. A brand new BMW X5. Russia was one of the largest markets in the world for luxury cars. Obviously working for the government was a big money-spinner.

I opened the driver's door and climbed in. I pushed the clutch with my foot and pressed the start button. The engine roared into life. As I reversed around to face the outer gates, I pulled out Chris's phone and went to the tracking app. The red blinking light was still there, still moving. I just hoped Schuster was going to be doing his own dirty work. If he was, he would lead me to Grainger. It was the only hope I had left.

Lena's words to me had been cryptic, but it didn't take much to figure what she'd meant. Schuster and the CIA thought they were getting Grainger on a plate. They thought they'd be able to kill her, or whisk her away and do what they wanted with her. And they'd been happy to trade me and to kill Mackie, supposedly an ally, to get that.

But Lena had other ideas. She wasn't going to let the CIA just walk away. My guess was that they were being set up for an ambush. Schuster, his men and Grainger were probably all on the list to go. Why would Lena pass up such a good opportunity to kill off her competition?

The tyres screeched as I sped away from the warehouse grounds. Time really wasn't on my side now. I had to catch up with Schuster and fast. The red dot had headed further out of town and was worming its way around the Tret'e Transportnoye Kol'tso,

265

the middle of three ring roads that circumvented the centre of Moscow.

The traffic was building as the working day drew to a close and I had to weave in and out of lanes to stop Schuster's vehicle edging further away. I'd been driving for twenty minutes when the dot, only about half a mile from me, pulled off the ring road and headed further out of town, toward the Khoroshyovo-Mnyovniki district.

I'd never been to the area before but it appeared to be mainly residential. After initially having a suburban feel, with detached and terraced houses, the area changed. Large residential towers rose upward on either side of the road. They were a mixture of modern and old, the Soviet-era concrete unmistakeable. Most of the buildings were much like the monoliths in Omsk where the safe house had been. Except these buildings were still in good shape and in full use.

Looking down at the phone, I saw the red dot had finally stopped. It was just a short distance from me. A couple of minutes' drive. Feeling the buzz of anticipation, I pushed down harder on the accelerator.

I took a left turning and headed toward the position where the dot had stopped. I followed a narrow, winding road that led up to two concrete apartment blocks. They were each about ten storeys tall, their L-shapes mirror images of each other, with a small car park and grass area between them.

The dot wasn't indicating the car park but the back of the nearest block. I carried on along the road, ignoring the turning that led to the car park and the main doors. I'd slowed so that I was crawling along, keeping alert for any signs of movement around me. The area was quiet, with few pedestrians. Most workers were probably only just beginning their evening commute.

As I rounded the corner of the block, I spotted Schuster's car in front. It had been parked on its own directly by a service entrance, in between industrial bins that were clustered along the back of the building. Parked side on, the driver's side faced me. I eased off the accelerator and the BMW rolled to a stop. I looked down at the phone and saw the red dot was still in position, not moving.

Because of the car's blacked-out windows, I couldn't see whether anyone was still inside. But seconds later, I knew the answer. The driver's door, the front passenger door and the back door on the driver's side opened in unison. Schuster stepped out of the front passenger door and began to walk around to the nearside of the vehicle. His two men stood and gazed around them. One of them spotted my car and said something to his friend, who turned in my direction.

The Glock was stuffed into the waistband of my trousers. I also had a SIG P226 in my pocket that had belonged to Lena that I'd picked up on my way out of the warehouse.

I didn't need either of them yet. I was already sitting in the best weapon available to me.

I slammed my foot down on the accelerator. The tyres skidded on the frosty ground but the four-wheel drive soon found traction. The car lurched forward, pinning me back against my seat. The engine whined and then growled, the revs pushing it to bursting point. The needle shot up on the speedometer.

The two men were still standing in position, pulling out weapons from inside their coats. Schuster had seemingly only just become aware of me and he slid down behind the far side of the car, out of view.

The two men opened fire. I ducked down as far as I could. I heard a succession of shots, only just audible over the engine noise. The windscreen of my car cracked, then shattered, sending glass flying through the air around me. I didn't let up. I kept my foot pressed down hard. And braced myself for the impact.

I heard shouts from the men. Then it came.

One thud. Then another.

Then the crash.

My body, weightless for just the briefest of moments, flew forward in the seat, nothing to stop my momentum. Then the seatbelt caught. My head snapped forward, then was thrust back as I was punched in the face by the rapidly inflated airbag. The whole car swung upward from the back, and I thought it might somersault right over. But it crashed back down to the ground again, bouncing and crunching on the broken suspension.

I don't know for sure – the impact had been brutal – but I think I lost consciousness for a few seconds. Certainly it took me a while to get my senses back.

When I found the strength to move, I punched down on the airbag, pushing it away from my face. I looked up and saw the carnage in front of me.

The front of the X5 had buckled and crumpled. It had inserted itself into the side of Schuster's car, which was being held in position on two wheels, having been pushed up and backward by the force of the crash. One of Schuster's men was wedged between the vehicles, his torso caught. He was slumped over the crumpled mess that had been the bonnet of the X5. He wasn't moving at all. No longer a threat.

I spotted movement in front, off to my right. Schuster. He was limping away from his vehicle, toward the service door to the apartment block. His movement was awkward but he didn't seem to be badly hurt. Being on the other side of the vehicle had saved his life, though his limp suggested he'd still been caught as his car was lifted through the air on impact.

I could see no sign of the other man. But I knew I'd hit him. He'd been one of the two thuds I'd heard before the crash.

I released my belt, then reached out and pulled on the handle of my door. It released but didn't open. The bending of the frame as the car had been pushed inwards had wedged it shut. I leaned on it, grimacing in pain as I did so. It moved but didn't open. I pulled back and thrust my weight against it, shoulder first. The same shoulder I'd landed on in the warehouse.

I shouted out in pain.

But it worked and the door flew open. Though I was unable to stop myself falling out of the car to the ground. My body twisted in the air and I landed flat on my front, my face scraping on the cold tarmac.

As I began to pick myself up, I spotted Schuster's other man. At least what was left of him. He was lying on the ground, his deathly eyes staring right at me. His limbs were twisted and bowed, the left leg still wrapped up in the wheel arch of the X5. His other leg was missing. He had a gaping hole in his mid-section, like something had sliced right through him. Blood and guts lay all around him and up on the car. He seemed to be breathing but I didn't fancy his chances.

I checked both of my weapons, then got the phone. The dot was still there, still moving. The problem was, I had no idea what floor Schuster would be on.

I darted off toward the door to the apartment block and entered a narrow corridor that soon opened out to the left and right. The dot was off to the left but I saw no sign of Schuster. I looked around and located the stairs, next to a bank of lifts. The stairs were the better option.

I checked the phone once more, then headed over to the first flight and ran up it. When I reached the top, I poked my head around, peering down the corridor. Still no sign of Schuster. I carried on and repeated the same move.

This time I got lucky.

Schuster was fifty yards in front, hobbling away from me. I took aim with the SIG but didn't fire. I began walking, a steady pace but enough to close the gap on him. He looked around and I heard him shout something. I couldn't make out the words but I knew they had been directed at me.

He was cupping his hands around his waist as though he'd been struck there. Or was it just from the damage I'd inflicted back on the train?

Then he swung around unexpectedly, gun in hand, and fired. The rushed shot missed me. I lifted an arm up to my face, pulled back against the near wall. I fired off one shot in response. At that range, having already been set, it was an easy shot to take. I hit him exactly where I'd intended.

Schuster screamed and fell to the floor, clutching at his left leg, the one he hadn't been limping on. He lifted his hand to fire at me again but I was too quick. I let off another round. This one caught him in the arm, the one that was holding the gun, which he dropped to the ground.

I closed the distance to him, my gun held out. Ready for anything else he had to offer. Nothing came. He was spent. When I got to him he was lying on his back, the elbow on his good arm propping him up. His nostrils were flaring, his determined eyes still glistening.

'Where is she?' I said.

'You really don't know what you're doing,' he said. 'You can't possibly expect to get away with this. Do you know who we are!'

'I could say the same thing to you. You should have thought more carefully before doing your dirty deals.'

'There was nothing dirty about it. Mackie had it coming. Grainger does too.'

'I'm not sure the Russians had quite the same idea as you.'

'No. There's nothing wrong with the Russians. At least you can deal with them. Negotiate with them. They always have something to offer. They understand how this game really works. They're not all out there trying to be goddamn heroes like you. They're realists.'

'You know, if this hadn't been personal for me, I'd have relished watching you get taken down by them.'

'Taken down?' Schuster said, confusion on his face.

'They've set you up. There was no deal. They've had you running around this country taking out people on your own side. There was no intention of ever letting you out of here alive with Grainger, your prized possession.'

Schuster didn't say anything to that. I gave him a moment to mull it over. Perhaps he finally understood.

'I'll help you get her out of here,' he said, a sudden change of tack. 'It's your only chance. You've got no-one else now. You help me, I'll help you.'

'Sure you would,' I said. 'But I learned my lesson a long time ago. Don't do deals with people you don't trust.'

I pulled up the gun and shot him in the face.

Chapter 50

I rummaged through Schuster's pockets and found what I was looking for. A piece of paper. That's what it had all come down to. Mackie's life. All the other people who'd lost theirs on the way. All the betrayal and the blood and the tears. The misery that had come to so many. All for the address that was scribbled on that one small piece of paper.

Apartment 406.

I looked up. All of the doors on this floor were numbered in the three hundreds. The four hundreds were one floor up. Angela was just one floor up.

After all this time, Angela.

I walked back to the stairwell and made my way to the next floor. Reaching the top, I peered cautiously around. Schuster and his men were all taken care of. But Lena's words were still reverberating in my head. The ambush. I didn't know when or how it would come, but she'd never intended that Schuster and Angela would leave alive. Would it be a sniper? A combat team? Was the apartment wired with a bomb that would go off the minute the door was opened? Was Angela really here at all, or was there one final deception from Lena still to come?

I didn't know the answer.

But I knew that I would soon find out.

I walked up to the door to 406, knocked three times and waited. I heard the faint sound of movement from inside but no-one opened the door.

I knocked three more times. This time I didn't hear anything at all.

But then came a voice.

Her voice.

'Who is it?' she said in Russian.

I didn't answer. I just stared at the spy-glass, noticing as a shadow crept over it on the other side. She was looking at me. Then the door was unlocked and pulled open.

And there she was.

'Carl?' she said. I saw confusion on her face, and fear and something else…hope?

I'd often wondered what it would feel like to come face to face with her again. I'd known the time would come. I'd told myself it had to. But I'd always been torn as to why I wanted to find her.

Did I want to be her lover again?

Did I want to turn her in for what she'd done?

Did I want to kill her?

Since the moment Schuster had said her name and I'd focused on getting to her, I hadn't given myself a chance to find the answer. But now, standing before her, I knew.

I wanted to protect her.

Because we were the same. Our own people had turned on us. First, my agency had left me for dead. They'd given up on me. The Americans had come in and they'd seen a chance to negotiate with my life. Grainger had been similarly wronged. It had started with the decision of her government to grant a life of freedom to the man who'd killed her father. Then the bloody quest that the CIA had embarked on to find and punish her for killing that same man.

We were both lost souls. We no longer had anywhere to call home. No longer had anyone that we could rely on. We had no jobs, no identities. We had nowhere left to go. All we had was our lives and the crowds of people behind us, our friends and enemies alike, trying to find us so they could take us down.

The future was a blank. How we'd get out of this alive, what we'd do next, I had no idea.

But I knew that whatever was to come, I would be facing it with her.

A note from the author

Thank you for reading *Rise of the Enemy*. I do hope you enjoyed it and would be very grateful if you could write a review. It needn't be long, just a few words. Reviews make a huge difference to writers and help other readers discover new books.

Look out for the return of Carl Logan in *Hunt for the Enemy* - out now!

To find out more about my other releases, just carry on reading, or head to www.robsinclairauthor.com, where you can also subscribe to my mailing list for up-to-date information on releases, promotions and competitions.

I also welcome your feedback, comments and questions. You can get in touch with me via my website or on social media:

> Twitter: @rsinclairauthor
> Facebook: fb.me/robsinclairauthor

The Hunt is on…

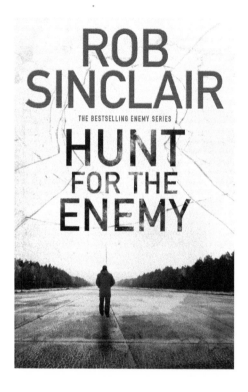

Hunt for the Enemy is the breathtaking and action-packed finale to the Enemy series

Read on for more details…

Chapter 1

It was summer. It was hot. No, not hot, scorching. The sun blazed down, heating the ground and everything around. Humid, sticky air seemed to seep through cracks in the road and from the walls of the sand-coloured buildings, rising upwards, choking everyone who breathed it. Carl Logan drove through the twisting city streets in a rusty old tin can of a car that clunked and jerked and whined every time he changed gear and every time the engine revved. He wore a pair of khaki linen trousers and a thin cotton shirt, but with the windows of the car fully wound down, the stifling air burst against his face and he was dripping wet. A thunderstorm had not long passed, leaving behind wispy grey clouds in the sky. Even though the fierce sun had done its best to burn away the remnants of the rain clouds, the humidity levels remained peaked.

And yet Logan was almost oblivious to the debilitating conditions. Because today was the day.

Three years of gruelling, agonising training had brought him to this point. The training had been more than tough; it had been life-changing, taking him to the brink physically on numerous occasions. He'd suffered terrible injuries, been hospitalised for weeks on end. It had been mentally draining too. From the intensive mock interrogations to the mind-bending psych evaluations, he'd felt like he was losing his mind. In many ways, he probably had. Numerous times during the training he'd questioned why he was going through it at all. Why he was committing his life to this cause that just three years before he'd not once considered.

But those thoughts were buried deep now.

Finally the training was over. It was time to show his true worth. Logan had been in Marrakech for four weeks, but the full details of his first assignment for the Joint Intelligence Agency had only been relayed the previous evening by his boss back in England, Mackie. No details or explanation had been offered as to why the targets were on the JIA's radar and Logan hadn't asked. The targets were on the blacklist and that was all Logan needed to know. The JIA had hammered into him that his job wasn't to ask questions. It was to carry out orders.

Sitting next to Logan in the passenger seat of the car was John Webb, a fellow JIA agent. Webb was a number of years more senior than Logan and had been a close mentor over the previous twelve months as Logan assimilated himself into the life of a field agent. The first two years with the JIA had been non-stop training, not even a hint of a real assignment. For the last year, he had been shadowing others in the field, learning.

Now it was his time to shine.

Logan had admired Webb from the very first time they'd met. After a troubled upbringing, like Logan's, Webb had come into his own since joining the JIA ten years previously. He had an air of respect and dignity and yet he was tough and ruthless. The job of an agent was a loner's one – there wasn't the time or capacity for close friendships. And yet Logan had enjoyed the time he'd spent with Webb and he could tell the older agent had relished the opportunity to act as guide and tutor.

'Take this next left,' Webb said in his bass voice.

Logan took his foot off the accelerator and the car slowed. He was beginning to turn the wheel when a moped came sweeping up on his inside. Logan slammed on the brakes, narrowly avoiding a collision. Oblivious, the moped driver sped off into the distance. Logan clenched his hands on the steering wheel, attempting to return his focus to the task at hand.

'Everything okay there? You seem a bit distant,' said Webb. It was the second time already on the short drive that Webb had questioned Logan's state of mind.

Logan shot him a look.

'I'm fine. I didn't see him. That's all.' 'Okay, okay, only asking.'

Logan put the car into first gear and eased around the corner, into a cramped side street. On one side it was lined with indus-trial bins and bags of rubbish from the various shops, cafes and restaurants that occupied the parallel street at the front of the buildings. On the other was a series of ramshackle buildings, anything from two to five storeys tall. Cars and mopeds were parked tightly up against the buildings here and there.

The alley was narrow and dank – and dark, which at least provided immediate relief from the ferocious sun. They drove for a couple of hundred yards, Logan keeping the pace slow, winding the car through the at times impossibly narrow gaps where other cars had parked a little too far from the side of the road.

'This is the place here,' Webb said, ducking down and looking up through the window at the building on the right-hand side. 'Pull up wherever you can.'

Logan drove just past the building and the nearest space, then put the car into reverse. He swung the vehicle back toward the wall, only stopping and re-aligning the steering when the rear of the car was a few inches from making contact. He misjudged it. As he turned the car in, there was a scraping noise: the bumper raking against the building.

'Easy there!' Webb shouted. 'Come on, man. Just keep it cool.'

'I am cool,' Logan said.

'Then straighten this thing up and let's get inside.'

Logan pulled the car forward a couple of feet, then eased it back into the space, this time missing the wall without any trouble. He and Webb opened their doors in unison. Webb squeezed his muscled frame through the six-inch gap that Logan had given him – it was the only way to park the car and still allow other vehicles to pass. They couldn't afford to block the street, which would cause unnecessary commotion.

Logan went around to the boot and opened it up. He picked up the larger of the two black aluminium cases that lay there. Webb took the smaller, lighter one. After shutting the boot, Logan followed Webb around to the door of the building. It was derelict, a set of apartments that was in the process of being sold on for refurbishment. Most of the other buildings either side were in a similar state of disrepair, including those that were still occupied. The worn door to the building had a simple lock. Logan stood watch, eyes darting up and down the street and over the surrounding buildings, as Webb expertly picked the lock. It took less than ten seconds. Webb pushed the door open, its warped wood creaking and straining.

'Come on, follow me,' Webb said, heading in.

The building was dusty and dark inside but the air felt cool and dry. Webb did a quick recce of the ground floor, looking for any signs of life. There were none. He headed for the bare wooden staircase and Logan followed, lugging the heavy case with him.

'You're sure you're ready for this?' Webb asked without turning. 'Yeah,' Logan responded.

'You know, it would be understandable if you were nervous. This isn't for everyone.'

'I'm not nervous.'

'I'm just saying, don't feel bad if you are. Training is one thing. But doing this for real? Not everyone can hack it.'

'Whatever you say.'

'But I know you can do it. I wouldn't have let Mackie pass this job to you otherwise.'

'Okay, I get it.'

'You ask me, I'd say you're a natural. Some people just don't have it. Others do. I'm sure you'll be fine.'

'I never said I wouldn't be.'

'Okay, okay. So let's just get this done.'

They passed the fifth and final floor, after which the staircase became narrower and steeper. At the top, they came to a stop at a gun-metal door. Webb pushed down the security bar and the door swung open to reveal the flat roof of the building.

Webb walked out and Logan followed, wincing as the blast of superheated air smacked him in the face. He followed Webb across the burning roof tiles to the far southerly corner. From there they had an unobstructed view toward the Kasbah district with its mix of old-world charm – the sumptuous colours of the rooftop gardens of luxury riads and the minarets from its many mosques poking proudly into the sky – together with the deep blue of the rooftop pools and gleaming glass of flash new hotels. Webb kneeled down and opened up his case, then took out his spotter's scope. Logan came down beside him and placed his larger case next to Webb's. He undid the thick clasps and opened the lid to reveal the green and black AWSM sniper rifle, snug in the deep foam interior of the box.

Logan took out the rifle and attached the bipod, then quickly gave the rifle a once-over, making sure the mounted scope was securely in place. He opened a pouch on the case lid to reveal five shiny .338 Lapua Magnum cartridges and placed them one at a time into the rifle's detachable magazine. With all five cartridges neatly inside, Logan clipped the magazine onto the assembled rifle and set it down on the ground.

'Fifteen forty,' Webb said, looking at his watch. 'The target isn't scheduled to arrive back until sixteen hundred.'

'May as well set up the spotting position now,' Logan said. 'Get our sights ready.'

'Agreed,' said Webb. He lay flat on the ground and pushed his scope through a gap in the worn concrete wall that lined the rooftop.

But Logan didn't lie down next to Webb to align the sights on the rifle. There was still plenty of time for that. Instead, he stood up, leaving the assembled rifle on the floor, and fished in his pocket for the plastic cord that he'd stashed there just a few minutes before the two agents had left the safe house.

'The distance to the front entrance of the hotel is six hundred and seventy-three yards,' Webb said. 'The drop is forty-three feet.'

Logan knew the measurements already. He and Webb had been through every last detail numerous times. Webb's repetition was just part of the routine. Everything had to be perfect for the shot. They would only get a few seconds. But Logan was confident he would take the shot exactly as planned. The distance wasn't that difficult. The rifle could handle twice with ease. Logan himself had managed close to two thousand yards in training. Six hundred and seventy-three yards wouldn't be a problem.

'Wind speed is close to zero,' Webb said, looking at his hand-held anemometer. 'But I'll keep rechecking. And we should take readings from different spots on the rooftop over the next hour just to make sure. If we get another storm coming over, it could change significantly.'

'Okay,' Logan said, as much to himself as to Webb. He took a deep breath.

And then he was ready.

Logan wrapped the cord tightly around both of his hands, leaving just two feet of flex in the middle. He was aware that his breathing and heart rate were speeding up, but he was sure it wasn't nerves. Just adrenaline and anticipation.

With Webb still preoccupied, Logan stepped over his colleague, one foot either side, then quickly dropped his weight to the ground, his knees pinning down Webb's arms. Webb immediately let go of the anemometer, squirming for just a second before Logan swept the flex under his colleague's neck. He used his left hand to wrap the cord around a full turn and then he pulled back and out, hard and fast.

Webb rasped, trying to shout out but unable to with the crushing pressure on his windpipe. He kicked and writhed and squirmed. But Logan had taken him by surprise. The experienced agent simply hadn't been ready and there was no way he was getting out.

Webb coiled and bucked but Logan held firm. He pulled on the cord, using every ounce of strength he could muster, his arms, his whole body tensing and straining. His face turned red, his knuckles white. Veins throbbed at the side of his head; his biceps bulged. But all the time he focused on just one thing: pulling as hard as he could.

Pained sounds escaped Webb's lips but they were quickly becoming weak, shallow. He clawed at the ligature cutting into his neck. Droplets of blood dripped onto the ground beneath him. It was wound so tightly there was nothing for him to grasp.

Soon, Webb began to scrape and rake at Logan, but he was too far gone already for it to make a difference.

When Logan felt the resistance from his associate wane, he only pulled harder. The cord dug into his hands, sending a shock of pain up through his arms. But he didn't let up – he just kept on tugging, harder and harder.

Webb's body went limp and it flopped down, melting into the rooftop. Even then, Logan held tight a few seconds longer, keeping Webb's lifeless head suspended in the air.

When Logan finally released the grip, unwinding the cord from around the neck, Webb's face thudded down against the hard floor with a sickening crack. And then he was completely still.

It was done.

Logan stood up, panting, sweat pouring down his brow. He unwound the cord from around his hands and a rush of blood coursed through them, making them throb and sting. He saw several lines of indented red flesh on his palms and the backs of his hands where the plastic had dug in and cut into his skin. Logan dropped the cord and put his hands to his knees for just a few seconds as he got his breathing back under control. His whole body ached from exertion.

When he was ready, he kneeled down next to Webb's body and rolled his former colleague onto his side, away from where he had been spotting.

After taking one last look at the man who had so readily mentored and guided him, Logan fished his phone out of his pocket and dialled Mackie. He picked up after just two rings.

'I'm in position,' Logan said.

'Good,' Mackie replied. 'And you're alone?' 'I am now.'

'Excellent. Then call me when it's done.'

Logan ended the call and put the phone back in his pocket. He didn't know why the targets had been chosen and he hadn't asked. They were on the JIA's blacklist and that was all he needed to know.

That was his job now.

He picked up the rifle and looked through the scope, eyeing the hotel entrance, six hundred and seventy-three yards away.

And then he lay down and waited for his second target to arrive.

***

To carry on reading head to Amazon.com where a longer sample is available.

Money. Murder. Revenge.

How much pressure can one man take, before he breaks?

DARK FRAGMENTS is the pulsating new thriller from Rob Sinclair.

Read on for more details...

Book description

Outwardly, Ben Stephens appears to be a normal, hard-working family man. In reality, his life has been in turmoil since the murder of his wife, Alice, seven years ago. The killer was never caught.

Now re-married - to the woman he was having an affair with while still married to Alice - Ben's life is once again spiralling out of control, and he's become heavily indebted to an unscrupulous criminal who is baying for Ben's blood.

When Ben's estranged twin sister, a police detective, unexpectedly returns to his life, asking too many questions for comfort, it becomes clear that without action, Ben's life will soon reach a crisis point from which there will be no return.

In order to avoid falling further into the mire, Ben must examine the past if he is to survive the present - but just how much pressure can one man take before he breaks?

Dark Fragments is a fast-paced thriller with a blend of mystery, suspense and action that will appeal to readers of psychological thrillers, as well as a broad section of crime, thriller and action fans.

DARK FRAGMENTS is available in ebook and paperback now! Head to amazon.com to find out more.

Lightning Source UK Ltd.
Milton Keynes UK
UKHW010630081020
371237UK00001B/175

9 780995 693319